D

Sandy rolled a six. She sat back with a smile, ran her tongue over her teeth and said, 'OK, Julie. I want you to open your legs. Stand there with 'em wide apart. Hands behind your head, too.'

Bitch! How could she have asked for something so embarrassing? Julie was standing; the others were sitting; her crotch would be right at their eye-level. God, they might even be able to smell her – smell that she was already turned-on. She said 'I –'

Rick said, 'I think you should do as you're told.'

Suddenly Julie realised the nature of the game. This wasn't about exhibitionism; it was about humiliation.

Other books by the same author:

CRASH COURSE

THE HAND OF AMUN

ARIA APPASSIONATA

WHITE ROSE ENSNARED

FORBIDDEN CRUSADE

DREAMING SPIRES

Down Under

JULIET HASTINGS

Black Lace novels contain sexual fantasies.
In real life, make sure you practise safe sex.

First published in 2002 by
Black Lace
Thames Wharf Studios,
Rainville Road, London W6 9HA

Typeset by SetSystems Ltd, Saffron Walden, Essex
Printed and bound by Mackays of Chatham PLC

ISBN 0 352 33663 3

Contents

1. Introductions . . . 1
2. Diva 13
3. Sandy 33
4. Rick 60
5. Zoe 78
6. Kathy 97
7. Jason 117
8. Julie 136
9. Alan 157
10. Jan 174
11. Greg 193
12. Sarah 212
13. Priss 234

Chapter One

Introductions

. . . were over, and their tour leader, Steven, got up and grinned and shouted in his strong Kiwi accent, 'OK, everyone, the bus is outside. Grab your bags, take them out with you, yeah?'

Priss looked around for Diva, but it was too late. If there was one thing absolutely guaranteed to get Diva moving, it was the prospect of being stuck in the wrong seat somewhere. She was already grabbing her trek bag and heading for the door, thick black ponytail whirling in her wake.

Since Priss would sit next to Diva wherever she chose, there really was no need to hurry, so she got to her feet and stretched. One of her new companions caught her eye and smiled. She smiled back, because he was probably the best-looking man on the trek: late thirties, fairly tall, dark eyes, brown hair, a brooding look. She concentrated and remembered his name: Rick.

'Looking forward to it?' he asked her, innocuously enough.

She smiled and said, 'Sure,' while she thought, I could look forward to it with you.

And then, out of the blue, the idea came to her. She walked over to her bag slowly, looking around at the faces of the people who were going to be with her, like it or lump it, for the next eight days. Two couples, and three pairs of single men and single women who had become involuntary tentmates. They ranged in age from early twenties to early fifties, all of them looked fit, none of them were ugly, and a few of them were strikingly good looking. The idea blossomed, and she smiled.

After the trek she and Diva would be headed for home, back across the other side of the world. She to her job, her flat, her single life, and Diva to her engagement. She wasn't happy about Diva's engagement, though Diva insisted that everything was fine. It sounded too much like an arranged marriage to Priss. Diva's parents were happy about it, and that was highly suspicious because they were very rarely happy about anything Diva did. Priss didn't like Diva's fiancé, and she didn't like the fact that when they were married they might not live in London, and she didn't want to lose her best friend.

OK, call her selfish. But when she had won this holiday in New Zealand, it had seemed like a wonderful opportunity to get Diva away from her family and her future, let her realise what she would be missing if she got herself hitched. A chance to be free and single: for Diva, perhaps, a last chance. But so far, in the city and on the beach, things had been, frankly, tame. A Kiwi surfer here and there, nothing to write home about. Now, in the middle of nowhere, there was a chance to spice it up. Fun, satisfaction – and perhaps a way to persuade Diva to stay single, at least for now.

Priss went out into the warm twilight, lugged her bag to the back of the bus and handed it to the driver to be stowed, then scrambled up the steps. It was a smallish bus, a half-size coach, really. The rear seats were higher than the front ones, and she wasn't surprised to see Diva sitting in the middle of the back seat, grinning and giving her the thumbs-up.

'Back seat bombers,' Diva crowed, as Priss approached.

The other trekkers were on board now, sitting in their pairs here and there, except that the two single men, Rick and a youngster whom Priss thought she remembered was Jason, were sitting apart. Rick glanced towards the rear of the coach, then settled down in a seat and arranged himself as if he wanted to get some sleep.

Steve jumped up behind the driver, the classic tour guide spot, and shouted, 'Can you all hear me?'

'Loud and clear,' Priss called back, and a few other voices responded from here and there.

'All right,' Steve yelled. 'Listen, we've got a couple of hours on this bus and then we arrive at the first night's hut. You'll meet our support team there, the guys who are going to drive the packhorses for us and look after your stuff, yeah? We've got three support guys for this trip: Josh, TJ and John. They're great blokes; you'll like them. TJ's a local guy, a Maori, and he knows all about the forest and the wildlife. You talk to him as much as you want. He's got some terrific stories.'

'A Maori?' Diva said, looking at Priss sideways. 'Think he's anything like those guys in the All Blacks who do the Haka, the war dance?'

'God, I hope so,' Priss said.

Diva slid a little further down in her seat. 'Wow. Perhaps he'll have tattoos.'

'Maybe,' Priss agreed, smiling. It sounded as if Diva was feeling frustrated. That would make her much, much more likely to be up for what Priss had in mind.

'... a long walk in front of you over the next few days,' Steve was saying, 'and this trek is a bit different from the usual New Zealand walking experience. We're not going to be using many marked trails, and you're not likely to meet any other trekkers or even a forest ranger.'

'Shame,' Diva muttered. 'I could just handle a forest ranger.'

'As well as a Maori?' Priss didn't take this type of comment from Diva too seriously. Usually it was just bravado, as in fact Diva was careful about appearances and private about her preferences.

'Hell, yes,' said Diva, with more bravado.

'So you may want to get a bit of shut-eye on the bus,' Steve went on. 'I'll be down here at the front if anyone has anything they want to ask. Otherwise, it's time to bid civilisation goodbye.'

The driver revved the engine and the bus lurched forward into the darkness. At the front one of the women, a thin, earnest-looking girl with glasses, hurried forward to engage Steve with what looked like very anxious questions.

'Bid civilisation goodbye,' Diva said, shaking her head. 'God, I hope this is a good idea.'

Priss grinned. Lifting her head, she ensured that there was nobody sitting in the rows directly in front of them. They were unlikely to be overheard, especially as the bus had seen better days and growled like a bronchitic lion with every squeeze of the accelerator.

'Tell you what,' she said, 'I think I know how to make sure that it is.'

Diva turned in her seat to look directly at her, eyebrows pulled down in sceptical enquiry. 'You mean you've got an idea? You? A blonde?'

Priss was past rising to Diva's Blonde jokes. 'Call it a challenge,' she suggested tantalisingly.

'Now let me think,' Diva said, tilting her head on one side and putting her finger to her lips in a parody of concentration. 'This holiday has been hideously short of men. On this trek there are some men. Could it be, could it possibly be that your idea involves –' she drew in a quick breath '– *men*?'

'Nearly right. Keep trying.'

Diva frowned and said more tentatively, 'Men and women?'

Priss smiled. 'Everybody.'

'Sorry?'

'The challenge is,' said Priss, 'that by the end of this walk we have been involved in sex with every single person on the tour. Including Steve and the Maori and the bush blokes with the horses.'

Diva's face didn't change. She said levelly, 'And what about the horses?'

'I draw the line at the horses,' Priss said. 'Consenting adults only.'

For a moment Diva looked as if she was going to laugh. Then she said, 'You're serious.'

She didn't look happy. Probably worrying about what her family and her future husband would say if they heard about this kind of suggestion. It was time for a bit of serious persuasion.

Outside it was nearly dark, but there was just enough light left to see the bus and the backs of people's heads. Priss stood up, leaning on the seat in front of her, and jerked her head. Diva got up too, stooping slightly because she was tall and the bus roof was low.

'Look,' Priss said, indicating the others. 'There's eleven people here, counting Steve, and three hunky blokes to join us at the other end. I've got a bagful of condoms we haven't had a chance to use. And we're going to be in the back of beyond. You heard Steve; we aren't even going to be on the main trails. We might as well be in a private playground. Nobody will ever hear about this.'

'They might,' Diva said. 'Most of these people are English. Six degrees of separation and all that.'

'Dee, didn't you listen to the introductions? Nobody else was from London, nobody at all. Hard to believe, but we're the only representatives of the capital on this whole trip. Nobody here is going to know anyone we know.' Priss looked down the bus. One of the couples, the younger couple, was snogging. They had their tongues down each other's throats. 'Look,' she whispered, pointing. 'Someone else has the same idea.'

'Yes, but they're married,' Diva said, reasonably.

But there was always another way to persuade Diva. And once she was persuaded, she would be committed, Priss knew that of old. 'Well,' Priss said, as if it didn't matter, 'if you don't want to, fair enough. I'll just have to handle it by myself.'

Diva swivelled to stare at her. 'What, on your own?'

Priss shrugged. 'Blondes have more fun, haven't you heard?'

'Without me? You wouldn't!'

'It would be easier with you. I suppose it's just possible that someone on this trip wouldn't prefer a blonde.'

Diva's face began to shade into a grin. 'Between us we've got it covered, haven't we?'

She was hooked. Delighted, Priss dropped back into the seat, pulling Diva with her into the corner. It was really dark now and they could only just see each other's faces. 'Great,' she said, 'great stuff, Dee!' She leaned forward conspiratorially and reached into her rucksack for a bag of trail mix. 'Here, get your energy up. Come on, let's plot and plan. Where shall we start?'

Diva arched upwards to look over the seat. 'Blimey,' she said between chews, 'that couple are really going for it, aren't they? Serious tonsil tennis. What were their names again?'

'Oh, God.' Priss shut her eyes and imagined the table where they had sat to do the introductions. She could see the two faces, early thirties, nice looking, the man fair and curly-haired, the woman a striking, ample redhead. 'Greg, I think, Greg and I can't remember.'

'Sandy,' Diva said positively. 'It goes with her hair, sort of. Greg and Sandy, a married couple. Ozzies, remember? Priss –' she reached down, catching at Priss's fleece. 'Priss, look,' she hissed.

Priss eased herself up and peered over the seats. She could just see what Diva meant. Greg had his hand inside Sandy's top. His fingers were moving beneath it, worrying at her nipple. She couldn't see any lower, but something about the way Sandy's shoulder was moving made her think that she was wanking Greg. They weren't making any noise, but the jerks of Sandy's torso showed how aroused she was. Priss swallowed and noticed the familiar symptoms of being turned on. A tight hollow ball under her breastbone, a fierce clenching between her legs, a sensation of warmth.

'Perhaps we should start with them,' she said as she

sat down. 'They're exhibitionists, if nothing else. Otherwise they might beat us to it.'

'Nah, I vote we start with the Maori,' Diva said, grinning.

'And then there's Rick,' Priss said. 'He'd be a good place to start, don't you think?'

Diva made an uncertain moue. 'You mean the tall dark one? Not sure, personally, Priss. I know he's your cup of tea, but he had the look of a game-player to me.'

Priss nodded slowly, accepting the comment. She wasn't particularly interested in sexual power games herself, but she knew that Diva had a strong streak of it in her make-up, which made her more sensitive to it in others. Priss freely accepted that she was only really likely to notice a dominant if they were wearing leather and carrying a whip; the little everyday nuances of expression and behaviour escaped her. 'I'll leave him up to you, then,' she said generously.

'All right. But I want to start with the Maori.'

'Diva, you haven't even seen him! What if he's seventeen stone?'

'Seventeen stone on a foot trek? I doubt it. You're not going to move me on this one, Priss.'

'May you not be disappointed. All right, then. Tomorrow you try what's his name, TJ, and I'll either pick one of the other guys or I'll make a move on Greg and Sandy.'

Diva peeped over the seat again. 'Can't see Sandy any more,' she commented. 'Reckon she's going down on him.'

'Uxorious beast,' Priss said. She could imagine, all too vividly, the excitement of going down on a man in this bus. The dark, the growl of the engine, all around the possibility of discovery, and every now and again the jar of a pothole to add a frisson of physical risk to the whole thing. She could almost taste him, feel the way she wrapped her lips around her teeth to cushion his cock against danger. She shifted awkwardly on the seat and turned her head to look at Diva. 'Don't fancy doing the same for me, I suppose?' she suggested, only half joking.

Diva grinned. 'I've been putting up with you for days. Now when there are men about you suggest it?' She made a thoughtful face. 'Though men find lesbianism very horny, don't they? Perhaps we ought to use it as a seduction device.'

'What, come into our tent and watch us getting it on? Yes, I imagine that could work.'

'Anyway, not right now, Priss. I'm saving myself for TJ and his tattoos.'

Priss sighed, then pushed herself across the back seat into the corner of the bus. Outside it had begun to rain, and drops starred the windows and ran down in shining trickles. It was black as pitch out there, black as prehistory. Apparently some of the forests they were going to see were made up of trees that had been around for millions and millions of years, survivors from the Cretaceous, *Jurassic Park* trees. Looking out into that wet darkness it was easy to believe.

What a place for a sexual odyssey. For a moment Priss felt almost depressed. What if the whole thing were rained off? What if they spent their week traipsing through mud and nobody wanted to do anything other than dry out and creep into their sleeping bags?

No, it wouldn't happen. She wouldn't let it happen. Besides which, there was that horny couple, and Rick the game-player, and then there would be the men with the horses. Surely they would be up for some high jinks? If they were like most of the men that Priss had ever met in the tourist trade, they would be on the lookout for encounters on every trip they accompanied.

Over the roar of the bus as it climbed a hill she was sure she heard a gasp from the seats in front, where Greg and Sandy were at it. She closed her eyes and felt slowly between her legs. Jeans were not the ideal wear for a quick private orgasm, but she had managed before under conditions just as difficult. She began to scratch her thumb against the central seam of the jeans, sending sharp, intense vibrations straight through her. The difficulty of getting the movement exactly right made the pleasure even more piercing when she did.

Her nipples were aching and, after a moment, she had to take hold of her right breast with her left hand and squeeze it, rubbing her palm against the areola, feeling the flesh tauten and harden even through layers of T-shirt and fleece.

She and Diva had hardly begun to talk about the group. They'd focused on only the most obvious targets: Rick, tall, dark and handsome; Sandy and Greg, at it like knives; and the unknown, bush-hardened, erotic totem of the Maori. What about the others in the group? The older couple, quiet and fit-looking, in their fifties? The thin, anxious-looking vet, what was her name, Sarah? Sally? And her tentmate, a black girl with a strikingly athletic body and a broad grin, whose name Priss had already forgotten? Or the two other single women, both looking as if they were in their mid- to late thirties – what would they make of this? Would they play the game?

She stroked herself again and shivered with the effort of repressing a sigh. And what about Steve, the tour leader? He was a typical Kiwi, lanky, tousle-haired, blond, so laid back that he seemed almost asleep. Some women's ideal. Not Priss's, but that didn't mean that she would ignore him. No, she was sure she would find something for him to do.

Her fingernail scratched harder and the vibrations set her clit on fire. Biting her lip with the effort of keeping quiet, she shut her eyes more tightly and squeezed harder at her breast, imagining herself on all fours by a blazing fire, gasping as she was vigorously fucked from behind by someone, it didn't matter who. All it needed was to be a man, a man with a big stiff cock to shaft her with while she flung back her head and howled. She imagined her breasts dangling bare in the firelight, her hair hanging around her face, her hand between her legs as she rubbed frantically at herself, bringing on a screaming orgasm even as now in the bus her body arched upwards from the seat with the desperate tension of keeping silent while the pulses flooded through her.

After a moment she let out a long breath and opened her eyes and there, standing in the aisle of the bus staring at her in the gloom was Steve. He looked as if he didn't know where to look, though it was too dark to see if he was blushing.

'Got to pass the time somehow,' she said, smiling slightly.

'Yeah. Right,' Steve said, rubbing his hand across his face as if he wanted to rub away what he had seen. He said, 'Yeah, ah, I just came to check everything was OK down here.'

'Everything's fine,' Priss purred.

'Bit bumpy,' Diva added innocently, 'but fine.'

'Not far to go now,' Steve said more brightly, as if this straightforward exchange had calmed him down a bit.

'Oh, I don't know,' Diva said. 'We could probably go farther than you imagine.'

Steve blinked at her, then turned away, shaking his head, and headed back towards the front of the bus. Priss looked across at Diva, shaking with laughter.

'Start as you mean to go on, huh?' Diva didn't look as if she disapproved. 'Anyway, if I were you I would chill out. Nothing to do for a while.'

In her post-orgasm relaxation Priss found it easy to doze off and she didn't wake until the bus juddered to a halt in a little pool of light beside a large wooden hut. Diva was sitting with her nose pressed to the window, and she grabbed Priss's arm and pulled her close.

'Look!' she whispered.

Standing beneath the light, reflected in the gleam of the wet ground, were three men. One was a young white guy, hardly more than twenty, tall and lean, with a tanned throat and big hands holding his jeans belt. One looked Chinese, medium height and slender, but with remarkably wide shoulders under his weatherproof jacket. And the third –

Unmistakably a Maori, broad and strong, thick blue-black hair standing back from his head in waving wings, dark intense eyes, and splendid slate-blue tattoos curving from his cheekbones to his brow, coiling in close snail-shell patterns on the side of his haughty nose, tracing the firm line of his jaw.

'Jesus,' Priss breathed.

Diva's hand tightened on her arm. 'Mine,' she hissed. *'Mine.'*

Chapter Two

Diva

She woke to the sound of birds and a thin dawn light seeping through the hut's grimy little windows. For a moment she felt stunned and couldn't make sense of her surroundings, but then she realised that the other sounds she could hear were of people moving around outside. She pushed herself up, careful not to hit her head on the bunk above her, and looked around the little room.

Everybody else was still asleep. All the women, anyway. Like a hostel, the hut had separate male and female dormitories. But if there were people awake, perhaps . . . She swung her feet to the floor, felt around until she found her flip-flops, and stood up.

At the window she glanced out. There was a fire lit in the barbecue circle and a big kettle steaming on top of it, and the three men of the support team were there, busy. Nobody else seemed to be with them.

Opportunity knocking! Diva jumped back to her bunk and pulled on the thick joggers and sweatshirt she had worn last night. Not very glamorous, but nobody was going to be looking glamorous on this trip. She looked at herself in the mirror, ran her tongue over her teeth and let her hair out of the thick plait she had coaxed it into before going to sleep. It obligingly separated into a mass of wavy, shiny locks, and she grinned. Priss was so jealous of her hair. Being blonde, according to her, was no compensation for having hair that was as fine as mist and as straight as rain.

Now, was she going to do this? Was she really going to try to seduce the Maori guy today? She made her way quietly to the door, trying to decide how she felt about it. There was no doubt at all what her body wanted to do, but she felt that her mind might think better of it. After all, what would happen if her family found out? What would happen if Kabir found out?

Come on, she told herself urgently, it's hardly likely. Remember what Priss said: there's nobody else even from London. And it's your last chance, your last chance to be wild and do whatever you feel like. After this it'll be married life for you, and you'll have to be respectable.

She really didn't want to chicken out, and she knew that mental argument alone wasn't going to be enough. She needed to engage her body in this debate. So she thought of the men she had seen last night by the fire, of TJ's strong cheekbones and Roman nose, the dark tattoos heightened by the dim, oblique light. Her spine tensed and she knew that she was ready.

She walked out into the morning. It was like walking into the heart of an opal, iridescent, glowing light, so beautiful that although she had meant to go straight to the campfire she stopped and stood still, gazing around her at the dense glossy green bush and the mossy rocks and the sky that was all the colours of blue from duck-egg at one horizon to velvet at the other and flecked with clouds the colour of roses.

Trees overhung the hut, dark and massive against the pearly sky. A bird was singing among them, making a strange, resonant call, and she looked to try to see it. She couldn't make it out and became distracted by the amazing branches of the tree, like the fronds of a giant fern. She reached up to touch one of the overhanging fronds and felt it rough underneath, just like a real fern.

'You find these in coal,' said a cheerful Kiwi voice beside her.

She jumped and looked round into the dark, bright eyes of TJ. Well, she hadn't tried at all, but she didn't mind the outcome. 'Coal?' she said blankly.

'Coal, you know, black shiny stuff? They're tree ferns. They've been around so long, the species is so old, they've been fossilised and turned into coal, plants just the same as these ones you see now.'

'Wow.' She didn't have to pretend to be impressed.

'And the bird you were listening to? That's a makomako. Pakehas call it a bellbird. See it up there, with the curved bill?'

'Is *pakeha* for a white person polite or not?' Diva asked with the free curiosity of someone who was herself a non-white person.

'Polite?' TJ looked uncertain. His thick brows pulled down, accentuated by the curving, swirling tattoos.

God, he was horny. 'I mean, is it like *honky*?'

He grinned. 'Oh, I getcha. No, it just means European. Perfectly straight up.' He jerked his head towards the fire. 'You want some breakfast? Porridge is nearly ready.' He must have noticed her expression, because he went on, 'Listen, a long day's tramping and wading through a few cold streams and you'll be glad you ate your nice porridge. Anyway, there's honey to put on it.'

'Well, who could resist?' Diva said, shaking her head.

But the porridge really was good, tasty and warm and filling. A few other people had emerged now to eat it, and Steve was in the huts, waking everybody else up. Diva wrapped her hands around the tin bowl to warm them and scooped up another spoonful.

'See?' said TJ, walking past her with the coffee pot. 'I told you so.' He hesitated, then went on, 'If you want to walk with me today, I could show you the birds and plants and whatnot if you're interested. Means you'd be at the back of the group, though, I've picked tail-end-Charlie for today.'

'I'd love to,' she said, hoping that he wasn't going to ask anybody else. 'But by the time everyone's walked past there won't be that many birds left, will there?'

He grinned again. It was a wonderful expression, making his dark, haughty face look like a warrior mask. 'Hey,' he said, 'this is New Zealand. Birds here aren't frightened of people the way they are back where you come from. Besides which, I know where to look.'

'That would be great,' Diva said, and TJ nodded and moved on. Diva glanced across the fire at Priss. Priss was standing nursing a tin mug of coffee, looking slightly pained. She was crap before her first caffeine injection. Even so, she lifted her eyebrows at Diva and gave a surprised, approving nod. Good! She was impressed. Sometimes Priss thought she was the only person in the whole world who knew how to get into a bloke's trousers. Well, she was wrong, wasn't she? And today she was going to be proved wrong.

Priss's expression of admiration widened into a

smile, and Diva chuckled. They had been friends a long time and Priss could read her like a book. No doubt her sense of purpose had showed. It was going to be a fair fight, anyway: Priss already seemed to have fallen into conversation with the youngest of the support guys, the lean one. Good luck to her.

'Beautiful, isn't it?' said an Australian voice beside her. She turned and raised her eyebrows. It was the guy who had been snogging his wife on the bus, what was his name, Greg?

'Sandy and me,' Greg said, 'were wondering if you'd like to walk with us this morning, get to know each other a bit.'

He was a nice-looking guy, slim and athletic-looking, but there was something vaguely slimy about him. Was it his rather pale eyes, or the set of his mouth, or the slightly rehearsed sound of his voice? Or that oh-so-coupley *Sandy and me*? Well, whatever, she was glad to be able to say, 'Another time, maybe. I'm going to have a lesson on birds today.' For God's sake, she thought, don't say you'll tag along.

'Maybe tomorrow, then,' he suggested. He looked a bit cheesed off. Why would that be? Anyway, she didn't want to think about it. Priss could figure it out, if she wanted a puzzle.

It looked as if more or less everybody was out of the hut now, so she went in to get dressed and cleaned up. There was running water, but the hut was simple and the water was cold only and she thought she could manage without washing her hair. It was usually fine for three or four days.

She looked out of the window at the sky. There were clouds, but more blue. From all everyone said, it was never certain not to rain in these parts, but she decided to take a risk and put her combat shorts on, along with a sleeveless top and a fleece. Then she hauled out her walking boots, scowled at them and tugged them on.

'Lara Croft, here I come,' she said, looking down at herself. There was quite a strong resemblance, given her long legs and high boobs. She couldn't resist enhancing the similarity by whipping her hair back into its tight, thick plait and fastening it with a camouflage-pattern scrunchie. Then she slung on her daypack, cleaned her teeth and packed her stuff. She left her bag with the others, where the Chinese-looking support bloke was loading them on to the horses. He glanced at her, but didn't smile or say anything. Which was OK, as her target for the day was TJ.

Breakfast was more or less over and the support team had begun to clear up. Diva didn't like watching other people work, so she got stuck in, collecting the tin plates and coffee cups. 'Where do you want these?' she said to the youngest guy as he passed her hauling the enormous kettle.

'TJ's got the washing up,' he said, 'over there.'

TJ was standing by the sinks at the back of the hut. Approaching from behind him, she noticed how sturdy and muscular his legs were, dark beneath faded khaki shorts. Juggling the washing up into one hand, she reached out and touched the back of his thigh and said, 'Boo.'

He jumped. 'Jesus, you crept up on me!' His eyes met hers, and they were dark and hot and hopeful and she knew that touch had done it. Just a touch, but in such a strange intimate place, on bare skin. He had felt hard, like wood or stone.

'Thought you were supposed to be some sort of a bushman,' she teased. 'Where are your super-sharp senses?'

'Just you wait until I have the jump on you,' he threatened.

'Later,' she said promisingly.

He grinned. Then his face changed as he saw someone coming up behind them. 'Hope you don't mind horses,' he said cheerfully.

Diva actually wasn't that fond of horses, being a town girl through and through, but she didn't want to look like a wuss. 'Horses are cool,' she said, throwing back her plait.

He smiled now, and she could see that he liked the plait. And the rest of her, she thought. It was as if they had made a contract, spat on the palms of their hands and shaken. It was just that she didn't know when exactly delivery would be.

It took surprisingly little time to load the gear on to the horses, and before the sun was strong enough to cast sharp shadows they were on their way. As always, Diva found the speed of walking deceptive. Looking ahead, at the string of people and horses moving ahead of her, they seemed to be going at no more than a crawl. But when she turned and looked back, in seemingly no time they had left the hut far behind and headed up the muddy track into the deep forest. They might be the only people alive in the world, and the dense vegetation muted the sounds they made, so that she could hardly hear the couple walking in front of her as they talked to each other. The only things she could hear clearly were the quiet sounds of her own footfalls and the jingling tack of the horse TJ was leading.

Because the woods were so dense they walked strung out and only occasionally did she see the front of the line. Priss was up there ahead of everybody else, her blonde hair glinting in the strengthening sun. She looked as if she was busy talking to the young support guy, what was his name? Josh, that was it.

'So,' said TJ, 'what brings you here, ah, Dee, was it?'

'Diva,' said Diva, because only Priss was allowed to call her Dee. 'Well, actually, Priss won this holiday. Just some stupid prize draw thing that you get entered for when you buy something. Nobody was more surprised than me.'

TJ looked surprised. 'Wow. So you're not a tramper usually, then?'

'Never done it before,' Diva admitted. 'But I'm pretty fit, so I'm not too worried.'

His grin broadened. 'Even fit people don't always like tramping. Too much roughing it, you know?'

She turned and paused in her step. 'I like roughing it,' she said.

Again that meeting of eyes, that chill through her spine. He was so horny, and sometime today she was going to have him. She was hollow and hungry just thinking of it. When would it be, and how? Would she choose the time, or would he? She hoped it would be her. She always liked to be in control, if possible.

And what if someone else saw them? Well, time to get over worrying about that, for a start. If Priss had her way they would all be at it by the end of the trek, so if anyone did watch her and TJ they would only be gaining a small time advantage on the rest of the group.

They came out of the trees on to an open area and she could see the rest of the group walking ahead of them. The path was narrow and they were strung out across the hillside like beads on a wire. Priss was still in front with Josh and a couple of the horses, and now the woman from the bus, Sandy, was walking with them. Behind them Rick, the tall, dark-haired guy she had marked out as a game-player, was walking alone, head turned to show off his fine jaw as he admired the landscape. Then came the Chinese guy with two more horses, and then Steve with the older couple, Alan and Jan, chatting to the youngster, Jason, who had been bunked up with Rick. Then the two younger women, the skinny one and the black one, walking with Greg. It looked as if Greg was hitting on the black girl now. He was probably one of those white guys who found non-white women attractive and thought he was supercool because of it. Diva disliked him even more, just on principle.

Then the two older women, falling back towards her and TJ. One of them, a petite, fit-looking woman with short hair and an attractive, mobile face, said, 'TJ, Steve says if we walk with you, you can tell us all about the birds and stuff.'

'That's right,' said TJ. He didn't look at Diva, but she could sense his mouth twitching ruefully. When were they going to get some solitude? How could it work?

She dropped back and to the side and walked where she could watch TJ's strong, muscular arse working beneath his shorts. He had tied the horse's reins to his belt, leaving his hands free to gesture, and his sleeveless T-shirt revealed big polished arms. There was another tattoo on his left bicep, an intricate coiled spiral, following the lines of the muscle. She wanted to run her fingers along it.

Before the other two women had joined them she had been enjoying the anticipation. Now that she didn't have the opportunity to do anything about it, it turned to frustration. Why had they interrupted? Sure, they were interested in the indigenous wildlife. Well, so was she, and she meant to get very close to it, and she wanted to do it soon.

The short-haired woman, whose name was Kathy, was chatting cheerfully to TJ, asking him about the Maori language and culture. He was telling her the names of all the plants in Maori and pointing out features of the landscape. Of course he would be a magnet to everyone on the tour, he was bound to be. Such an interesting background, and gorgeous too! All the more reason to lay claim to him fast. The other woman, Kathy's bunkmate, had hardly said a word, other than to introduce herself as Julie. She was tall and willowy, with soft brown eyes and an expression of passivity which the predator in Diva recognised as a signal. She wondered briefly if anyone else on the tour would be aware of it. Rick the game-player, for sure. And anyone else? Not that she had noticed so far, but she didn't want to rule anything out.

They walked for a couple of hours and then took a short break during which people sat on rocks and ate energy bars and the horses tilted their hooves and snatched at the lush vegetation around them. Then they set off to walk the second stage before lunch. Kathy and Julie seemed to be glued to them like limpets. Diva scowled and marched along in the shelter of the horse, muttering, 'Fuck off, fuck off,' beneath her breath.

They didn't get the message. But time passed, and the countryside was beautiful, and eventually she simply settled down to wait, like a cat at a mousehole.

And, like a cat at a mousehole, eventually she was rewarded. Steve ambled back along the line, all lean tanned legs and droopy sunstreaked hair, looking rather like an amiable Afghan hound. He pointed at a tall rock outcrop ahead of them, high over the landscape and backed by tall trees. 'Lunch up there,' he said.

TJ said, 'Steve, mate, I know there's a bit of water up behind the crag there, but you never know whether there'll be enough for everything. I'll stop at the next stream and let this horse drink. Catch you up in a while, yeah?'

'Don't miss out on lunch; this lot look like right vultures,' Steve warned with a grin, then set off back towards the front of the line, long legs eating up the trail.

There was nothing in TJ's expression to suggest that he had taken this action on purpose, but Diva was convinced that he had. She concealed her grin and shook herself into talking to Kathy and Julie, seeing that it wouldn't be long now. They seemed nice people, interesting, but not exactly brimming over with erotic possibility. For a while she wondered just how Priss proposed to carry this off. Then she saw a stream ahead of them, lying across the path in a spill of silver, and she knew that this would be it.

All her pent-up excitement released itself, flooding her body with heat. She felt full, generous, brimming over. Her breasts lifted and through three layers of clothing her nipples began to show. She caught her lower lip in her teeth to keep in a sharp breath and jammed her hands into the pockets of her shorts. How long was it since she had had sex in the open air? There weren't that many opportunities for a London dweller. The last time had been at some office party, years ago, in a shrubbery around the back of a marquee at the Hurlingham Club. Not quite as al fresco as this, with the sun streaming through the leaves and water rushing down from the mountains.

'You go on up,' TJ said vaguely, in the direction of all of them, when they reached the stream. 'This horse takes his time; I'll be a while.'

Kathy and Julie nodded and splashed across the stream. They had all been told that there was no point in trying to keep their boots dry; there was just too much water in New Zealand, and everybody seemed quite relaxed about it. Diva said, 'I'll wait here and walk up with you,' and the others didn't miss a beat.

As Kathy and Julie walked away TJ walked the horse into the stream and gave him his head. The horse stuck his nose into the clear water and began to drink, making snuffling, hoovering noises. TJ looked down at the horse. Had she missed something? Was he not interested?

Perhaps he was waiting for her to make the first move. Well, that was fine by her. She stepped up behind him, into the cold stream, and glanced up the path. Kathy and Julie were still just in sight, making their way up the hill. The water found its way over the top of her already wet boots, and she didn't care. She smiled and let out a long, satisfied breath and put both her hands on the splendid curves of TJ's arse.

This time he didn't jump. He didn't move. He said in a low voice, 'You can't possibly know what it's like walking for half the morning with a stiffy like a dinosaur bone.'

Mmm, that sounded very nice. 'You can't possibly know what it's like walking for half the morning with wet knickers.'

He began to turn towards her, but she put her hands on his back to keep him still. 'No, don't move.' She returned her hands to his arse and then moved them down to the bottom of his shorts, on to the skin of his thighs, up inside the shorts, where his skin was warm and slightly damp –

And strangely ridged. She caught her breath, unsure of what she had felt and wanting to see before she did anything more. She moved her hands to the front of his shorts, reaching for his fly.

He wasn't kidding about the stiffy. There it was beneath the zip of the shorts, hot and bulging. Were Maoris rumoured to have cocks as huge as African black men? She hoped so. Her personal lifetime sample of two black guys had been extremely satisfactory from that standpoint.

He still didn't move, which pleased her. She liked a bloke who knew how to stand and take it. A quick look up the path told her that the others were out of sight, screened from them by rocks and trees. She smiled and quickly, deftly unbuttoned the shorts and whizzed the zip open.

When she touched him he dropped the horse's leading rein and sucked in a quick breath. She wrapped one hand around him and weighed his cock thoughtfully, testing its weight, its springy thickness. It was hot and hard and she couldn't wait any longer to see it, so she squeezed around in front of him, between him and the warm bulk of the horse, too eager even to be nervous. The horse snorted and moved away slightly and she put her other hand on the nape of his neck and looked down.

It was gorgeous, dark and thick and proud, and gleaming with urgency. She slowly lifted her eyes, knowing that he would be looking at her, and he was – with the expression of a man wrestling with the fact that he had too much pride to beg.

He still didn't move, and his silent, implicit acknowledgement of her control made her shiver with wanting him. She leaned forward, lifting her face, and let her lips hover in front of his, making him wait. He closed his eyes and she felt his breath hiss in and out. After a few tormenting seconds she let her mouth brush his, no tongue yet, just a delicate touch, and he let out a little moan. Then she pressed her lips on to his a little more firmly and now the tip of her tongue just slipped into his open mouth, questing and withdrawing almost at once.

'Jesus,' he whispered, and she smiled and let her lips move to his cheek, the flat haughty plane of his cheek where the tattoos coiled and twisted. They felt strange, corrugated, and suddenly she thought that that was what the skin of his thighs had felt like and she frowned and pushed both hands inside his shorts and looked down.

He was tattooed there too, beneath his shorts, over his buttocks and the top inch or so of his strong thighs, deep curving grooves of blue-black parting the brown gloss of his skin. For a moment she was shocked, and she looked up into his face, knowing that she had lost her composure, knowing that it would show.

He smiled, though he was still breathing quickly. 'Important place for a warrior to carry *moko*,' he said. 'Got to be able to insult your enemies good and proper, yeah?'

She couldn't help but imagine how much it must have hurt. The thought made her gentle, sorry for him. She didn't want to torment him any longer. She let her fingers trace the strange furrows across his buttocks, and slowly, steadily she dropped to her knees, letting the cold stream of water run over her calves and up her thighs, concentrating only on opening her mouth and extending her tongue to lap at the broad shining head of his cock.

His breath hissed again as she licked him, and she shut her eyes tightly, completely absorbed by the extraordinary sensation of tasting him, smelling him, while all the time the stream licked at her thighs and crept chillingly up her shorts.

He had a lot of self-control. She liked that and, instead of taking him in her mouth at once, she licked him delicately, gently, slipping the tip of her tongue under the shelf of his cock head, waiting for the bead of dew to appear and then lifting it off as lightly as a bee sucking nectar, flickering the blade up and down the length of his shaft until he was shiny and wet with her saliva. When she glanced up she saw his eyes tight shut and his nostrils flaring like a racehorse's.

What now, what now? She was torn. She really was wet for him, aching, but she also wanted to make him come in her mouth. She wasn't sure if they would have the time to do it twice. It was easy to imagine someone wandering back down the path to find out what had become of them, and she still felt uncomfortable about being discovered *in flagrante*.

Better make it quick, then. Take the opportunity to demonstrate her skill, her control. She brushed her lips against the whole length of his quivering cock, opened her mouth and took him in.

When he felt her lips close around him he let out a suffocated cry and his whole body tensed. She sensed that he was trying not to thrust into her mouth and, although she appreciated that he was letting her stay in charge, she wanted to feel that strength surging towards her. So she caught hold of his buttocks and tugged at them. He got her drift immediately and pushed his thick cock deep into her mouth, right to the back of her throat, almost making her gag. Quickly she compressed her lips on him, holding him tightly, sucking hard to acknowledge his urgency. He thrust again and this time she just touched him with her teeth, letting him feel the danger, and she squeezed hard with one hand at the base of his cock, massaging his taut balls. He groaned again and his cock twitched and shuddered and she gave it to him hard, sliding her lips up and down as fast as she could and sucking at the end of each stroke. She knew he wouldn't last long and after only a few moments he gasped and staggered and his cock jerked and pulsed in her mouth. She swallowed quickly, once, twice, and then again. There was plenty of come in him. It tasted good, salty and pleasant, without any tinge of bitterness. She released him gently and looked up into his astonished face.

'Bloody hell,' he said. 'Do you do that for a living?'

Without doubt that was a compliment. She smiled and tried to stand up and found that the freezing water had drained all sensation from her legs, so that what was meant to be a sirenesque slither became an undignified stagger. He caught her arm, looking concerned. 'Jesus, you all right?'

'My legs have gone to sleep,' she said. He helped her across to the bank, sat her down on a patch of sand, then began to chafe her knees and calves, rubbing them hard all over with his big hands. The sensation of warmth returning was delicious. She lay back on the sand, letting her legs part, feeling the sun and his touch bring her frozen limbs back towards their normal temperature, her skin one big shiver of delight. The cold seemed to have left her acutely sensitised, and she was so desperate to come that she would have humped herself against a rock if he hadn't been there. When he let his hands stray to the edges of her damp shorts, rubbing the insides of her still-chilly thighs, she arched her back and moaned, 'For fuck's sake, TJ, go down on me.'

He gave her one quick startled glance then grabbed at her shorts, tugging them open so fast she was afraid he would burst the button. He pulled them down, wrestled them over one boot and left them dangling from her other ankle as he threw himself to the sand and buried his face between her spread thighs.

In such a feverish hurry she was afraid he would be greedy, gobble and suck and make her flinch when her whole body was so sensitive that a single touch would probably be enough. But she needn't have worried. He drew in one long, luxurious breath, as if he wanted to inhale the very essence of her. Then he brushed his nose against her bush just where it adjoined her clit, swishing the curling fur this way and that. He leaned his cheek against her thigh and she closed her eyes tightly as she felt the ridges of his tattoos grate ever so slightly against her skin.

For a moment she thought that he was going to make her wait the way she had kept him waiting, tease and torment her in revenge. But almost as the thought crossed her mind he touched her clit with his tongue, so gently that she couldn't restrain a cry of agony and delight.

It was so simple. He didn't do anything fancy like sticking his tongue up her or touching her arsehole or putting his fingers inside her. He just lapped at her clit, very gently, very steadily, until the waves of pleasure built up inside her and her body tightened and her head fell back and she grasped at the sand with both hands as she tried to keep still, to keep quiet, to draw out the moment, not push herself against him like the rutting bitch she was. And he went on, and it was so exquisite that she knew she was going to come and she couldn't keep silent any more. She arched up from the sand, clutching at his head with both hands and crying out, one desperate shout of fulfilment.

She let go of him and sat panting and shaking. He

drew back and sat on his haunches, looking into her face, and then up the track. 'Someone's going to have heard that,' he said quickly. 'They'll come down to see what's up.'

Looking where he looked, she saw the bushes moving. Some quick thinking was required. She scrambled up from the sand, tugged up her shorts, ran two steps to the river and let herself fall into a deep pool. The horse, grazing at the edge of the stream, snorted and pranced away, and TJ laughed and ran after it to catch it as she pulled herself from the water, dripping and shivering and fastening her shorts.

Steve emerged on the track, looking anxious. 'Hey, is everything OK? I didn't know where you'd got to and then I heard –' He saw Diva's soaked state and grinned. 'Oh, I get it. Take a dip, did you?'

'I slipped,' Diva said, panting. The shock of the icy water so soon after her warm delicious orgasm had almost driven the breath from her. 'I was trying to lead the horse over, and I slipped.'

He grinned. 'What's TJ doing letting you take risks like that?' This was clearly not a serious remark. 'Come on up to the camp; there's lunch and the tea's nearly made. There's sun up there too; you can warm up. Take your boots off and let them dry out.'

'Sounds great,' Diva said, shivering.

Steve headed up the track ahead of them and, as they climbed, TJ whispered, 'Are you all right?'

She glanced sideways at him. 'Absolutely terrific,' she said, 'if a bit cold right now.'

'Here.' He pulled a fleece from behind the horse's pack and draped it over her shoulders. 'You don't want to catch cold.'

She'd achieved her task for the day, but perhaps she could do more. TJ hadn't bothered with small talk;

they'd hardly exchanged a word. He'd clearly been up for straightforward sex, no complications. 'TJ,' she said, keeping her voice low, 'you know what Priss and I have in mind?' No need to tell him that it had been Priss's idea. 'We thought it would be fun to try to get everyone in the group having some sex before the end of the trek. Like a relay race, if you like.' His eyes widened, but he didn't look shocked, only amused. 'Would be nice to be able to rely on some male help. You've got the baton now, and I was wondering if you'd pass it on. Are you up for it?'

He hesitated, and she knew that he was thinking his way through the women on the trek. Who knows, perhaps the men too. After a while his face cleared and he said, 'Yeah, count me in.'

'I'll let you know the plans,' Diva said, and then they were at the lunch site and she had done it!

People were solicitous, bringing her plates and cups and dry socks. She sat down by the fire on a flat rock and marvelled for a few moments at the view. The lunch site was high up and on a small plateau of open rock, commanding a great vista of the valley laced with streams that they had just walked through. She warmed herself up by the fire and wrapped herself around some food, and after a while Priss came and sat next to her. 'You OK?'

Diva grinned. 'Just a quick cover-up. I wouldn't recommend it straight after though, it's a bit of a shock.'

'Lucky bugger. I haven't managed Josh yet; we couldn't get the opportunity. He's gagging for it though.'

'TJ's up for helping out with the Grand Plan,' Diva said proudly.

Priss looked impressed. 'Hey, great! Is he any good?'

Diva nodded judiciously. 'I would say so.'

'Great. I reckon Josh is likely to be a bit callow, if you know what I mean.'

Diva glanced over to where Josh was sitting drinking a cup of tea and looking at Priss with ill-disguised hunger. Callow was an accurate description. She nodded, and Priss went on, 'Well, if you get the chance, tell him we might need him tomorrow. I think we could have a go at Sandy.'

'Sandy by all means,' Diva said, 'but not her other half. He's a creep.'

'He is, isn't he? He's been making up to Zoe all morning.'

'Only after he failed with me.'

'Well, we'll leave him till later. Perhaps someone else will fancy him,' Priss said hopefully.

'Anyway, he's already had sex,' Diva pointed out.

'Yeah, but that was with his *wife*. That doesn't count.'

Diva took another bite of food and stretched. She was warming up and feeling ready for anything. TJ was eating on the other side of the fire, ostentatiously avoiding her eyes. She tilted her head back to look up at the brilliant blue sky and the lush green of the forest canopy.

'I am looking forward to this,' she said, and smiled.

Chapter Three

Sandy

She came slowly awake, puzzled by a really weird combination of familiar and unfamiliar things. The unfamiliar ones were all around her: the greenish light filtering through the sides of the tent, the sounds of birds in the canopy, the rushing of water from the nearby stream, the snap and sweet smoky smell of wood burning on the campfire nearby. The familiar, well, that was the warmth of Greg pressed up against her, the smell of his aroused body, the feel of his hand between her legs, fingers exploring, seeking out the places he knew well, the special spots that would drive her wild.

'Greg,' she hissed, arching her back to try to squeeze away from him, 'for God's sake, someone will hear us.'

'You didn't care about that last night, did you?' His fingers settled on her clit, teasing and pressing, making her shut her eyes tight and struggle against the urge to moan.

'Last night was different,' Sandy insisted. 'Everybody must have heard those two girls at it. I even think that other couple was doing it as well, and anyway night time is – *different*! Oh, Jesus!' His thumb slipped around her clit, avoiding the supersensitive tip, and then the ball of his thumb just brushed over it and she almost sobbed. 'Greg, please, don't.'

'This trip is going to be great,' Greg hissed, pressing himself closer to her and easing the tip of one finger into her cunt. She was still sticky from last night and her damp flesh offered no resistance. 'Those two, Priss and Diva, they're really up for it. It's going to be one big long party.'

She couldn't stop herself from pushing towards his finger, wanting to feel it slide right up inside her. At once he withdrew it. He was such a bastard, such a tease: he always liked to make her beg for it. She gritted her teeth and tried to pretend that she wasn't turned on. 'It's different at a party,' she said, and her reluctance was genuine. 'If people come to a party to swing everybody knows what they're getting into. People came here expecting to walk, Greg, for God's sake.'

He grinned down at her and flicked his fingers against her clit, one-two one-two one-two, and with his other hand he caressed the ample curve of her breast. 'If people don't want to join in, they don't have to,' he said. 'There's plenty of bush, isn't there? Plenty of places to go.'

'Can you imagine having sex in the bush back home?' she asked, still amazed by it. 'You'd be stepping on a snake or lying on a funnelweb before you knew it. I still can't believe that nothing out here will hurt you. One poisonous spider! One! How about that?'

'Make the most of it, then,' he said. He caught her erect nipple between thumb and forefinger and squeezed it, gently first, then hard, and as she gasped he pushed two fingers into her cunt and moved them in and out, fast, rubbing at her clit with his thumb. The suddenness of the pleasure made her moan and jerk her hips towards his working hand, orgasm hovering only a few inches away and any second now she would be able to reach out and grasp it. 'God,' she whispered under her breath. 'God, God –'

He stopped as suddenly as he had started, pulling his fingers out of her, teasing them through the red curls of her pubes, tormenting her. 'Greg,' she whimpered, 'Greg!'

'You gotta beg me,' he smiled, tugging at her nipple. 'Oh yeah, baby, you gotta beg me.'

Although she was so aroused that she would do practically anything, she still felt a tinge of irritation at him. Why did he have to talk like a bloke out of a corny porno video? He only ever called her *baby* when they were having sex and she hated it. And she never told him because when she hated it she always wanted him more and she didn't want him to stop. Now, the same as all the other times, she lifted herself towards his hand and moaned, 'Please, Greg.'

His fingers returned to her clit, touching her so lightly that it was more frustrating than satisfying. 'Louder.'

'Please!' she hissed, trying to rub herself against his hand.

'Louder!' he insisted, running the tip of one finger down her lips to her bottom, circling her arsehole and then returning to her clit.

Everybody in the camp would know they were having sex. Well, shit, right now she didn't care. 'Please!' she said, almost loud enough to make him jump.

'Keep saying it, baby,' Greg said, as his finger began to flick against her throbbing clit. 'Keep saying it.'

'Please,' she moaned, letting her head fall back as the touch of his fingers began to make her come. 'Please, please, please.' God, he was so good at this, she could put up with him being a bit of a prick sometimes as long as he could do this to her. He finger-fucked her better even than she could do it to herself; there was something about the way his fingers squirmed inside her and curled against her clit that was totally irresistible. 'Please!' she wailed, letting her body sink into orgasm and shudder helplessly.

'God, baby, you look so good when you come.' He caught hold of her legs and pushed them apart, climbed on top of her and slid his cock inside her. She didn't care what he did now; she was completely relaxed, letting him do anything he wanted. He pushed himself into her to the hilt and then began to thrust, jerky stabbing movements, clutching at her breasts and hissing, 'Baby, baby.'

She thought he would come quickly, but he didn't. He put his hands under her thighs and lifted them, rolling her back until her knees were over his shoulders and she was completely open to him. 'You look so dirty,' he hissed as he fucked her. 'You look as if you'd let anybody fuck you. You would, baby, if I asked you, wouldn't you? You'd fuck anyone, wouldn't you?'

Suddenly she had an image of herself on hands and knees, taking one man from behind as another fucked her in her mouth. Despite all the parties and the clubs and the staged events it still had the power to turn her on. She knew that if she told Greg about it, it would really excite him too. But she didn't want to tell him. It was her fantasy; she wanted to keep it. Greg wanted to own her fantasies, own everything about her. This vision was private – it was hers. She just murmured, 'Yes, Greg, yes,' because she knew that that was what he liked to hear.

He leaned forward and hissed, 'I'd like to see that Maori guy fuck you. I'd like to see him slide his big black cock into you. I'll fuck that black girl Zoe while he does it. Jesus, can you imagine, you're so pale, it would be –' He stopped, teeth bared, caught unawares by his climax. After a moment he let her slump down and lay on top of her, whispering, 'Christ.'

Sandy closed her eyes. She enjoyed this moment, when she felt how she had made him weak, how all his strength had been poured in to her. It made her feel powerful. Greg thought he was the top dog in their relationship, just because it was him that suggested things, her that accepted them. But she knew that he needed to exert his power over her more than she needed to feel it. Having her, watching her with other people, made him feel as if he was strong. Underneath it, she didn't really think that he was. She thought he was weak and, once he had come inside her, she saw his weakness and enjoyed it.

Eventually she said, 'Greg, I can hear people moving around. It must be breakfast time.'

He shook himself out of his daze and said, 'Yeah. Yeah, I could eat too.'

By the time they got out of the tent, most of the rest of the party were gathered around the fire, eating breakfast, which was cereal this morning. Sandy tried to look as if she felt embarrassed about the noise she had been making, but she didn't really. Really she was quite pleased that people would know that she was highly sexed, that she enjoyed herself in the sack. That was the other good thing about Greg, the way he pushed her to do things that she felt she ought not to do but got a real kick out of when she did them. It wasn't as if she didn't know what she would do without him or anything, but after all these years – and it had been a few – she was still excited by being with him.

Greg came and sat down next to her. He'd got himself a cup of coffee but hadn't brought her one, which was typical. He said in a low voice, 'Listen, I'm going to have another go at Diva today. If she's as hot as she sounded last night I can't believe she wouldn't be interested in us.'

Sandy thought that Diva had already found her fun in the Maori guy, but she didn't say so. All she said was, 'I thought you fancied Zoe.'

'Yeah, I do, sure, but she's too uptight for me.' That was code for *she turned me down*, of course. 'So I'll concentrate on Diva again, and you can have a go at her friend – what's her name?'

'Priss.'

'Yeah, Priss. Bloody stupid Pom name, isn't it?'

'Don't know, I think it's nice.' Sandy actually rather admired Priss, her confident stride, her strong stance and direct look. She seemed like a woman who didn't need a man to give her ideas. In fact, it seemed more likely that she had plans for Greg rather than vice versa.

'Well, you won't mind keeping her out of my way then, will you?' Greg said with a grin.

'D'you want to fetch me a coffee?' she demanded, nettled.

'Hey, I thought you wouldn't want one,' he said.

Typical, always trying to make himself look thoughtful. 'Well, I do,' she contradicted him.

'No sweat. Be right back.'

He went over to the kettle and Sandy looked around for Priss and Diva. There they were, standing across by the horses with TJ and the other kid who was carrying the bags, she couldn't remember his name. There was something about the way they were standing, something about the distances between them that made her sure that something was going on. The kid was clearly smitten with Priss – he looked at her the way a puppy looks at its owner when it wants to play with its favourite toy – and Diva and TJ were laughing together with peculiar intimacy. They made a handsome couple, certainly, Diva's perfect café-au-lait skin smooth against the gleam and furrows of TJ's tattoos. Diva had her hair loose today and it was magnificent, halfway down her back in shining waves. Sandy wasn't actually jealous because she liked her own red-gold hair, but you had to admire the sheer gorgeousness and resilience of Diva's locks. She would have looked like a princess if she hadn't been wearing the same battered shorts as yesterday and a khaki fleece over a camouflage-pattern singlet, as if they were on a military exercise rather than a holiday.

Priss glanced in her direction and saw her looking. She smiled welcomingly and Sandy felt encouraged. She got up and went over to join the group.

'Hi,' Priss said. She looked intensely amused. 'Sounds like it's a good morning.'

Sandy lifted her eyebrows. 'Sounded like last night was a good night.'

The kid – what was his name? – shuffled his feet and made an uncertain face. 'Ah, think I'd better go and check all the tents are packed,' he said. 'TJ, you coming?'

TJ hesitated and Diva said, 'I'll come and help out.'

'Right,' TJ said, and Diva grinned at Priss and followed the two men towards the horse pickets.

'We'll be off in a few minutes,' Priss said, tucking her chin-length blonde hair behind one ear. 'Want to walk with me this morning?'

This was a very innocuous comment, but something about Priss's look told Sandy that it had a real meaning behind it. Priss was wearing cut-off jean shorts and a white T-shirt with long sleeves, and she had an air of, well, energy. She didn't exactly look predatory, but she did look distinctly interested. She definitely had plans of some sort. Sandy smiled and said, 'Yeah.'

'Got your water and everything?'

'Yeah –' Sandy rummaged rather uncertainly in her rucksack to check that her two big water bottles were there. She held up a rather crushed snack bar. 'Goodies,' she said.

'Good plan. I've got about half a ton of trail mix in my rucksack. Can't risk running out of food, can we?'

Thank God she wasn't one of those women who look on walking miles every day as a reason to eat even less and lose weight. 'You sound like my kind of girl,' Sandy said with approval.

They set off quite soon. For the first few minutes there wasn't a lot of conversation because people moved around, sorting themselves out into a string to walk along the narrow trail, easing towards the front or the back depending on their pace and inclination. Sandy and Priss were quite near the front, not far behind Steve, who was leading today with the silent Chinese guy, and the two younger girls, the athletic-looking black Zoe and her skinny friend Sarah. Sandy glanced over her shoulder as they climbed the first hill and saw to her surprise that Diva was not far behind them, and that she was walking with Greg. They were even talking together.

'Well, there's one for the record books,' she said, loud enough to be overheard.

Priss looked curious and followed the direction of her glance and, when she saw Diva and Greg in conversation, Sandy thought that her reaction was a bit odd. She didn't actually look surprised.

What did she know that Sandy didn't? 'I thought,' she fished, 'that Diva was getting on rather well with TJ yesterday.'

'Well,' Priss replied, rather cautiously Sandy thought, 'she was, yes.'

There was absolutely no doubt that Sandy and Greg had overheard Priss and Diva having sex last night, and two women who were prepared to have sex loud enough to be overheard by a bunch of complete strangers had to be pretty bloody upfront about this kind of thing, so Sandy felt emboldened to say, 'I was so sure of it that I almost told Greg this morning that he wouldn't stand a chance with her.'

There was a little silence. Priss looked at her attentively, as if measuring her up, and then frowned slightly. 'You two are swingers, I take it.'

If she knew the term enough to use it so easily, Sandy was relaxed about it. She smiled broadly, as to another kindred spirit. 'Yeah, we are. You?'

Priss shook her head. 'No. Well, not exactly. Not to date.'

What was she getting at? Bloody English people always talked around things rather than just saying what they meant. Impatiently, Sandy said, 'So, do you reckon Greg stands a chance with her?'

Priss's smile was suddenly like a good-natured shark's. 'I wouldn't think so. I asked her to talk to him to keep him occupied. So that I could have a free rein with you.'

Sandy opened her mouth, then closed it. All of a sudden she found herself speechless.

She didn't know what to say. All these years she had been with Greg, swinging round the clock and having sex with all sorts of people; all these years, she'd been doing what he asked. Never, not once, had she made the decision for herself.

She'd had sex with men because he asked her, and with women because he wanted to watch. She'd dressed up in kinky gear and crawled around and done whatever he wanted because she loved him and because it was the best sex she had ever had, and because he made it fun and interesting and always praised her for it.

But she'd never chosen, not really. And now this little English woman, with her bright eyes and her direct stare, had decoyed Greg away from her and offered herself. And she could choose!

'Did I shock you?' Priss sounded puzzled. 'I thought this would be no big deal.'

She didn't want Priss to realise that it had always been Greg with the ideas! 'No, no, I'm not shocked,' Sandy said hastily. 'I was just feeling sorry for Greg. He thinks Diva's really horny.'

'Got a bit of a thing for women of colour, has he?'

Sandy looked intently at Priss and saw someone who looked as if she could take pretty much anything. 'Definitely,' she said, 'and to be honest, I think he'd love to see me with TJ.'

Priss's Cheshire cat grin appeared again, crinkling her eyes and spreading slowly over her face. 'Well,' she said, 'if you fancy TJ personally, I'm sure something could be arranged. Though I'm not sure what he'd think about Greg being involved.'

'So Diva did get him yesterday!' Sandy was delighted that her intuition had been right. 'I knew it.'

'Absolutely spot on, sweetie,' Priss said. 'And –' She hesitated, then stopped.

'What?' Sandy was eaten up with curiosity. 'What?'

'Nothing.' Priss looked down at the path, shook her head a little.

'No, what? You gotta tell me. About Diva and TJ? What about them?' Sandy knew she was sounding like a little girl, tugging at a grown-up's hand and whimpering, but that had always worked with Greg.

It didn't seem to work with Priss, who was busy with her water bottle and taking a drink. 'Why won't you tell me?' Sandy whined.

'Because it's a secret,' Priss said, with a sudden direct look, 'and I don't know if you can keep secrets.'

'Sure I can!' Sandy exclaimed, hurt. 'I keep loads of secrets. For girlfriends and stuff.'

'Even from Greg?'

That was harder, and she hesitated, frowning.

'You'd have to keep it from Greg, you see,' Priss went on calmly, 'because, quite frankly, Diva thinks he's a creep.'

Sandy opened her mouth, then closed it.

A creep! Who was this Pommy cow to call her husband a creep?

And yet, didn't she think he was a bit of a creep herself, sometimes? The way things always had to go his way, the way he didn't think to fetch her a cup of coffee and then covered it up? The way he called her 'baby' in that awful corny way, and always left the kitchen in a mess and never put his socks in the washing basket? Was it such a big deal that someone called him a creep and asked her to keep a secret from him?

She said with sudden decisiveness, 'You can trust me all right. I won't tell Greg anything. I promise.'

Priss looked thoughtful and for a moment Sandy thought she was going to refuse all the same. But then she said, 'OK. It wasn't about TJ and Diva, actually. It was about the other guy, Josh.'

'The tall kid, is that his name, Josh?' Priss nodded, and Sandy chuckled. 'He's got the hots for you, that's for sure.'

'Only because I told him yesterday that I'd like to suck his dick,' Priss said with a grin. 'That often works.'

Sandy glanced around, wondering if Josh was in sight, but he wasn't. They were surrounded by dense, green forest. She called him to mind and said musingly, 'He's pretty cute, I suppose. As long as Diva's got TJ, that is.'

'Oh sure, TJ's the one I would prefer, but Diva sort of booked him,' Priss said. 'For the moment, anyway.'

Sandy shrugged. 'So what about Josh? Did you suck his dick?' She thought she sounded pretty cool, but in fact talking like this about sex, without Greg, talking in this matter-of-fact, woman-to-woman way, felt quite new and exciting. She suppressed a shiver.

'I didn't get a chance, actually. So he's all excited about the prospect today. And then I thought about you and, well, I really fancied you.' Priss's eyes met Sandy's, bright with frank admiration. 'But I'd sort of promised Josh. So I wondered if you'd, well, if you'd mind if we worked it out so that he could join us.'

'Join us,' Sandy repeated. She felt a bit weak now and if it hadn't been for the knowledge of the others behind her she would have stopped walking.

'I hoped,' Priss said, 'that when we stop for lunch, you might come away with me and, well . . .' She hesitated, but her eyes said everything.

Sandy licked her lips and swallowed. How long was it since someone had gone after her, just her, rather than her as Greg's wife, his sexual sidekick? She couldn't remember. Not since before Greg. It made her feel so good, to be pursued.

And she could say no if she wanted! She could choose! There was no arguing with it: it was a real turn-on.

So what she said was, 'I'd like that.'

Priss smiled. She had a great smile, which started slowly and then spread to light up her whole face. She glanced up and down the track and then, very swiftly, stepped in front of Sandy and steadied her face with her hand and kissed her.

Sandy just closed her eyes as Priss's warm tongue slipped into her mouth. She was shaky with lust, but also vividly conscious of the other members of the trek approaching from behind them, about to appear around the turn in the track, about to see them, two women standing in the middle of a forest kissing.

Priss must have thought about that too, because after only a moment she stepped back, still smiling. 'More later,' she said. 'Let's walk.'

Sandy nodded and set off, her heart pounding. She turned to look behind and saw that they were only just in time because the others were coming into sight behind them. Greg was still walking with Diva, she saw, but now they had been joined by the older single guy, she couldn't remember his name. He was talking to Diva, and Greg was looking sulky.

For a moment she felt sorry for him. Perhaps she

ought to drop back and talk to him and make him feel better, get him involved.

But only for a moment. This was her sex adventure; she didn't want to share it with Greg.

'Let's not make it look obvious,' Priss said. 'Come on, let's go and catch up the guys in front, just for now.'

Sandy would rather have had sex right away, that minute, but she could see the point, so she just speeded up to follow Priss. As she walked she thought it was quite funny that Greg had asked her to talk to Priss so that he would have a chance with Diva, and all the time Diva and Priss had been planning just the opposite. It was funny, and it was flattering too. She watched Priss's strong bare legs walking ahead of her, her firm arse shifting under her shorts, and imagined herself unfastening the shorts and pulling them down and putting her face between Priss's legs, smelling her, licking her. Normally she only went with women because it turned Greg on, but now the idea was turning her on too. She couldn't wait.

Of course, she had to wait while they walked for miles. It was a beautiful walk, and a beautiful day too, without a cloud in the sky, never mind rain. Sandy searched in her pack for her sun hat and her factor 50 and wondered whether they would find somewhere shady to go.

Priss was talking to Steve and the two girls. Sandy didn't really feel like talking, because she was too horny, so she looked at the men instead. Steve was chatting in his laid-back way. He looked like any old beach bum; she could easily see him on a surf board back home. And the Chinese guy was walking with Priss and the others and never saying a word. Odd, that. She hadn't seen him speak to anyone. If his face had had some life in it he would have been nice looking too, with that very smooth Chinese skin, and he looked as though his physique would be good. But he was either really stupid or really quiet, and either way she wouldn't be interested in him.

It seemed like forever, but at last they stopped by a stream and Steve said, 'Here's our lunch spot.'

Priss shrugged off her daypack and looked around with a smile. 'Lovely place, Steve, you know how to choose them.'

Sandy took off her own pack and looked around too. It was lovely, a sort of glade, with grass and moss and ferns underneath the trees and the little stream gurgling and chuckling through it. There were trees on every side, broad branches outspread, letting the sunlight through in little patches that shifted as the wind blew.

'There's some nice pools up and down the stream,' Steve said. 'We're here in good time so there'll be a chance for a dip if you want.'

Priss caught Sandy's eye. 'I wouldn't mind one now. Before lunch is better for me. Upstream or down?'

Steve said, 'Either, really. There's more spots downstream.'

'Well, look, I tell you what,' Priss said, 'send the others down, would you? I'll go up, and I haven't got a cossie with me.'

'Me neither,' Sandy said quickly. 'Would you mind, Steve?'

For a moment she thought Steve was going to say no, but then he shrugged. 'OK, if you like.'

'Cool,' said Priss, and she smiled at Sandy and set off upstream, jumping from rock to rock. Sandy followed her and when they were out of sight and earshot of the others Priss said, 'I thought for a minute he was going to suggest he came with us.'

'That wouldn't have been the plan,' Sandy said. Her breath was coming quickly, and it wasn't from the climb. The anticipation was killing her.

'And did you see Sarah's face?' Priss went on. 'She looked as if she was going to have a heart attack. Someone sewed up her arsehole for sure, she's so tight. All I was suggesting was skinny-dipping, for God's sake.' She laughed. 'Imagine how she'd have looked if she'd known what we really meant to do!'

How could she laugh? Did she want to get it on, or what? Sandy suddenly felt helpless: she was so unused to grabbing what she wanted. She looked around and saw them surrounded by green, no sounds of the others reaching them over the sound of the stream, and she said, 'Priss.'

Priss looked down the stream and shook her head. 'We need a pool as cover. Come on.' She stretched out and caught Sandy's hand and tugged her up the stream.

Sandy followed, stumbling over the rocks, feeling the warmth of Priss's hand seeping right through her. Priss was surefooted and a couple of times Sandy stumbled and was glad she was hanging on to her. But she didn't fall and at last the ground flattened and they were beside a wide, still pool with a little mossy beach and a narrow rocky neck where the water leaped away down the hillside.

Priss dropped her hand and turned to face her. 'Now,' she said.

Sandy didn't feel hesitant, didn't feel anxious. She stepped forward to meet Priss with a sense almost of joy and pressed her body against Priss's and searched for her lips and when she found them she actually pushed her tongue into Priss's mouth, probing deeply, almost as if she were a man, and it made her shudder.

Priss moaned and pushed both hands deep into Sandy's hair, forcing her lips away. 'Wow,' she said.

'Priss, I'm so horny,' Sandy whispered. 'I can't wait another minute, come on, please.'

Priss kissed her on the lips, a quick kiss, and then reached for the buttons on her shirt. As she unfastened them, one by one, she let her mouth rest on the creamy skin that was slowly revealed. Sandy shivered and let her head fall back, hearing the rustle of the fabric and the sound of the stream and the birds singing in the canopy above her and hardly believing it.

The shirt was open and Priss slowly pushed it back, exposing Sandy's shoulders and her sensible sports bra. For a moment Sandy wished it was something sexier, but then she realised that she didn't care. The bra was made of soft cotton and her small tight nipples stood up through it almost as if she were naked, and all she wanted was to get rid of it anyway.

'You're so fair.' Priss spoke almost in a whisper. 'You're as pale as milk. You must burn like nobody's business.'

'Factor 50,' Sandy said. 'You can't teach an Australian anything about sun protection.'

'And your hair.' Priss slid one hand under the fine red-gold mass and lifted it and Sandy arched her neck like a preening cat. 'You're a Pre-Raphaelite wet dream.'

Sandy wasn't sure what that meant, but she was sure it was supposed to be a compliment. She reached behind her back and unfastened her bra and pulled it off, then pushed her breasts towards Priss and whispered, 'Kiss them, please kiss them.'

'God, they're gorgeous,' Priss said, in what sounded

like genuine admiration. She stooped and cupped Sandy's breasts in her hands and lifted one nipple to her mouth, extended her tongue and just touched the aching peak with the tip of it. Sandy gasped in frustration and pushed forward, wanting to feel the sweet pain of a sucking mouth fastened to her breast. Priss smiled and ignored her, turning her head so that she could lap at the point of the other nipple, flickering between them until they were deliciously cold with saliva and stiff and aching and Sandy was grinding her hips against Priss's thigh and moaning with pleasure and eagerness.

'OK,' Priss whispered, 'OK, Sandy,' and at last Sandy felt strong fingers unfastening her pants button, dragging the zipper down, pushing pants and panties downwards in one quick motion and, although she was hobbled by the trousers around her ankles and by her heavy walking boots, she cried out as Priss pressed her face to her bush and extended her tongue and explored until she found Sandy's swollen clit and flickered the tip of her tongue against it until Sandy whimpered and staggered and fell slowly backwards, hands extended to catch herself, half-sitting, half-lying on the little mossy beach and moaning to Priss to go on, go on.

'Jesus, these boots,' Priss hissed, fumbling with Sandy's laces, pulling the boots off, dragging Sandy's pants and knickers and socks down her pale thighs and chucking them to one side, then suddenly stopping.

Sandy pushed herself a little more upright, very aware all of a sudden of her nakedness in this strange open place. She felt alone, exposed, cold, although there was no wind and the patches of sunlight on her bare skin were warm. Priss was still fully dressed, and it made Sandy feel vulnerable.

Priss was breathing quickly. She looked really excited. 'Lie back, Sandy,' she said.

'But –' Sandy hesitated, one hand scrabbling beside her for her clothes. 'I don't think –'

'Don't think. Just lie back.' Priss kneeled between Sandy's feet and leaned forward to push her back and back until she was lying naked on the cool moss. Then she reached into the back pocket of her jeans and pulled out a little camera. 'Smile,' she said.

For a moment Sandy almost protested. Then she thought of herself reflected in the camera lens, glowing white against the forest green, her hair tumbling across the moss, her nipples erect, and she smiled a little and arched her back and parted her thighs.

The camera clicked. Priss said, 'Wider,' and Sandy closed her eyes with a long breath of delight. She opened her legs and put her hands between them to part the lips of her cunt.

Priss took another picture, then shut the camera. Sandy opened her eyes and saw Priss looking at something beyond her. Priss smiled and said, 'Hi, Josh.'

Josh? Jesus! Although they had planned it, Sandy gasped and tried to sit up, but Priss leaned forward and put her hand on her belly, holding her down. Unbelieving, Sandy craned her neck and saw Josh behind her, upside down in her vision, approaching slowly with his hands in his pockets. From her position she couldn't see how he looked, if he looked angry or shocked or what, and she wriggled and grabbed her clothes and pulled them on top of her.

Josh came closer and Sandy twisted round so that she could make sense of his expression. He looked flushed and his eyes were dark in his lean ranger's face. He licked his lips as he approached and suddenly she saw how turned on he was. She glanced at Priss and saw her smiling and then she wasn't scared any more; she knew this was going to be exciting, fun, and that what she did would be up to her.

'I sure would like one of those pictures,' Josh said.

Priss said, 'Sorry. They're for my private delectation.' She stroked one hand down Sandy's belly, took her clothes from her limp hand and laid them back on the ground. Then she smiled into her eyes. 'Now,' she said, 'I'm busy.'

She began to stoop down between Sandy's thighs, easing them apart with the flats of her hands. Sandy closed her eyes and drew in a deep breath, waiting to feel that first touch on her damp flesh. When Josh said, 'Hey, what about me?' she felt really angry with him.

'Sorry,' said Priss, 'what about you?' Sandy concealed a smile.

'What about my blow job?'

He sounded like a kid, but then he wasn't much older than a boy anyway. Sandy opened her eyes again and saw his upside-down face, puzzled and resentful, as if he couldn't understand how anybody could be more important than him. Just like Greg. Well, fuck him. Let him wait.

'Sorry,' said Priss, 'I have a subsequent engagement.' She kneeled again and at last, at last, Sandy felt the tickle of soft hair brushing against her thighs and then the coolness of Priss's breath on her pubes. She moaned and spread her legs wider and Priss's hands were cool on the insides of her thighs and there was her mouth, warm and wet, lips brushing against Sandy's aching pussy lips, fingers probing very gently into her wet anxious cunt.

'Oh,' Sandy whispered, 'oh, please.' And for once

somebody listened to her and Priss's tongue was lapping against her clit, soft and persistent. 'That's so good,' Sandy said, stretching her hands out and letting her head roll to one side in ecstasy. 'Oh, that's good.'

There was movement above her and she opened her eyes and found herself looking up at a strangely foreshortened view of Josh, kneeling over her face, hands busy at his fly. 'Jesus,' he whispered, 'come on, come on, please.'

He fumbled with his pants and she thought, I don't have to do this. I can say no if I want. But then he pulled his cock out and it was a beauty, straight and stiff and smelling so hot and ready that it made her breath catch in her throat, and although she knew that she could say no, she didn't want to. She sighed and opened her mouth and tilted her head back and heard him groan as he slid his cock between her parted lips.

God, it was bliss, with Priss's warm wet mouth working at her throbbing clit and Josh's hard dick sliding into her mouth, in and in until she thought she would choke and didn't care. She wanted it to go on for ever, but it seemed only a few strokes before Josh made a strangled sound and his cock jerked and twitched and suddenly her mouth was full of his come. She swallowed violently and moaned with disappointment and Priss heard her and stopped for just long enough to say, 'Josh, make yourself useful, suck her tits or something,' and then returned to her gentle, gentle lapping.

Sandy closed her eyes, hoping that Josh would do as he was told, and she heard him shift position and then his hands were on her breasts, big strong hands, hard with calluses from leather reins, and he tugged and squeezed her nipples and then began to suck them. He had not shaved that morning and his face scoured the tender skin of her tits as he suckled and pinched. She moaned with pleasure and arched her hips towards Priss's face, and obediently Priss licked her a little harder and slipped one finger into her cunt and reached forward, searching.

'Oh, God,' Sandy cried, because something that Priss had done filled her with such piercing sensation that it jerked her immediately into orgasm. She gasped and heaved, pierced by Priss's finger, held still by Josh's strong hands, and it was long seconds before she subsided to the moss with a quivering moan.

She didn't subside for long though. After one orgasm she was always ready for another, and she quickly opened her eyes and reached down for Josh. He was young, he would be bound to have got it up again by now.

She wasn't disappointed. Josh's dick was back to its erect state, stiff and eager, even weeping a little leftover come. She took hold of it, smiled at him and reached down with her tongue to lick him clean. Then she said to him, 'Fuck me.'

He looked as if he wanted to, but his eyes shifted to Priss. What was this? He didn't prefer Priss, did he? Sandy frowned at Priss, hoping that she wouldn't ask for Josh for herself. But Priss just reached into another pocket, pulled out a condom and held it out to Josh. Then she looked at Sandy and said, 'No problem, as long as you'll do something for me.'

Sandy would do anything to feel that cock inside her and, besides, she would enjoy pleasuring Priss. She said, 'Sure, whatever you like,' and caressed Josh's taut heavy balls and watched in hungry anticipation as he tore the condom packet open with his teeth and rolled the rubber on.

Priss ripped off her T-shirt and began on her shorts.

She said, 'Josh, kneel down, pull her on to your knees, OK?' And when Josh looked puzzled she said with a wicked smile, 'She needs to be face up, Josh, so she can do something for me.'

Josh looked as though light was dawning. His expression of bemused delight would normally have had Sandy chuckling, but she wanted him too much to find things funny right now. She said, 'Josh,' and ran her hand up his taut lean thigh and on to his flat belly, warm through his open fly. He growled and leaned forward, over her, the fabric of his shirt scratching at her face. For a moment he laid his face to her belly and inhaled deeply, drawing in her scent while she whimpered at the feel of his prickles and the chill of his moving breath. Then he came around and kneeled between her legs and caught hold of her hips, lifting them high so that he could inch forward until her thighs were resting across his legs, her backside on his knees. The hot head of his cock was brushing against her pubes, teasing her. She said, 'Oh, yes,' and tried to wriggle a little closer to him.

Priss pulled off her panties and bra. Sandy noticed almost despite herself that she had a tidy little body, compact and strong, with a tight rounded belly and toned muscles in her thighs and arms. She looked as if she worked out, maybe lifted weights. Her breasts were OK, but a bit flat, and Sandy felt a pleasing frisson of superiority as Priss kneeled beside her and leaned forward. Then the head of Josh's dick nudged her again and she couldn't think about Priss any more for wanting him. What was the matter with him: why didn't he just shove it up her? She sighed in frustration and Josh shifted again and she looked at his anxious face and realised that perhaps, with both his hands holding her hips, he just couldn't manouevre himself inside her. He was only young, maybe he hadn't got to the Look-No-Hands stage yet.

'Priss,' she said, and Priss seemed to catch on straight away. She slid her hand down Sandy's belly, down between her parted thighs, caressing her clit most deliciously en route, and then she must have got hold of Josh and put him in the right position because all of a sudden that big fat head was lodged right there, in just the right spot, and Sandy knew that with one good thrust it would go all the way up inside her.

She arched her back, lifting her hips to put herself in the perfect position and heard herself let out a long, long sigh of anticipation. Then Josh hissed something and his hands tensed on her thighs and he pushed hard, penetrating her with the single thrust of her dreams, and her sigh turned into a harsh moan of pleasure.

'That's it,' she heard Priss muttering, 'go on, Josh, give it to her.' And, to her delight, Priss's hand was back between her legs, touching, stroking, tickling her clit until the sensations blazed in her head and her nipples felt as if they would burst.

Then she felt Priss move and opened her eyes. Priss was approaching her, straddling her, spreading her legs around her face. She hadn't enjoyed this much in the past, but now she was filled with an urgent need to give back some of the pleasure that she was getting from the touch of Priss's hand and the quick urgent strokes of Josh's cock as he fucked her and fucked her. She stretched up, extending her tongue, reaching for the soft folds of Priss's cunt. The slight, salty taste shivered right through her. Burrowing through the dense damp flesh she quickly found the little hard nodule of Priss's clit and quivered the very tip of her tongue against it, echoing the very caress that she most yearned to feel from Priss's hand.

Priss gasped, 'Oh, God,' and responded as if she had heard Sandy tell her what to do, the rhythm of her tickling finger speeding to match the quick deft quiver of Sandy's searching tongue. Sandy tried not to let her own cries prevent her from keeping up the movement. She knew she was going to come very quickly and she desperately wanted to take Priss with her. She felt the body above her begin to shudder as if little waves were passing through it and she knew that Priss was almost there, so she lapped harder and slightly more slowly, strong pulses that exactly mirrored the strong hard thrusts of Josh's cock. Priss responded and the three of them began to heave in unison, a single ripple of movement beginning with Josh's dick lunging into Sandy's cunt, flowing through Sandy's soft determined tongue, finishing with the delicate maddening touch of Priss's finger on Sandy's clit. Faster, faster, and then Sandy couldn't wait any longer and cried out as her body arced into orgasm. Priss twisted above her, pressing her spasming flesh down hard on to Sandy's mouth, and somewhere far away Sandy vaguely felt Josh's fingers clawing at her thighs as he came deep inside her.

Too soon, much too soon, she felt Josh withdrawing. 'Jesus,' he said. Then he glanced up at the bushes above their heads. 'Y'know,' he muttered, 'I could have sworn I heard something just then.'

Priss moved away from Sandy's mouth, letting her sit up. 'Probably just a bird,' she said. 'Everything else seems to be OK.'

'I dunno.' Josh was beginning to look embarrassed now. He shuffled his big feet and said, 'I got to get back. I told them I was going for a dump; they'll wonder where I've been.'

Sandy rubbed her eyes, catching a bit of Josh's anxiety at the thought of returning to the others. Priss said with a reassuring grin, 'Say you thought we were skinny-dipping. That might explain why you took your time coming back.'

Josh looked as though this wasn't helpful. He shook his head, fastened his trousers and headed off into the bush. It was amazing how quickly the sounds he made just vanished, leaving them alone with the birds and the sunlight through the leaves.

Priss smiled at her. 'You OK? Not sunburned?'

'Yeah, I'm good.' She felt good too. Satisfied, stroked, happy. And all without Greg! Aware of what she must smell like, she crawled on the mossy rocks over to the stream and washed her face and between her legs with the cold clear water. It tingled like a slap.

Priss kneeled down beside her to wash herself and said as she splashed her face, 'D'you want to hear another secret?'

Instantly Sandy was alert again, excited. 'Go on,' she said, as she reached for her clothes.

'Well,' Priss said, 'I had this idea, to keep things interesting. I want to get everyone on the trek having sex with each other. And with me and Diva, of course. And I wondered if you'd like to help.'

For a moment Sandy felt a twinge of reluctance, though she wasn't quite sure why. Perhaps it was something to do with other people's ideas, like being a passenger. She hesitated and Priss said, 'The thing is, Sandy, you're just so sexy. I know that loads of people would want to get involved if it meant getting it on with you.'

Sandy agreed with that completely. And then she

thought of TJ, and Rick, and Zoe, and Diva, and all the other people on the trek that she could easily fancy, and the possibilities got the better of her. 'Yeah,' she said, and then more strongly, 'Yeah! Count me in, Priss. I'm up for it.'

'Excellent!' Priss nudged her in a chummy, confidential way. 'Come on, let's get back to camp. On the way I'll tell you what I've got in mind.'

Chapter Four

Rick

That tosspot Greg was almost unbelievably dense. He'd walked with Diva all morning, either completely unaware of or blatantly ignoring her signals that she did not find him attractive, and his presence had prevented Rick from engaging the Asian girl in the sort of conversation that he would have enjoyed. When they set off for the after-lunch stint and Greg came over again to join them, Rick knew he would have to do something drastic, and soon.

The answer was immediately apparent. Greg was an unpleasant specimen. He had resolutely kept the conversation on sex the entire time, even though it might have been interesting to talk about other things as well. And he was disparaging about his wife in her absence, outspoken about his own (dubious) prowess, greedily demanding of Diva's attention, insistent on the importance of male decisiveness and the attractions of observing lesbianism, totally ignoring the possibilities of men with men. To Rick he came across as spineless, unattractive and someone whose homophobia quite possibly disguised a repressed submissiveness, potentially even an attraction to other men.

This in itself presented possibilities, but they could wait for later. For now Rick was much more interested in Diva and her friend Priss. Did they really believe that they were being subtle in what they were attempting? He couldn't credit it. More probably they were intending that their machinations would be obvious. Certainly they were obvious to him, and he thought that Greg's wife Sandy had probably noticed for herself too. Nobody else seemed to be aware of it at the moment, but that was probably the usual prudish closing of eyes to anything remotely sexual, just pretending it wasn't happening rather than dealing with it. At least Sandy and Greg were uncontaminated by prudery, although they were appallingly crude.

Greg was busy now, speculating on what might have happened between Sandy and Priss while everybody else had been setting up lunch. 'I guess they might have been getting it on,' he said, laughably trying to sound judicious, 'but, y'know, Sandy isn't really keen on going with other women. She really only does it to please me, y'know, because I like watching. I mean, she wouldn't just want to do it on her own.'

Diva's almond-shaped, long-lashed dark eyes flashed towards Rick and held his gaze just long enough for him to pick up that she had spoken to Priss over lunch and that Greg was most definitely mistaken about his wife's predilections. But after all, that was no surprise. Priss and Diva had clearly set out to conquer everyone on this trip and Sandy was an obvious place to start. She was a sexual peony, garish, tumbled, blowsy.

'There again,' Greg rambled on, 'I guess that kid, the young guy, I guess he might have followed them.' His mouth looked pinched, as if he had bitten a lemon. 'I suppose Sandy might have fancied getting it on with him. I suppose, maybe.'

He obviously didn't like to think that his wife really enjoyed sex with anyone other than him, despite putting her up for it so many times. His conversation really was becoming tedious. It was time for action.

'You know, Greg,' Rick said, 'I've been really interested listening to you. You obviously know a lot about this kind of stuff.'

Greg looked startled, as if he hadn't expected Rick to speak. He'd been focused on Diva, certainly. After a moment he looked as if he had decided to be flattered and said, with a set of his shoulders, 'Yeah, well, I'd say I had a pretty wide experience, y'know?'

'It puzzles me though,' Rick said silkily, 'that you haven't talked much about the other men who must be involved.'

'The other men?' Greg frowned.

'Well, don't you find that it's just as stimulating – in a different way, of course – making contact with the other men at events like this?'

Greg's eyes bugged.

'Personally, I've always found that women really enjoy watching two men together, just the way men so often enjoy watching two women together. Wouldn't you agree, Diva?'

Diva picked up the thread instantly. 'Oh yes, absolutely,' she said. 'There's something about seeing a man with another man's, well, another man's cock in his mouth.' He didn't believe that she was speaking from experience, but she had certainly picked up the appropriate cue.

'You're kidding,' Greg said faintly.

'You don't think so?' Rick sounded surprised. 'Well,

look, why don't we try an experiment?' He let himself glow in Greg's direction and was satisfied to observe a look almost of terror come across Greg's face. 'I'd be delighted to offer my services,' he finished, lifting arch eyebrows, 'in whichever role you prefer.'

Greg didn't speak for a good few seconds. Then he said, 'Well, gee, I, ah, I'm doubled up for a slash.' And without another word he walked off the track into the bush, glancing once behind him as if he was afraid that Rick would chase him.

'Excellent move,' Diva said with approval. 'I don't think he'll be back.'

'I doubt it,' Rick agreed, and added, 'But I'll settle scores with him another time.'

Now it was Diva's turn to look shocked. 'What, you don't mean you'd –'

Had she not noticed what Greg's reaction of abhorrence might conceal? She wasn't as much of a game-player as she thought herself to be. Rick said mildly, 'He needs to know himself better.'

Diva smiled at him. She was extremely attractive, and the smile told him that she knew it. She had been holding back while Greg was with them and now she was unleashing her full armoury against him. It was rather charming to watch her believing that she was irresistible. She probably thought she was going to be able to make him pay suit to her.

She would find that she was mistaken. Rick never begged anybody for anything. He made sure that they always begged him. He didn't ask for pleasure, he gave it, and took it when he wanted to – and Diva would be no different.

'Would you really –' She hesitated. 'I mean, Greg's attractive enough, but he's such a dickhead. Would you really, I don't know –'

She hesitated again and he put her out of her misery. 'Have sex with him?' She looked relieved, as if even speaking of it would have been distasteful. Well, if she didn't grasp the appeal of compelling someone to understand the true nature of his sexuality, he had no interest in explaining it to her. 'I might,' he said, 'under the appropriate circumstances.'

She shook her head. 'Well, I can't imagine it.' Her eyes slid across to him again, a sidelong, come-hither look that said *But I could imagine it with you.*

Now he was supposed to come on to her. But he wasn't going to, of course. He smiled, a smile that he knew was both attractive and mysterious, and said nothing.

Diva's face betrayed pique for a fraction of a second, then cleared. He waited with interest to see what Plan B was.

She looked up at the sky, where the clear blue of the morning was beginning to be overlaid with a veil of cloud. 'Getting pretty warm,' she commented.

Oh, we English, reverting to the weather! 'Steve said he thought it might thunder tomorrow,' Rick said equably, as if this were the most natural topic possible which, after all, it was for a group of walkers. 'It'll probably get pretty humid.'

Diva fished in her pocket for a scrunchie and began to run her hands through and around her cascade of black hair, stroking it into line. She had lovely long arms and must have been well aware of how attractive the movement was. Rick watched her with grave attention, finding her desirable. Not as desirable as she would have been if she had ignored him or, even better, been slightly afraid of him. But desirable certainly, and he would be very content to have her, as long as it was on his terms.

She pulled her hair through the scrunchie and up into a high doubled ponytail. The nape of her neck, thus revealed, glistened with a fine dew of sweat. She ran her hand across her nape, down her throat, and commented, 'Sticky.'

He could see from the slightly heightened colour on her throat that she was not just feeling the heat. Her attempts to arouse his sexual interest were having precisely the effect on her that they were supposed to have on him. Soon he would have her grovelling, and he would barely have to lift a finger.

'I should have taken a dip at lunchtime,' Diva said. She ran her hand down her front, almost imperceptibly cupping the curve of her breast, one finger faintly tracing the outline of her nipple, which was becoming erect. 'I didn't realise how hot it was going to get.'

'You'd never have got to a pool without Greg following you,' Rick said, watching her breasts rise and fall. He knew instinctively that as she touched her nipple she was shuddering with desire, the wet flesh between her legs clenching emptily.

'I thought Priss had got the best of it at lunchtime.' Diva reached behind her for a water bottle and glanced at Rick. 'But now I'm not so sure.'

'Did you notice,' Rick said, ignoring her innuendo, 'that Zoe and Sarah disappeared too? I thought they set off in the same direction.'

'Really?' Diva looked interested. 'Priss didn't say they were there. I wonder what became of them.'

'I doubt that Sarah would countenance anything. She's as repressed a specimen as you could hope to meet.'

'You don't sound repressed at all,' Diva said meaningfully, lifting her water bottle. Yes, she was going to do the spilling-water-down-herself bit. And, yes, she took a gulp from the bottle and then let the cool water splash over her face, down her brown throat, on to the front of her camouflage top, dampening it, allowing her tight nipples to show sharply through. It did look attractive, but it was a desperate cliché. She clearly hadn't realised that she would have been better advised to behave with him as if she felt no arousal at all, which, perversely, he would have found much more arousing.

All the same, he was not immune to her. She was exceptionally attractive, and she was hot, and the smell of her warm, damp skin played insistently on his senses. His belly tightened and for a moment he almost thought that he was going to get an erection. That would have been very undesirable, a far too obvious sign of his interest, and he concentrated briefly on the pattern of stones and mud in the path ahead of him until he had regained control over his recalcitrant body.

Diva hadn't noticed his brief retreat. She was frowning slightly, revealing her frustration. Almost with a pout she said, 'I need a pee. Hang on a moment while I step off the track.'

'I'll walk on,' he said easily. 'The others'll be up with you in a minute.'

Her face was a picture – *how can he ignore me?* – but she said nothing, just tossed her head a little and disappeared into the bushes.

He glanced up and down the track. They were towards the rear of the group; he could just see Alan and Jan walking with Jason and TJ, right at the back, more than a hundred yards away. If he was quick, they would never notice. Moving smoothly, watching where he trod, he stepped in amongst the leaves.

It was amazing how quickly the forest closed around

him. He had seen the direction that Diva had gone but even so, he thought for a few seconds that he would not be able to find her. He glanced behind him, identifying a couple of big trees to help him find his way back to the track, checking the position of the sun.

There was Diva, standing between a couple of tall glossy-leaves bushes, scowling down at herself. She muttered, unaware of him, 'God, what's the matter with him? You'd almost think there was something wrong with me.'

She cupped her breasts and sighed, and in a moment he knew that she would succumb to her arousal and masturbate. He didn't want her to have that relief, so he stepped out of his shelter and leaned against a tree, saying, 'I thought you said you wanted a pee, not a wank.'

She jumped like a deer, and her face showed that she was delighted that he had followed her, that she thought she had him on the run. 'I can't imagine what you mean,' she said. 'And I'm certainly not going to have a pee while you're standing there, am I?'

'Aren't you?' he said, innocently smiling. He was glad that she was exhibiting some distaste, something he could work against. 'Well, I'll just join the others then.'

He turned his back, and for a couple of seconds he thought he might have miscalculated. But then she said, 'Rick.'

Slowly he turned back. All the sex-goddess smoulder had gone from her face. She looked unsure, reluctant and anxious, and he felt an immediate pang of arousal. Shamelessness had never been attractive to him, he much preferred the subtle, shimmering pangs of shame.

'Are you serious?' she asked hesitantly. 'You, you actually want me to pee?'

'You need to pee,' he said. 'And you want me to stay.'

Now if she was still playing for superiority, she would deny at once that she wanted him to stay. She would let him go hang, rather than admit that she wanted something from him. But she didn't deny it. She looked down at the ground and whispered, 'Oh.'

He said nothing, letting her come to her own conclusions. For a while she stood completely still, her face lowered, so that it was hard for him to see the emotions coming and going. Then she flung her head back, and there was resolution in her eyes.

'OK,' she said brazenly, 'if that's what you want.' She unfastened her shorts and pulled them down, barely revealing her flat brown belly and a wisp of black fur before she squatted there, right in front of him, and let go.

Her urine smelled strong, hot, as if she hadn't been drinking enough. She finished, pulled a wisp of paper from the strap of her top and wiped herself, then stood up, holding his eyes challengingly as she pulled up her shorts and fastened them.

What was he supposed to do now, fall on her, so inflamed by the sight of her that he was unable to control himself? He couldn't keep back a little smile. 'Now,' he said, 'I think that you were going to masturbate.'

A spasm of anger crossed her face. 'God,' she expostulated, 'you're –'

He was what? Better at this than she was? He said nothing, just crossed his arms as he leaned against the tree trunk, lifted his eyebrows and looked.

She set her fine jaw defiantly, then pulled the scrunchie from her hair and shook her head, slowly, sweeping the magnificent black mane from side to side. Glancing down at where the earth under her boots gleamed and steamed, she moved away, across the little clearing towards him. Then she put both hands to her singlet and hoisted it up and off in one smooth movement.

She was standing in a patch of sunlight and the glow of the sun on her fine pale-brown skin was wonderful. Her breasts were high and quite full, and their stiff nipples were dark rose-pink. She put her hands on her belly and ran them up her body, flicking against her nipples, caressing her shoulders, her throat, sweeping into the rich dark mass of her hair.

All of this was designed to make him want her, and he had to admit that he did want her. His erection had returned, and this time it would not be willed away. But he was not going to have her until she begged him, and then he was going to have her in a way she did not expect, a way that elicited that delicious reluctance from her again. She was trying to come across as experienced, but he thought that she was faking it. And she had been shy of peeing in front of him. No doubt she would have one or two taboos left that he might enjoy breaking.

She unfastened her shorts again and slid her hand inside them, beneath her panties, down the flat plane of her belly. Her eyes still held his, but when she found the spot and touched herself they closed in a wince of delicious response. She let out a little sound, almost a grunt, and her left hand caught hold of her breast and began to squeeze her nipple in a rhythm, which he could tell was born of long habit. This was what she did to herself in the quiet of her own room, when she was alone.

If he let her go too much into her own world, he would lose control. He needed to remind her of him, remind her of her desire for him. He unzipped his own trousers and brought his cock out, stroking it slowly, barely hinting at its possibilities of sensation. Her eyes were closed; he needed her attention. Quite sharply he said, 'Tell me what you're thinking.'

Her eyes snapped open and her hand left her breast and covered her face as she saw him standing in front of her, erect cock in his hand. Her dark eyes were huge. She liked what she saw, but she was afraid that he was going to masturbate too, that his erection would go to waste. It was all written on her face.

'Tell me what you're thinking,' he said again.

She licked her lips and shifted her body from side to side, rubbing herself against her fingers. 'Just the usual,' she whispered, and her eyes shifted again from his face to his cock.

She had done what he asked her. Did she realise how significant that was? Probably not – she wasn't subtle. But he knew, and he could build on it. He ran his hand lazily from the root of his cock to the tip, thumb and forefinger delicately ringed, encouraging it to become even stiffer, even thicker. 'Take off your shorts,' he said.

Her eyes met his, and he saw that she understood the significance of his order. If she was naked and he was not, then he was in charge. Her eyes dropped again, and he resisted the urge to smile. She wanted his cock, and he thought that she wanted it so much that she would allow herself to be controlled, at least on this occasion.

He was right. She breathed quickly, bit her lip, and then pushed her shorts down around her ankles, struggled briefly with her boots and socks, and at last kicked everything off and stood before him in just her black thong, barefoot, vulnerable.

'And the panties,' he said, sliding his hand again along his cock and relishing the sensation.

She hesitated, then let out a long breath and pulled the panties off.

Her body was beautiful, and she had trimmed her pubic hair into a neat triangle, short enough to show the glistening lips of her pussy. He nodded in admiration, but it was time to find out how he might extend the envelope of her experience. He had a theory, and it was easy to test it.

'Turn round,' he said, and when she didn't obey immediately, 'Let me see all of you.'

At this she turned, but he did not think that she quite knew what 'all of you' might mean. Her back was cello-shaped, with a deep, sensual groove along the spine, a high, full arse and lush thighs. 'Bend over,' he said.

She should have been well in the habit of obeying him by now, but she did not respond to this order, and that told him all he needed to know. Again he said, 'Diva, bend over.'

There was a little pause and then, instead of doing as he said, she turned and came up to him, her face beseeching. 'Let me go down on you,' she offered, reaching out to take hold of him.

He caught her wrist and pushed her hand away, shaking his head. 'No,' he said. He held on to her wrist and with the other hand touched her nipple, testing its tension, its fullness, watching her eyes tense and her breath hiss. Then he ran his hand down her belly and slipped two fingers between her legs.

'You don't need to do anything to me,' he said,

letting his fingers just stir against her wet flesh. 'You're ready for anything, aren't you?'

Her lips were parted and she was gasping. The tip of her clit throbbed beneath his finger. 'I'd just like to go down on you,' she whispered.

Again he shook his head. 'I don't think so. Now.' Still holding her wrist, he turned her, gently but firmly, until she stood with her back to him. Her body tensed slightly, stiffening with apprehension. To soothe her, he stepped closer to her until his hard cock brushed against her warm buttocks, then released her wrist and reached around in front of her, cupping her breasts in his hands. She sighed and leaned her head back and he smelled the perfume of her hair and her scalp, heavy with her warm damp scent. She smelled of the jungle. His cock ached for her.

'You're very lovely,' he said, and with his left hand he held her left breast and with his right he reached down her body, mimicking the movements he had seen her make when she masturbated. She relaxed, her head heavy on his shoulder, moaning as he squeezed her nipple and worried her wet entrance with searching fingers.

She was so ready that he almost misjudged it and brought her to orgasm, but just in time he realised the signals and stopped what he was doing. She whimpered in protest and moaned, 'Please.'

That was good to hear, but 'Please don't' would have been better. He buried his hand in her thick hair and pushed her head forward, holding her hips so that she had to bend at the waist. His cock nudged between her thighs. It had a mind of its own; left to itself it would just have got stuck in. Fortunately he knew how to control it and he made himself draw back a little.

She was in position now, and when he let go of her

she didn't move, just stood there, long legs slightly parted, her hair sweeping the ground, the dark gleaming furrow of her pussy splitting her smooth backside like the cleft in a fruit. He reached into a pocket for a condom, tore it open and rolled it on with one hand, while with the other he probed slightly between the swollen damp lips of her cunt, making her whimper. His fingers heavy with moisture, he drew them out and slid them backwards, anointing her perineum, her arsehole.

She twitched as he touched her and made as if she would pull away; he had to catch hold of her waist to keep her still. 'Don't move,' he commanded her, and let the tip of his sheathed cock brush against her pussy, lodge itself at her entrance, slide a little way up into her.

'Oh, yes,' she sighed, her relief very obvious. 'Yes, please.'

His fingers returned, slipping around the buried shaft of his cock, flickering against her clit, then returning again to the back of her slit to moisten the delicate puckered mouth of her arse. She whimpered, and he put one hand back on her clit and tickled it, teasing her until she whined for mercy and her cunt twitched and clenched around the half-buried length of his cock. Then, with his other hand, he stroked the entrance to her arse, easing one finger into the little hole, all the while tickling her clit, bringing her to within an inch of orgasm, then stopped so that she cried out in frustration.

'Oh, Jesus,' she moaned, 'please make me come, please, Rick.'

His finger was deep inside her arse now. It was tight, desperately tight, but he knew he could fuck her there. Slowly he withdrew his finger, then pulled his cock out of her and positioned it. He didn't enter her yet. He wanted her to know what was coming.

Her whole body stiffened. 'Don't,' she said.

He touched her clit, just once, delicately bringing her back to the edge of orgasm, holding her there.

'Please don't,' she whimpered, and he let out a long sigh of delight and began to press, to ease himself inside her, squeezing and pushing until she opened to him.

'Please don't,' she moaned again, and then, 'Please, please.'

The head was inside her now, and it was so tight that he had to grit his teeth to keep control over himself as he forced himself deeper and deeper. A strangled sound escaped him and she responded with a gasping, desperate, 'Yes.'

He was nearly there now, and the tight grip of her sphincter on his buried cock was so delicious that he knew he wouldn't have to do anything once he was in there, just relax into the velvet grasp of her arse and let her contractions milk him into oblivion. But he had to know that he was fully inside her, the whole length of him sheathed in the one place she had not wanted him to go. Setting his jaw against the pleasure, he pushed again and again until at last he felt his balls rest against the soft pouch of her pussy lips and knew that he could go no further.

'Oh God,' Diva moaned, squirming beneath him, fixed on the invading spike of his body. 'Oh God, make me come; make me come.'

He leaned forward, arching himself over her body, reaching around to cup one dangling breast and tug and squeeze the swollen nipple. 'I want to feel you come,' he hissed. 'I want to feel you coming round me. Come now, Diva, come now.'

His searching finger settled on her clit, pressing and stroking, and her peachy backside quivered and surged as she reached for her orgasm. She gasped and cried out and he stroked her harder, resting the tip of his finger on the little hard nub, rubbing it hard, and waves began to shimmer through her body, quaking in her belly, forcing her thighs back against his balls, tightening her nipples even further. She swung her head from side to side and her long hair dragged in the dirt and then she flung back her head and yelped helplessly as she came, shuddering with orgasm, convulsing around him. He closed his eyes and let the pulses of pressure suck the juices out of him, gasping as he released himself into her.

He would have liked to stay in there longer, to wait until he became fully hard again and then to make her beg for a proper fucking, but if they were away too long they might not easily rejoin the group without attracting attention. So, reluctantly, he eased backwards until his softening cock slipped out of her. He slid off the condom and wrapped it in a twist of paper and stuffed it in his pocket, not wanting to litter the virgin forest with unbiodegradable latex.

She straightened, her face hidden by her tumbled hair and her shielding hands. He cleaned himself up, saying nothing, waiting for her. After a little while she turned her head away from him and went across to pick up her panties and shorts and pull them on. She found her top hanging from a bush and slid into it, still not looking at him.

After a little while he said, 'You enjoyed that.' It was not a question.

She glanced at him, but only a glance. 'We'd better find a pool or something on the way back to join the others. I must look as if –' She didn't finish, just sat down to wrestle her way into her socks and boots.

'As if you've been buggered?' He regarded her candidly. Her hair was tangled and her coffee-and-cream skin was flushed. 'Yes, I suppose you do.'

They were silent for a while as they found their way back to the track, where they could see the footprints of the others clearly in the soft mud. After a little while they crossed a stream and Diva took the opportunity to tidy herself up a bit. When she had splashed her face and fixed her hair she seemed calmer and, eventually, she gave a little chuckle.

'Something funny?' he enquired.

She smiled ruefully. 'I imagine that you've guessed what Priss and I are up to. I was going to ask you if you wanted to help, but I think we should probably be asking you for help rather than the other way around.'

That was sweet to hear, and he smiled. 'Thank you for the accolade,' he said. She waited, and he knew that she was hoping that he would volunteer information about the other people on the trek, and so he waited for her to ask.

'Jesus,' she exclaimed after a moment, 'you don't give anything away, do you? What else do you think about our fellow walkers, apart from the fact that Greg's a wanker and Sarah's seriously repressed?'

He laughed. 'Not much else, to be honest. I think they're quite ordinary, and that means that you ought to be able to bend them pretty much to your will. Except,' he added as an afterthought, 'except possibly Julie.'

'Julie?' Diva frowned, not remembering.

'The other two women who have been put to share a tent, you remember. Kathy and Julie.'

'I remember Kathy.'

'Julie's slipped your mind, eh? I'm not surprised. She likes to blend into the background.' He imagined Julie's distress at being required to come forward from the background, and smiled. 'I think with a little help Kathy might find herself quite in charge there. And then, perhaps, I might take over.'

Diva frowned. 'You want Julie?'

'I'm staking a claim, yes.'

Her face became a little more animated. 'And if I agree, will you help us?'

What on earth made her think that she was in a position to strike bargains? Had she established some sort of right over Julie, to allow her to negotiate? But he was actually quite interested in whether she and Priss would succeed in their plan, and not averse to being involved either. So he decided to let her think that she had won this round, as she had lost so spectacularly earlier.

'Leave Julie to me,' he said, 'and I'll play along.'

Chapter Five

Zoe

'Do you know,' Sarah hissed, 'I actually think that there's something going on between Diva and Rick now. Honestly, those women are –'

Zoe really didn't want to hear one more word about what Sarah thought of Diva and Priss. Not one more single solitary word. What had she done to get saddled with a convent tight-ass for a tentmate? She got to her feet and said, 'Listen, I'm just going off into the bush for a minute, OK?' She knew it was rude, and Sarah's face told her that Sarah thought it was rude, and she didn't give a stuff. If she listened for a second longer she would tell Sarah just what she thought of her, and then they wouldn't speak for the rest of the trek, and that would be a real drag, and it was better just to get away.

Camp that night was in a beech glade. Much of the day had been a gradual climb and the glade was just below a ridge leading up to tomorrow's early highlight, a mountain crest with what, according to Steve, was a fantastic view. There was a stiff, gusty wind up on the ridge. Zoe could see the tops of the trees up there thrashing, but the tall trees around the glade gave good shelter and the smooth branches of the beeches around her hardly moved. It was still stickily hot and clouds of midges were dancing under the trees. The horses, picketed in one corner of the glade, were shaking their manes and twitching their hides and stamping. People were busy around the camp, finishing with the tents, washing whatever they had worn today, and making dinner. But Zoe thought that if she stayed there a moment longer she would start twitching her hide and stamping just like the horses, so she took off, leaving Sarah sitting on her rock like a goblin on a toadstool, sliding between the tall beech trunks towards the ridge above the camp.

She climbed briskly to begin with. The pace had been slow today and she'd found it frustrating; not the only thing that had frustrated her either. Stretching her long legs, she reached her way up the slope, moving quickly from rock to rock between the tree ferns and the thick green undergrowth. A little stream bounded down in front of her and she found a flattish place and jumped it and went on, up and up, as fast as she could, losing herself in the exercise the way she did when she trained on the track.

After a little while she felt less hemmed in and she stopped, belly heaving, and looked around. Her hair clip was in the top pocket of her shorts and she took it out and pulled the front sections of her braids back and clipped them behind her head for coolness. Where was she? She needed to be sensible – it would be easy to get lost in the forest. But it looked OK; the track she had made through the brush was as clear as if it had been signposted.

She moved on, climbing slowly now, heading

towards a glow of brighter daylight ahead which might be the ridge or might just be an open space between the trees. Sweat formed on her shoulders and under her breasts and trickled down, unable to evaporate in the sticky warmth. She stopped at the next stream to splash herself and rubbed the water along her limbs and throat.

That morning she'd followed Priss and Sandy, attracted by the idea of a skinny-dip, and had seen them by the little beach. She'd been about to join them when they'd starting kissing. Two women, standing in the middle of a forest snogging! It was unbelievable. She'd had views about Priss – everyone had heard the noises coming out of her and Diva's tent at night – but Sandy was married, for God's sake, and here she was with her tongue down Priss's throat. Unbelievable, and incredibly, astonishingly horny, like watching a blue movie.

She'd settled down in the undergrowth, ready to watch, feeling sexual energy building up in her body. Priss and Sandy had got right down to it and then, from the other side of the stream, Josh had appeared, and Zoe's tongue had started hanging right out. Not that she fancied Josh, but just the thought of that kind of scene, three people together, was wholly amazing. She'd been getting her nerve up to get up from the bushes and go and join in, because frankly it looked as though anybody would be welcome, when of all the bloody things Sarah had appeared at her elbow, astonished and shocked and horrified, and had started making such a fuss beneath her breath that the three of them would have heard in a minute and then it would all have been over and Zoe would never get the chance to join in, so she had grabbed Sarah by the elbow and piloted her back towards the camp, absolutely weak with frustration.

And that was how she still felt. Weak with frustration, and furious. It wasn't as if she had come on this holiday with the intention of getting laid. She hadn't. She had wanted to get away from a stressful job and indulge in some great exercise in a beautiful place, somewhere people didn't often go. But she had been blokeless and short of sex for a couple of months before coming away, and if someone else out there was getting some, she wanted some too. Lots of it, preferably.

Apart from anything else, her competitive instincts were aroused. She was younger than Priss and Sandy, and a bloody sight better looking too. Priss was OK, and her friend Diva was really gorgeous, but how could any bloke really fancy Sandy, with her soft squidgy body and her washed-out skin and red hair? Wouldn't any red-blooded guy prefer Zoe, whose body was lean and hard and whose dark slender legs went on for miles?

But the only bloke who had made a move was Greg, and she'd sort of written him off because he was married. Mistake! If she had known then what she knew now, what Sandy had been getting up to, she might have felt differently. Why hadn't Josh followed her instead of Sandy and Priss? Did it all come down to the fact that her tits were too small?

The bright patch was close now and she was able to make out that it was a big clearing in the forest. Much bigger than the glade where they were camped, this was big enough to play sport in and was partly rocky outcrop, partly grass and ferns. It looked inviting, as if it would hold clearer, fresher air.

Unfortunately she wasn't the only person to have

found it. There was someone else there already. She was irritated. She couldn't quite make out who it was and she moved closer, walking more quietly now in case it was someone she would rather not meet.

The person had been standing quietly on the rock outcrop. She decided it was a man and, as she squeezed closer and closer, trying with every bone in her townie body not to step on any twigs, he lifted both hands high above his head in a stretch, then folded forward, his head practically on his knees.

He was doing yoga. Which of the men in the group would come up here to do yoga? And which would be so bloody flexible? He was as limber as a diver.

Just as she recognised him, she realised who it must be. John. Silent, Chinese John, with his smooth skin and impassive face. She had suspected that there was an excellent body concealed under his loose clothes, and she had wondered how she might engineer a closer look. Well, now was her chance. Moving with painful slowness, trying to be as stealthy as she could, she crept around towards a spot where the forest was quite close to the rock outcrop, where she would be able to have a good view.

As she moved, John continued with his exercise. He was doing the first Sun Salutation series, and his moves were clean, positive and strong. When he went into the bent-arm plank, supporting all the weight of his stretched-out body on his arms, he held the pose for a staggeringly long time. Yes, it would definitely be worth taking a good look at this bod.

He was wearing loose, soft trousers and a loose T-shirt. As she approached her final spot, she was close enough to see him really well. As he stretched upwards the breadth of his chest and shoulders was amazingly apparent, and as he took his weight on his arms she could make out the muscles of his forearms flexing and tensing, the tendons standing out like wires.

Zoe had always been athletic and she kept herself very fit, and she admired athleticism and good physique in men as she did in women. She enjoyed doing sport and she also really enjoyed watching it. She settled herself on a moss-covered rock behind the shelter of a tall overhanging bracken plant and prepared to be entertained. Watching John repeating the Sun Salutation again and again, she recognised that this was a warm-up exercise, and she hoped that there would be more dramatic stuff to come. She also hoped that he would take off his T-shirt.

After another ten repetitions John stretched upwards one last time and then shook out his arms and legs. Good; he was warmed up. Now it was time for what Zoe hoped would be quite a show.

To begin with it was impressive, but relatively dull. John started off with a sequence of squats and bends, followed them with a surprisingly long set of press-ups, and then a pile of sit-ups fit to tax the strongest abdomen. OK, all very well, nothing exciting there.

But then things got more interesting. John pushed his hands through his hair and then, in one quick movement, pulled off his T-shirt.

His physique was remarkable. His waist was as narrow as hers and, above the top of his trousers, his belly was as hard as a board and resplendent with a perfectly defined six-pack. And, as if that in itself wasn't admirable enough, his chest was incredibly broad and the width of his back and shoulders was astonishing, and everywhere the muscles were carved and drawn as if on honey-coloured marble. She knew who he reminded her of: it was Bruce Lee, at the height of his powers, honed and smooth as a racehorse. He was taller than Lee, but the shape, the overall effect, was the same. She salivated just looking at him.

And now, the fireworks. She had wondered what his sport was, and the next moments showed her, and also showed her how he had come to resemble Bruce Lee. He began a sequence of martial arts moves that left her open-mouthed. Punches so quick she couldn't really see them, leaps, kicks that came from nowhere and seemed to reach up into the air twice as high as you could possibly expect, an incredible display of strength and speed and razor-sharp co-ordination. And everything was done in absolute silence, no screams or shouts, not even a grunt as that amazing body did things that no body was supposed to do, seemingly without any particular difficulty.

Not without effort though, or concentration. John's face was set in a forbidding frown and his whole body was soon covered with a sheen of sweat, like oil on polished wood. Gradually his sequence changed its emphasis, away from combat moves and towards purer gymnastics. He tumbled, flipped, somersaulted, all on a rock surface that would probably break his back if he fell. She rested her chin on her hands and gazed, wondering how soon she might be able to get her hands on that gorgeous body.

Gradually the speed of the routine became slower and the moves turned from tumbling to strength. After such a long workout she could hardly believe how much power he still had left. He held a handstand for what must have been a full minute, while sweat slowly trickled down his torso and arms and dripped from his hair, and then slowly lowered his perfectly poised body until his head touched the rock, lifted it, lowered it again.

Handstand press-ups! She had heard about them,

seen them in movies, and never seen anyone do one for real. Awed, she watched the muscles flex and shimmer on John's shoulders and back. It wasn't that they were big muscles; they were just, well, perfect. A perfect physical machine. When he gradually lowered himself to the ground, extended his legs and began to perform push-ups balanced just on his fingertips, and then just on the fingertips of one hand, she was beyond doing anything but gasping.

It seemed, however, that three-finger push-ups were John's *pièce de résistance*. Once he had completed two sets he lowered himself to the ground and began a series of cooling stretches. His breathing was already almost normal, as if he had hardly been exerting himself at all.

Stretching meant that he was nearly finished. She didn't want to interrupt him until he had cooled down properly; anyone that skilled was bound to be really intense and serious about the whole thing, from warm-up to the final stretch, and she would have been angry being interrupted if she was him. She just watched him, enjoying every aspect of his movement from the muscles on his strong neck to the way his toes stretched and gripped at the rock. When he was done, she would step out of the bushes, say how much she admired him, and offer herself. A man like him would be bound to like strong athletic women. He'd pick her up, perhaps, hold her so that she could wrap her legs around his lean waist while he lifted her up and down on his cock. She didn't have a condom, and he wouldn't have one either, and she didn't care. She wanted to touch him, feel the smooth carved hardness of his body, give herself to him as the prize for his prowess. It would be such a pleasure to submit to so complete a male.

He began the Sun Salutation sequence again, and she knew that this was the last. Getting up off the rock, she loosened her hair from its clip so that her braids swung forward, framing her face, beads echoing the strong line of her jaw. She glanced at herself, at her flat belly framed between crop top and shorts, long legs that looked great even finished with a pair of sports sandals. Yes, he would have to find her irresistible, because watching him had made her so horny that she absolutely had to have it, and now.

To her surprise though, instead of stopping and relaxing as she would have done at the end of a workout, John sat down on the bare rock, folding his legs easily into the full lotus position, his heels resting on his flexed thighs. He laid the backs of his hands on his knees, thumb and first finger touching, and closed his eyes.

Jesus, he wasn't meditating, was he?

He bloody well was. His lips moved, and she just heard him breathing, 'Om.'

Meditating? *Meditating*? After that workout? Wasn't his body just humming with energy, wired on endorphins, just ready for another type of workout? Hers was, and she'd hardly moved. How could he sit there with his eyes closed and bloody *meditate*?

She was totally foxed, stymied. She simply didn't dare break in on him now, and she didn't know how long he was going to be. While she had the patience to watch him for as long as he was working out, she didn't have the patience just to sit and watch him sitting and humming Buddhist mantras with his eyes shut, especially not when she wanted to be getting it on with him. He was gorgeous, but he wasn't that gorgeous. And to be honest, this level of intensity was a bit much, even for her. She could take dedication to a sport: she could understand that. But to go straight from a workout into meditation took a level of self-absorption and concentration that was way beyond her and which she found vaguely freaky. To be brutally frank, she thought it would just drive her nuts. What on earth would there be to say to a man like that? And he hadn't said a word to anyone on the trek as far as she knew. Amazing body, but a bit of a weirdo.

So what was she going to do now? She put her hand over her face and scowled as she tried to come to terms with her disappointment and frustration. All this time she had been waiting for him, and now this!

Just as she had felt she had to get away from the camp, now she knew that she had to get away from John. If she stayed she would do something dumb, like barge out of the bushes and challenge him to single combat. As if she'd stand a chance; he would have her on the ground in two seconds flat.

Oh, if only . . .

But no, he was too weird. Shaking her head, she turned away and followed her own tracks back down the hillside, heading for the camp. At least there would be people there, someone to talk to, some way to take her mind off it. She could stop somewhere and have a wank, but she really didn't fancy it. It was a sweaty physical encounter she wanted, some real grappling and shoving, something to get her blood going. And she certainly wasn't going to get it from John.

It hadn't seemed like that far coming up from the camp, but going back seemed to take ages. The sun-light was slanting now over the canopy and beneath it was becoming gloomy. A couple of times she was afraid that she might have missed the way, but the track that she was following, the track she had made, was very clear. It would be pretty hard to go wrong.

Once she wondered how long John was going to meditate for, and how he would find his way back to the camp if it had got dark before he finished. But she decided that he would know the place better than her, so he would be bound to be able to find his way back, and besides, if he couldn't, she didn't care.

She crossed the little stream that she had jumped earlier and sighed because, now she was nearly back at the camp, she felt as if she had really missed an opportunity, something that perhaps wouldn't offer itself again. Should she have interrupted him while he was working out? Would he have stopped, would he have responded to her?

Well, you never found out that kind of thing, and she didn't think it was that likely, anyway. Best just to commit his amazing display of prowess to memory and write the whole thing down to experience. It would make a great story to tell over a drink anyway. She could imagine it now, sitting in a bar with a bunch of friends from the gym. *There was this time when I was in New Zealand and I saw something really incredible, I mean, something you wouldn't believe . . .*

'Zoe,' said an Australian voice. 'Hiya. I thought you headed up this way. And that was ages ago, and I was kinda worried because you were gone so long, y'know?'

Greg. Greg, standing on the track with his hands on his hips, grinning up at her.

As a physical specimen he couldn't compete with John. Not many men she had ever seen could, and she was a gymworm. But he was reasonable, a good height, a few inches taller than her, with a decent body on him, the sort of body that a bloke who works in an office has if he takes good care of himself and gets plenty of exercise. He was Australian; he probably swam and ran and did that kind of healthy outdoor thing. He was tanned and his curly blond hair gave him a very boyish look, and he was looking at her with the sort of frank admiration that she had hoped to see on John's face when she walked out of the bushes.

He would do. She knew he was keen – he'd tried a couple of times before. And this time, he was going to get lucky. The way she felt right now, she would have sex with a squirrel as long as it was male.

'I just thought I'd get away from camp for a bit,' she said, shaking her head so that her braids danced. 'I wanted a bit more exercise, yeah?'

He grinned. 'Jeez, you must be fit. Most people are sitting around the fire waiting for tea and complaining about the climb today.'

'That wasn't a climb,' she said. They were looking at each other with that hot, direct contact that meant that sparks were flying, and she could feel the sparks too. All it had taken was that sense of a man wanting her, and the arousal which John's body had begun was revived as if someone had blown on the embers of a fire. Her limbs tingled with excitement, her back straightened, her shoulders went back; she preened. She felt great and gorgeous.

Greg had seemed a little hesitant to begin with. Probably afraid that he was going to get rebuffed again. But he seemed to have picked up now that she was interested, that things were different, and his face brightened and he came a little closer to her.

'You look amazing,' he said. 'I mean, amazing. Exercise must agree with you.'

'It does,' she said, circling her shoulderblades and stretching her neck. 'But I could do with some more.'

Shameless, obvious flirtation, and he was lapping it up. He came a couple of steps closer and her heart began to speed up. 'I reckon,' he said, in a rather hoarse voice, 'I reckon I could manage some sort of a workout myself.'

Her nipples were so erect that they were standing out through the shiny fabric of her crop top like two thimbles. 'Maybe we should pair up,' she said, and licked her lips.

'What,' he said, still slowly approaching, 'like work-out partners?'

'Something like that,' she said. She took a couple of steps back, until her back rested against the smooth silver-grey trunk of one of the beeches by the path. She lifted her hands above her head to grip the trunk and lowered her head, looking up at him through the screen of her braids. 'Something like that.'

That was clear enough. Decision flashed across his face and he almost jumped the rest of the distance towards her. That was just what she wanted, a man so eager that he couldn't keep his hands off her. She arched her back and turned her face up towards him and he flung himself against her, pressing the whole length of his body against hers, his hands over hers on the trunk of the tree, frantically searching until he found her lips and gasped, 'Christ, you're so gorgeous,' into her open mouth and then pushed his tongue between her lips, hard, so that she gasped and kissed him back with all the pent-up frustration flooding out as their tongues twisted and thrust.

'God, I've got to have you,' he muttered. He slid his hands down her long bare arms, caressed the soft insides of her elbows, kissed her bicep, moved his lips to her armpit and actually kissed her there, where she was sweaty and pungent. She cried out with surprise and delight that he would want to touch her, to kiss her, even there.

'What a woman,' he hissed, and he got hold of her top and pulled it up, over her head, up her arms to her wrists. He left it there, so that her wrists were held by the twisted stretchy fabric and her shallow breasts were bare, the dark stiff nipples rising and falling swiftly as she panted with eagerness.

'Lovely tits,' he muttered, 'beautiful little tits, look at them, they're perfect; look at how they turn up.' He palmed them, letting the nipples peep through his fingers, and briefly looked into her face. 'Do you like having them sucked?' he asked, squeezing slightly. 'Do you want me to suck them?'

'Oh yes,' she said. 'Yes.' She did, too. She wanted him to worship her, to adore her, to recharge her self-esteem. He lowered his head to one breast and slowly, deliciously drew the nipple into his mouth and sucked, then nibbled at the resilient flesh with his front teeth, flickered his tongue against the puckered tip, sucked again. She groaned with pleasure, clutching more tightly at the trunk of the tree and thrusting her hips against his. His cock was stiff inside his shorts; she could feel it hot against the skin of her thigh, and she lifted one leg and draped it over his hip so that she could rub herself against him more easily. Her clit was swollen and burning with eagerness and her whole belly felt empty, hungry to be filled.

He sucked her breasts for what seemed like hours, until the nipples were so swollen that they were almost painful and she was sure that her juices would start trickling down her legs at any moment, she was so wet. Then as he sucked he deftly unfastened her shorts. She lowered her leg to let them fall, stepped out of them, trampled them. He sank to his knees, reached up to cup her breasts in his hands, and kissed the tight black curls of her pubic hair.

'You're so beautiful,' he said, brushing his nose against her mound. 'God, baby, I can't wait to watch myself going into you. I can't wait. But I'm going to make you come first.'

A little part of her was almost surprised at how giving he was, at how he seemed to want to celebrate her being a woman rather than take what a man normally wanted. She'd thought he would be more selfish than that. But it suited her down to the ground and she didn't question it, just held on more tightly to the tree and closed her eyes with a whimper of delight as he pressed his face to the join of her thighs and extended his questing tongue.

Oh, God, it was good to feel him licking her, to feel the petals of her pussy lips slowly parted by the firm dampness of his tongue, the soft delicious pressure on her clit, the deliberate nipping of his fingers on the peaks of her breasts. She gave herself up to it, leaned back against the smooth hard tree trunk, closed her eyes and, on the insides of her eyelids, painted once again the vision of John working out, his wonderful body spinning, leaping, his muscles flexing and gleaming with sweat. But this time she walked out from among the bushes and he saw her and came to a dead stop, shivering like a greyhound just before the off, watching in heaving silence as she stripped off her clothes and walked towards him, lean and naked and magnificent. She got closer and he tensed, and then he leaped, catching hold of her and bearing her down to the ground with such violence that the breath was knocked out of her, holding her down so that she could feel his strength and power, then pushing himself into her and arching his body high over hers so that she could watch his abs working as he thrust into her over and over again, until she twisted and writhed and screamed and came.

'Was that good?' Greg whispered, rubbing his gleaming face against her belly, leaving a shining streak. 'Was that good, baby?'

She almost said *Don't call me baby*, because it really irritated her, but she hadn't finished with him yet. All she said was, 'Yeah, great,' and then, because she could fancy it, 'Do you want some?'

'Hey, no, babe, it's OK.' Now that really surprised her. How many men turn down head? But Greg was rubbing his cheek against her body as he stood up, nursing at her breasts, clutching at her buttocks. 'No, baby, I just want to have you. I want to feel my cock inside you. Do you want that, baby?'

Of course she bloody wanted it. She said, 'I hope you've got a condom.'

'Never without one, babe,' Greg said, reaching into the pocket of his shorts and flourishing the little packet.

'Thank God,' Zoe said, licking her lips. 'Come on, Greg, don't keep me waiting.'

He smiled, rather smugly, she thought. 'Jeez, you're hot for me, aren't you, baby?'

Not for you, dickhead, just for your dick. 'Come on,' was all she said, and as he unfastened his shorts and pulled his cock out she glanced down to check out whether there was enough there to be worthwhile. There was. In fact, he had quite a nice one, not terribly long but a good thickness and as stiff as a tent peg. As he rolled the condom on she hooked her thigh over his hip again and said, 'Now.'

She wanted that feeling of being held and, as he looked down and guided the head of his cock to the right spot, she poised herself. He began to enter her, and she reached down for a moment and grabbed his hands and put them under her bum and then she jumped up and wrapped her legs around his waist. He grunted with surprise, but then he seemed to get the picture and took her weight, leaning forward slightly to press her back against the tree and moaning as his cock slipped up inside her.

Oh, it felt good, to have that thick hardness filling her up. She reached up again to grip the trunk above her head. The sensation of her breasts lifting, of the cool air on her armpits, turned her on. Greg moaned, 'Baby,' and withdrew slowly, then thrust in again.

'Go on,' she said. 'Greg, go on.' Then she shut her eyes again and arched her hips towards him each time he thrust and changed him in her mind's eye to John, imagined John's muscles of golden marble twitching and flexing as he supported her weight, as he slid her up and down on his penetrating shaft, imagined John's impassive face softening, relaxing into a gasp of pleasure as she gripped him tight with the muscles of her cunt, squeezing him, milking him, showing him that there, where it mattered, she was as strong as he was.

'Oh God, baby, that's good, yeah, squeeze me,' Greg muttered, and she wished he would shut up because she was sure that John wouldn't say anything. She arched her back and tensed her hips and squeezed as hard as she could. There wasn't enough pressure on her clit to give her another orgasm, but tightening her inner muscles as Greg thrust sent deep pulses of pleasure through her, as if she was still coming. It felt so good, she was content, at least for now.

'Yeah, baby.' It sounded and felt as if Greg was going to come soon, and he did, fingertips clutching at her buttocks, breath rasping in her ear. She waited a few moments, then let her legs slip back down to the ground.

'I didn't come again,' she said, letting herself sound hard done by.

Greg looked distressed, as if this was a slight on his manhood. 'Don't worry, baby,' he said, panting slightly. 'Don't worry, I'll do it for you.' He slipped back to his knees in front of her, but to her surprise he didn't use his mouth again. He looked at her very carefully and then slowly slipped one finger between her legs, exploring until her hiss of pleasure told him that he had found her clit. Then he began to stroke her.

Now this he was really good at. She could hardly believe how sensitively he touched her. He seemed alive to every movement, every twitch of reaction. Within moments he had her panting, and then he pushed her thighs apart and began to stroke and squeeze the soft inner flesh with his other hand, and when she moaned he moved his hand so that while his dextrous finger still quivered against her clit he could slide his fingers inside her, first one, then two, then three, then all the fingers of his left hand forcing their way past the outer lips of her cunt, like the thickest cock that ever existed, stretching her and tormenting her until she came with a gasp that was almost a scream.

That time, she noticed as she recovered, she hadn't thought of John. Greg was looking up at her as if he expected some praise, and she just said, 'Wow.'

He stood up. 'Want to do it again sometime, baby?'

'Maybe,' she said cautiously, and then couldn't resist adding, 'but only if you don't call me *baby*.'

He looked absolutely astonished. 'Hey, don't get hot and bothered, yeah?'

'I'm not hot and bothered,' she said, pulling her shorts up. 'I just don't like it.'

'Hey, whatever.' He fastened his shorts, still looking at her admiringly. 'You know, you really are a babe, whatever you say. You're so fit. I can't keep my hands off you.'

'Thanks,' she said. But this guy was married, wasn't he? She had to ask, 'Listen, Greg, does Sandy know you get up to this?'

'Oh, Sandy's cool. We swing, y'know?'

Never in all her life had Zoe heard anyone actually say *we swing*. But that would explain Sandy and Priss, in any case. She nodded, then said, 'I think this might be quite an interesting trip for the pair of you then.'

'Yeah, I reckon.' Greg looked pleased with himself. 'I got a plan, actually. I reckon that by the end of this tramp maybe me and Sandy'll have got to have sex with everyone. Like a kind of relay race, y'know? Don't you think that would be cool?'

'What, everyone?'

'Should be possible.' God, he was a smug twat. Was he suggesting that all the women on the trip would find him irresistible? And did he really believe that someone like John would want to fuck Sandy? Get real, Greg.

She just said, 'I'll watch with interest.'

'You'll take part, won't you?' He was grinning at her. 'I mean, we had a good time, yeah? You'll want to do that again?'

He had certainly been adequate. But she had been so horny that she would have settled for a lot less, and she didn't know whether in the cold light of day she would want to do it again. She didn't reply, just pulled her top back on and began to head back down the track towards the camp.

'Zoe,' he called after her, sounding anxious now, 'you would want to, wouldn't you?'

'Maybe,' she called over her shoulder. Maybe she would, but it would depend on who else was involved. 'Maybe.'

Chapter Six
Kathy

The night had been as hot and sticky as the day. Kathy had ended up on top of her sleeping bag rather than in it, risking the mosquitoes and sandflies, and she'd still woken up sweaty and uncomfortable.

Mind you, that hadn't just been the heat. Julie stirred on the mat beside her, and Kathy said in a low voice, 'Julie, are you awake?'

'Mm.' Julie sat up, pushing both hands through her long, soft hair. She blinked. 'I hope we stay at a hut tonight. I really have to change my lenses and I just don't like to do it where there isn't nice clean running water.'

Kathy really didn't want to talk about sanitary arrangements of any kind. She had spent a bad night and now she wanted to discuss just what had kept her awake. She leaned a little closer and said in a low voice, 'You know, Julie, I'm sure there's something going on on this trek.'

Julie blinked her big eyes. 'What d'you mean?'

'I mean,' Kathy said, dropping her voice even further,

'I mean between people, if you get my drift. Last night, for example. There was a lot of noise last night, and it wasn't all Greg and Sandy.' Julie looked puzzled, and Kathy hissed, 'Obviously Greg and Sandy are at it like rabbits, but I think it's not just with each other! I'm sure I heard Diva and Priss, ah, having sex. And not just them either. I think TJ is involved, and I thought Zoe was looking pretty smug as well. What was all that crap she and Greg were talking over dinner about workouts, and all the significant looks? And why did Diva and Priss join in? I'm sure there's something going on. It's as if everybody on this damn trip apart from us is leaping into bed with everybody else at the slightest opportunity. Which, given how hard the mattresses are, must mean they have pretty bloody high sex drives!'

Julie looked away. She was practically blushing. 'I don't think so,' she said, shaking her head. 'I mean, I didn't hear anything. Honestly.'

Kathy frowned. Julie was by no means stupid, so what was all this about? Why should she pretend not to have heard something you'd have to be stone deaf to have missed? Perhaps she was easily embarrassed and didn't like talking about things like that, but for God's sake, they were both grown women. It was odd, this sharing a tent with someone you'd never met before. You were thrown together so much that you became intimate really before you became close, which was by no means the usual order. Sometimes she wasn't quite sure how to handle it.

There was no point in worrying anyway. If Julie was offended, she ought to say so. 'Well,' Kathy said decisively, sitting on her sleeping bag to flatten it before she rolled it up, 'I think something's afoot. And I tell you, while we're on the subject, I wouldn't say no to a bit of a workout with TJ, if it was on offer. He is just gorgeous. And those tattoos, wow.'

Julie shook her head as she started on her own sleeping bag. 'I don't know,' she said, sounding shy. 'He's not my cup of tea, really. A bit too, well, earthy.'

'Earthy? Sounds good to me!' Kathy rammed the sleeping bag down into its stuffsac. Why would they never fit back in? What was it she was doing wrong? The damn thing seemed to have as many corners as an icosahedron and as many tentacles as an octopus. 'Who would you go for then?' she asked, puffing as she forced a corner down and watched another one pop up.

There was a long silence and she glanced across at Julie, wondering if she had offended her. Again. But no, Julie's long face was thoughtful; she was obviously mulling the question over.

'Steve?' Kathy suggested. 'Greg?'

'Oh, not Greg,' Julie said, with what was almost a pout. 'And Steve, well ... No, the one I would –' She hesitated, then stopped and pressed her lips tightly together and addressed herself to her sleeping bag.

'Oh, go on,' Kathy urged. 'I told you mine.'

Julie's heavy eyelids swept down over her eyes. 'Well,' she said, in what was scarcely more than a whisper, 'Rick.'

'Mm,' Kathy said, musing. Rick: tall, dark eyes, dark hair, bit of a Heathcliff sort of look. 'Interesting choice. He is nice looking, for sure. But don't you think he's a bit, I don't know, a bit cold?'

'Cold?' The big eyes fixed on her for a minute, wide open. 'No. I don't think he's cold at all.'

Kathy sat by herself at breakfast, taking the opportunity to watch what was going on. A careful study of the dynamics of the group would tell her a lot, she was sure. So she nursed her bowl of porridge, which she hardly wanted to eat on such a sticky morning anyway, and let her eyes roam from group to group.

Zoe, for example. Zoe had started off with Greg, who was behaving almost possessively towards her. But then Greg went to get a coffee and at once Priss went over to Zoe and sat down on Greg's rock beside her, saying something that made her laugh. They talked for a while, Priss's face alert and eager, Zoe's first frowning, then delighted. After a while they began giggling like a couple of schoolgirls and Zoe gestured with her eyes towards the horses. Kathy followed the lead and saw the Chinese guy, John, dealing with one of the pack saddles. Was he involved, then? What was going on there? And now Priss was saying something funny and glancing towards the youngest kid on the support team. Gordon Bennett, how many of them were up to this?

Greg returned, carrying two cups of coffee, handed one to Zoe and looked at Priss as if he expected her to get up and let him sit down. But she looked up at him with a bland, blank face and didn't move, and Zoe blanked him too.

Now what? Kathy looked across the camp and saw Diva sitting with Greg's wife Sandy, looking as thick as thieves. So they were up to something as well. What were they planning? From where she sat it looked as if they might be sizing up Jason, the youngest of the trekkers, but she couldn't be sure.

And Rick, Julie's object of desire, was standing not far behind them, watching them with an expression that was hard to read, but might have been amused tolerance. In which case he would know what was going on. He lifted his head as if he had felt her eyes, looked directly at her, and smiled. A subtle smile, a conspiratorial smile, but a secret one. It told her that something was up, but didn't invite her to join in.

Looked as though Julie had missed her chance then. Obviously if you wanted a man on this trip, you had to act fast!

Kathy let out a long sigh and went to wash up her plate and cup. She felt strange and not at all happy. Watching all these goings-on around her, listening to them at night, made her acutely aware of what she was missing.

She had been single for a while, and at forty that was not so easy to fix. There weren't a lot of single men of her age on the market, and those that there were fell in to two types: those who had always been single, in which case there was always a damn good reason, and those who had been attached and were now single, who universally carried baggage. Plus, as she had got older, she had become more choosy. Any man who could walk and talk wasn't good enough for her any more: she wanted the type of man she wanted. So, for a start, there weren't very many, and then half of them were write-offs before she started, and of the half that remained she would be bound not to fancy at least three-quarters for one reason or another, and altogether that meant that there were pretty lean pickings.

Plus there was that creeping, insidious suspicion that perhaps she was getting past her sell-by date. For a start, why did the few single men her age so often want to go out with women who were ten years younger than them? Were wrinkle-free skin and high boobs really so important? She knew that she was fit, that she had a decent body, that she was attractive: but that didn't seem to mean that she was a prime target.

On this holiday she'd have been delighted to settle for some uncomplicated sex, if she had guessed that it was on offer. As it was, the people around her all seemed to be having uncomplicated sex, and every one of them was younger than her, and altogether it made her feel pretty bad.

She picked up her daypack and slung it on with a sigh. A few years ago she'd have found it amusing to watch the goings-on all day and speculate about who was the ringleader and who were the followers. Now she felt left out, passed over, dismissed.

On the trail she found herself walking beside Sarah, the thin, earnest-looking young vet who shared a tent with Zoe. Sarah seemed to take everything terribly seriously. She had read up on all the flora and fauna before she came, and she waxed her boots and wrote up her journal every night, and she always went a long way away from the camp to pee, and she sat in the mess tent after dark reading Dickens by the light of the gas lantern, and according to Zoe she did yoga exercises in her tent every morning and every evening. It seemed entirely possible that at some stage in her young life she had received a fun bypass. What on earth would she make of all the high jinks?

Perhaps it would be easier not to mention it. In fact, that would definitely be the line of least resistance. Kathy hadn't talked to Sarah much, so she just said, 'Enjoying the trip so far?'

Sarah looked at her for a moment before replying. She had wide, rabbit-in-the-headlights eyes, so that she looked permanently startled, or scared. It made Kathy feel as if she was being assessed as a potential predator. Eventually Sarah said in her slightly breathless voice, 'The mountains are absolutely incredible. They've really exceeded my expectations, really.'

Kathy nodded thoughtfully. Sarah was quite right, the landscape was beyond belief and, as they climbed towards the ridge that was the highest point of the tramp, the views became ever more spectacular. That's why she had come, wasn't it? To look at the beautiful country? So why was she getting so upset about what other people had decided to do with their holidays?

'You're absolutely right,' she said to Sarah, with decision. 'It's wonderful.'

'Bit sticky today,' Sarah went on. This was no exaggeration; they were both of them visibly sweating even though they were only on a gentle climb. 'But TJ said that there would be a storm before too long.' Her wide eyes widened further. 'Can you imagine a storm in these mountains? I'm really looking forward to it.'

That surprised Kathy. 'Not scared of thunder?' she asked with a smile.

'Oh no, I love it. It makes me feel really alive.'

Well, there was a turn up for the books. 'I just hope there's a hut tonight, if it's going to rain,' Kathy said practically.

Sarah's face looked pinched. 'I hope not.'

'You hope not? What, you like the tents?'

Sarah hesitated, then her lips tightened. 'Well,' she said, in a low voice, 'I just don't like to think what people will get up to once they've got a roof over their heads.'

She had a point, but Kathy didn't like the censorious tone. She said judiciously, 'I think that, as long as nobody tries to do anything to anyone who doesn't want to, it's up to them, really.'

Sarah looked as if she would either explode with anger or burst out crying. 'I really don't agree,' she said. 'If I'm sleeping in a hut, it's my bedroom as well, isn't it? I ought to have a say on what goes on in there.

It would be like Zoe bringing a, bringing a man into our tent if I didn't want to.'

She sounded as though this was really getting to her.

'And you don't want to.'

Kathy had tried to keep her tone neutral, but Sarah flared up. 'I know what you're thinking. I know what everybody's thinking. You think I'm a prude, an old maid, someone with a thing about sex, a sort of nun. Don't you?'

'I didn't mean that,' Kathy said, although she had to admit that that was how Sarah came across.

'I don't have a problem with sex *per se*,' Sarah insisted. 'I just think that it ought to be special. Something –' she seemed to struggle for the words. 'Something, something almost divine, something two people experience when they are truly in tune with each other. That's what I think sex ought to be about. Not something physical, like scratching an itch, or a competitive sport, the way Zoe seems to see it.' Her voice was heavy with scorn. 'Particularly,' she finished, 'in particular, I think it's private. And I don't enjoy being surrounded by it, like wallpaper.'

'Well, wow.' Kathy lifted her eyebrows. 'You have fairly high expectations of sex then?'

'That's right,' said Sarah definitely.

'And you've actually –' Kathy considered how she might put this '– you have personal experience of this, ah, transcendental union?'

Sarah looked blank, then blushed. The blush started at her throat and climbed quickly all the way up her pale cheeks and right into her hairline. She didn't say anything, but Kathy knew for certain that far from experiencing any transcendental union, Sarah had never had sex with anyone at all.

She didn't want to seem to be taking the piss, but

she couldn't ignore Sarah's reaction either. She said quite gently, 'Sarah, you can believe anything about sex you want. That's your right. But I think you're going to find yourself in the minority on this trip. You'd better just keep out of the way of the people who think it's a sport because I get the feeling that they're going to be quite busy.'

'I suppose that includes you,' Sarah said with what appeared to be an attempt at defiance.

Kathy grinned. 'Chance would be a fine thing.'

'I thought you might understand.' Sarah looked really distressed. She turned her head away and dropped back.

Kathy let her go. She looked over her shoulder and saw her waiting to be caught up by the rear of the column, where TJ was walking with the older couple, Alan and Jan. That was likely to prove less challenging company.

When she turned back to the trail she was surprised to find Rick at her shoulder, smiling his dark smile at her. Her immediate reaction was one of excitement. Why was he there? Was he just being friendly, or did he carry the key to getting involved in whatever was going on? She smiled back at him and said, 'Well, hello.'

'I couldn't help but overhear a bit of that,' Rick said, falling into step beside her. 'She's not finding this to her taste, is she?'

'Not finding what to her taste?' Kathy asked, with mock innocence.

'Don't try that with me,' said Rick, smiling again. 'I saw you at the camp, watching the faces. I think you must have formed a pretty good idea of the proceedings.'

Kathy shrugged. 'I'm not so sure. I can tell that there

are a lot of proceedings, if that's what you want to call them. I'm not sure how they fit together though.' She looked up at him, hopeful. 'If you're in a position to enlighten me, I'd be particularly grateful.' Oops, that was careless language. Would he interpret it as a come-on? She hadn't meant it that way.

He raised his eyebrows at her and she realised that he had followed the whole of her thought process. Well, he was a subtle one. Not her cup of tea, really, good-looking though he was. He said, 'Have you guessed the instigators?'

She glanced up the track to where Zoe was walking with Priss and Diva, Greg trailing along a little way behind her, a sulky shadow. 'I was thinking earlier that it might have been Greg and Sandy,' she said, 'but now I think it's Priss and Diva. I think their nocturnal activities are some kind of a signal, if you like.'

'Well done,' he said, nodding seriously. 'They have an idea of a sort of relay race, everybody on the trip getting involved over the course of the eight days. I think they're making fair progress, so far.'

'Including you?' she speculated.

He wagged his head. 'I think you should see me as on the periphery. I did have a brief encounter, as you might say, with Diva, but neither of those girls are really my type. But I admire their presumption, so I've allowed myself to be talked into playing along.'

Everybody. *Everybody.* That meant that she wasn't going to be excluded! A surge of eagerness filled her, a sudden resurgence of sexual adventure. 'Do you have to wait to be picked,' she asked boldly, 'or can anyone volunteer?'

'Oh, volunteers are absolutely welcome.' Rick grinned. 'And I don't think they've quite got the rules settled. So if you wanted to start with someone else entirely, that would be your privilege.'

Kathy bit her lip, thought for a moment, then laughed out loud at her own excitement, her own boldness. 'My God, the world is my mollusc! Where shall I start?'

'Wherever you choose, of course. If you wanted to talk to Priss and Diva, I'm sure they would have some ideas. At the moment they're planning –'

She frowned and interrupted him. 'No, I want to think about it for myself.' It was funny: he didn't seem as if he would be offended by her not considering him. It was as if they were partners in crime. She said confidentially, 'To be honest, the one I really fancy is TJ.'

He lifted his eyebrows, then fished a little packet out of his shorts pocket and held it out to her, saying, 'God be with you, my child.'

A condom! She stared, then laughed, then said, 'What's your drift?'

'I dare you,' he said. 'Take the condom. Take TJ. Do it by dinnertime.'

She nearly said, Yeah, sure, nice try, funny joke. She nearly laughed it off. But she was so excited, so possessed by the idea of a dare, she couldn't. For a moment she just looked and thought. Too old? Past it? Forty and out of the race?

And then she reached out and took the condom.

'Very good,' Rick said. 'Priss and Diva will be delighted.'

'So will I, if I get anywhere.' She remembered that she had interrupted him, and said, 'And by the way, you were going to say what Priss and Diva had in mind for now.'

'Oh, yes. Well, I mentioned your tentmate. They're going to have a go at mine.'

'Oh, Jason!' She couldn't stop herself from laughing. Everybody laughed at Jason. He was a frightfully nice boy, well educated, well brought up, apparently intelligent, in that he held down a good job in a government scientific institution. But he was either unbelievably naïve or as dense in other respects as several bricks, and he seemed to have no general knowledge or understanding of the world whatsoever. 'Good grief,' she said, 'what d'you think he'll make of that?'

'I think he'll be astonished. He doesn't have a clue that any of this is happening.'

Kathy shook her head in delighted disbelief. 'That boy is incredible! Doesn't he have ears?'

'He did say this morning that he thought a lot of people seemed to be having nightmares.'

Kathy snorted. 'D'you reckon he knows which end is up?'

'Debatable. Anyway, Priss and Diva are looking forward to finding out. They've even lined me up to assist.'

Now that made Kathy lift her eyebrows. 'How exactly?'

Rick smiled. 'On this occasion, just getting him out of our tent. On this occasion.'

'Well, I await the outcome with interest.'

They walked on for a moment in silence, while Kathy contemplated the enormity of her dare. Then Rick said, 'By the way, while we're talking about tentmates. I don't know what your inclinations are, but you strike me as someone who knows her own mind. I'd just like to make the observation that, if you wanted to, I'm sure you could seduce yours.'

'My tentmate? *Julie?*' Kathy boggled. 'Are you serious?'

'Oh, absolutely. She strikes me as distinctly – pliant. Try it and see.'

Pliant? He sounded almost hungry. Did she recognise an echo of that hunger in herself? She didn't like to think so, and she frowned. 'I think that's a bit out of my depth, to be honest. I'll stick with TJ.'

'As you wish.' Rick lifted an admonitory finger. 'Remember though. By dinnertime.'

Dinnertime! And after lunch she hadn't done anything about it, and the condom was burning a hole in her pocket.

Well, she hadn't exactly done *nothing*. She had changed her position among the group, so that she was now walking at the back with Alan and Jan and TJ. Sarah had scowled at her and gone somewhere else, and good riddance.

It was easy to feel irritable, as the weather still hadn't broken. Great blue-black thunderclouds hung overhead, pregnant with rain, and sudden strong gusts of wind whipped across the ridge where they climbed, and the horses trailing behind TJ had flat ears and rolling eyes. But still there was no storm.

'It may hold off just until we reach the top of the ridge,' TJ said.

'I hope so,' said Jan. 'I'm looking forward to the view. Curtains of rain would spoil it rather.'

'Not far now,' Alan said, pointing ahead. 'Look, you can see it.'

Kathy really rather liked Alan and Jan. They were in their mid-fifties, fit and well preserved, and had apparently taken to going on long trekking holidays when the last of their three children left the nest a couple of years back. Now they spent four or five months of every year travelling, on a shoestring budget like a couple of students, and it was really refreshing to meet people their age who didn't think that enjoying themselves needed a cruise ship or a five-star hotel with attached golf course.

They were a good-looking couple too. Alan was tall and lean, with receding close-cropped grey hair and a short neat beard, which he said was much easier than trying to shave with cold water in yet another backpackers' hostel. Jan was small and slim and wore her hair shoulder-length with a heavy fringe. She walked in an Indian cotton skirt, rather than trousers, and tended to have knot-fringed scarves draped here and there about her person, and it was altogether very easy to imagine her as an early 70s hippie chick with eyeliner and Joan Baez records. Kathy would also be prepared to lay money on the pair of them being no strangers to the kinds of illegal substances that were often to be had in backpackers' hostels, at least in the past.

Altogether she thought that Priss and Diva would be a lot more likely to find success with Jan and Alan than they were with Sarah, whom she personally bet would prove to be the fly in the sexual ointment, so to speak. However, right now, nice as they were, Alan and Jan were in the way. Seriously in the way.

All the same, it was hard to think about getting her hands on TJ when they were approaching the top of the ridge. On either side the stunning South Island mountains stretched away and, despite the thunderheads above them, the air was crystal clear, so that when they looked back at switchback ridge they had climbed they could see beyond it, faintly gleaming, the ocean.

It was obvious that they had to sit and look at the view for a bit. People broke out chocolate bars and bags of dried fruit and someone suggested brewing up, but Steve didn't think it was a good idea. 'More like get your waterproofs out,' he suggested.

Alan shook his head. 'It's so damn hot, I think I'll just let myself get wet.'

'Might get cold later, Al,' Jan said warningly.

They could all have looked at the view for hours, but Steve seemed anxious to move them on before the storm broke. 'It's not far to the next camp,' he said, 'and you try putting the tents up in a storm; it's a real pain, much better to get there and get it done.'

So they left the vista and went on, downhill now, walking quite quickly, and there was no chance at all for her to talk to TJ alone, never mind get him alone. It wasn't her fault, but she felt bad about the possibility that she might not achieve the dare. What would she say to Rick?

Above them the sky darkened and the wind increased, but it still didn't feel cold. In the dense humidity she sweated, her T-shirt soaked, her shorts leaden. At one point she found herself walking beside TJ, but she couldn't think of the right thing to say, the thing that would seem innocuous and in fact carry the inference that he would be able to grasp. And would he fancy her anyway? Would he want to have sex with her? He had a choice, after all, and he'd had either the vigorous Priss or the beautiful Diva already, possibly both, so why would he want her?

That kind of thinking was not likely to be helpful. OK, TJ hadn't exactly been all over her, but he'd been friendly and sparky and they'd been with other people the whole time anyway. Even if he'd been dying for it he might not have shown it. She was in with a chance. She just had to wait.

So she waited, waited all the way to camp, and then she helped TJ picket the horses, and she knew that if she let him get involved in the next task her whole chance would have been lost. So, as he clapped the last horse on the neck, she said, 'TJ, I wonder –'

He glanced up at her, and she thought that his expression changed slightly. Had he caught something in her tone? But it was hard to say; the tattoos made him seem to be snarling even when he wasn't. She just said, 'Could I show you something?'

'Sure,' he said, looking a little confused.

'It's over this way,' she said, leading the way into the forest undergrowth beyond the camp clearing.

'D'you mind getting wet?' he asked her, as a few fat drops of rain made the leaves around them shiver and rattle.

Did she? No, she bloody didn't. She hadn't let herself get aroused during the walk, but knowing what she had planned now was really doing it for her. The tension was terrible, not knowing if he would want to, how he would react. If he turned her down –

'The rain feels good,' she said, and it did. It was cool and fresh, delicious after the long hot day.

'There's going to be a lot more of it,' TJ said, and followed her down a scramble of rocks. 'Where is whatever it is?'

'Here,' she said, stopping in a gap in the undergrowth between three or four great tall trees, whose widespread leaves trembled as the rain continued to fall.

'Where?' He looked puzzled.

Now or never. She swallowed, then reached up

behind her, unclipped her bra through her T-shirt, and stripped T-shirt and bra off together. 'Here,' she said.

TJ's black eyes flashed immediately to her breasts, remained there for a moment, then returned to her face. He was smiling, and she felt as if a weight had been taken from her. He liked what he saw; he liked it! His eyebrows arced upwards, highlighted by the tattoos. 'And?'

Raindrops filtered through the leaves and struck her skin, making her shiver and come out in goosebumps. Her nipples tautened, the rosy skin crinkling as a single cold trickle of rain ran down between her breasts. 'And I wanted you to show me your tattoos.'

He put his head on one side. 'I don't show them to just anyone, you know.'

She nodded slowly, pushed her way out of her boots and began to unfasten her shorts. Now her shivering wasn't just the rain – it was the thought of having him, of feeling that smooth Maori skin pressed against her naked body. She said, 'I'm sure I can make it worth your while.'

Lightning flashed and moments later a huge thunderclap rolled over them, making them start and look up. The rain began to fall harder, pelting its way through the canopy of leaves.

She pushed off her shorts and panties. 'I don't think we need to worry about anyone overhearing us.'

He took a step closer. 'I didn't realise that you were part of this game too.'

'Just inducted,' she said, and now she felt bold enough to go to meet him and put her hand on his strong bare forearm, stroking it, sensing the hard muscle under the skin. She slid her hand up his arm, on to the bulge of his bicep under his sleeve. 'And you?'

'Just going along for the ride,' he said.

She stepped closer and as she moved her hand to cup his crotch and feel the stirring of his cock the lightning and the thunder came again, absolutely together, and the heavens opened.

Lances of rain hurled themselves through the canopy, making streaks in the suddenly darkened air. Shocked, soaked, she pressed herself against him for a moment, seeking the shelter of his big body. She turned up her face and he kissed her chin, her throat, cupped her breasts in his hands.

She realised that she wanted him to please her, even though she was the one who was asking. She wanted to take, not give. So she twisted her hands in the coarse shining waves of blue-black hair and tugged, pulling him down in front of her, making him kneel on the wet moss, and she held his head still and pushed her body against him, demanding the services of his lips and tongue.

If he had had any other ideas, he didn't insist. His hands went around to hold her buttocks and at once he began to eat her, hungrily, noisily, as if he had been starved. She held on to his hair and arched backwards, offering her face and throat and breasts to the lashing rain, every drop like a cold needle on her skin, whipping against her tender nipples, stinging her lips and eyelids.

TJ's thirsty tongue slavered between her legs, lapping like a beast at a waterhole, and she grunted and jerked her hips against his face, willing him to go on. The tip of his tongue latched on to her clit and flickered there and she cried out and tightened her fingers in his hair, forcing herself forward, grinding her pussy against him, frigging herself on his face as he teased her clit with his tongue. The rain streamed down her shoulders and back, coursed in rivulets along the curves of belly and haunches, and the heat of her approaching orgasm was so intense that she didn't even feel the cold. She gasped, 'Yes!' and arced backwards, holding herself up with her death-grip on his hair, shuddering as she came.

Then she reached for her shorts and pulled the condom from the pocket and grabbed him as he got to his feet, shirt plastered to his body, face gleaming with her juice. She pulled his shorts open and reached inside to grab his cock, let out a quick gasp of delight as she felt its thick stiffness, and rolled the condom on. Then she sat down on the wet moss and pulled him down on top of her and he didn't hesitate, just poised himself between her spread legs and positioned his cock and thrust so that it slipped right up her, filling her.

It felt so good to be fucked by him, just straightforward simple fucking, and she looked up past his dark face and closed eyes to the thrashing leaves and the pillars of rain and beyond the leaves the dark towering clouds and the thunder and the lightning, and all she wanted was for him to shaft her as hard as he could. No subtlety, no technique, just fast brutal in-out in-out, primeval and wonderful. The moss beneath her was cold and beneath it the rock was hard and she felt herself bruise and chill and didn't care, because the cock in her cunt was strong and stiff and TJ had wanted to do it to her and she wasn't past it.

The furious tempo of his shafting increased; she knew he would come soon, and she dug her fingernails into his shoulders and lifted her head to bite his neck and he shouted and froze, his whole body shaking, eyes tight shut, mouth twisted into a snarl of pleasure-pain.

Then he fell forward on to her, and the rain dripped

from the eaves of his thick hair and trickled down her face, and she was panting and completely happy.

After a moment he pushed himself back and withdrew from her, removing the condom and stashing it in a pocket somewhere. His chest heaved.

'I still haven't seen your tattoos,' she said.

He grinned. 'Another time. What will I say at camp?'

'Say I took you on a wild goose chase and we got caught in the rain.' She reached for her clothes, though it was hardly worth putting on wet dishrags. 'And don't think I'll forget about the tattoos.'

He gave her a hand to pull her up. 'Come on, we ought to get back.'

He led the way back through the rain. The storm was passing over now and behind it the sun was beginning to come out. Brilliant shafts of light danced through the steaming air and every leaf glistened. In her post-coital state it was as if the forest had been sprinkled with diamonds.

The whole experience had raised her confidence. If she could foist herself on TJ in that way, then –

Then what about Julie?

She'd never had sex with a woman before, let alone seduced one. But Rick had said it would be possible, and he seemed to be a good judge of such matters. How had he described Julie? That she was likely to be – *pliant*, that was it.

Pliant. Someone who would do what they were told. Kathy drew in a deep breath, realising that she found the concept very appealing. She imagined herself in the man's role, pushing Julie back, tilting back her head until her lips parted, forcing her tongue between those parted lips, holding Julie down to subject her to her will.

The thought was arousing her all over again. She'd have to give it a try.

Chapter Seven

Jason

Sometimes he wondered whether there was any rhyme or reason in the way the tents got put up. Obviously some pitches were better than others, less slopy or smoother or with a better view for whoever crawled out of the flap in the morning, but at most of the pitches there didn't seem to be that much to choose between most spots and yet people still ended up sort of moving round, so you never knew whose guy ropes you would be tripping over during the night.

Anyway, at least the neighbours would be the same two nights running, as tomorrow they weren't going to shift camp at all. The horses would get a rest day, any people who felt like a rest got one too, and anyone who wanted a challenge could climb a nearby peak, overlooking the ridge they had crested today, and spend the night at a hut close to the summit. Jason was definitely going to do it. He was determined to squeeze every ounce of adventure out of his first ever foreign holiday.

He sat in the mess tent for a while, reading the

guidebook. People seemed to be coming and going a lot this evening. Maybe there'd been some dodgy food or something; they seemed to have that furtive look that usually meant a bad poo was on the way. And if he hadn't known better he might have thought that his tentmate Rick was striking up some sort of a relationship with Kathy. They were talking together, heads bowed towards each other in an intimate sort of way. But that didn't really seem very likely. Who would bother with that, with a bunch of people who'd only be together for a week? It wouldn't be worth the trouble. Jason certainly couldn't be arsed. He hadn't come away for that kind of thing.

Eventually it felt like bedtime. He wanted to be fresh for tomorrow, so he finished his beer and said goodnight to Jan and Alan, who were reading too, and headed across towards his tent. It was a dark night, still cloudy after the storm, and there was only just enough light from the mess tent to show him the way. He counted tents, so as to be sure not to stumble into Kathy and Julie's by mistake. They had already gone to bed, and breaking in on them would be embarrassing, to say the least.

Rick was lying on his sleeping bag in his underpants, reading with a torch. The storm had cleared the air a bit, but it was still very warm, probably too warm to get into a sleeping bag until you absolutely had to. Rick nodded at Jason and said, 'All right?'

'Yeah. Time for beddy byes,' Jason said, wriggling out of everything but his boxers and heading for the sack. 'You know,' he added, 'I hope we have a quieter night tonight. I –'

As if on cue, there was a moan from Kathy and Julie's tent. Jason made a despairing noise and said, 'Oh, no.'

Rick turned on to his elbow and put his book down. Looking at Jason in the light of the torch, he looked vaguely scary, all hollow eyes and cheekbones highlighted the wrong way up. He didn't say anything for a moment, and Jason felt uncomfortable. Then he said, 'More nightmares?'

'I don't understand it,' Jason said, genuinely frustrated. 'It must be the hard ground, or the food, or something. People don't have nightmares this often normally, do they?'

After another little silence, Rick said, 'Jason, I can't help but wonder if you are deliberately trying to wind everybody up.'

'Wind people up?' Jason was astonished. 'Me? What d'you mean? Why would I do that?'

Rick frowned slightly, as if he was thinking, or weighing up what Jason had said. Then he said, 'All right. I'll take you at face value, for now.'

'Well, thanks very much,' Jason said, trying to sound sarcastic. To be honest, he didn't really like Rick terribly much. He didn't seem to be a very straightforward person, and Jason preferred things to be straightforward.

'So,' Rick went on, 'if you're not trying to wind people up, then you are either preternaturally slow on the uptake, or extraordinarily unobservant.'

'What?' Jason was getting a bit cross by now, and he certainly didn't like the way this conversation seemed to be going. Apart from anything, Rick was talking down to him, and it was bloody annoying. Just because he was the youngest person on the trip didn't mean that everyone could treat him like a child. 'Listen, Rick, what are you getting at?'

'All right,' Rick said. 'Jason, I want you just to be quiet for a moment. Listen.'

Jason frowned, but did as Rick suggested.

There was the silence of the bush, the noise of the horses stamping and snorting underneath the trees, the rustle of people settling down in their tents, and, from the next door tent, a murmur, and then another long moan.

The sound made him uncomfortable, but he didn't know why. It made his bowels clench and his balls twitch. He didn't like what it did to him and, now he was really listening, he knew why. He had to admit that it sounded more like someone having sex than someone having a nightmare. He opened his mouth to say something, but Rick held up a warning finger and he subsided.

From next door there was movement, and then a voice saying softly, 'No. Lie back. Lie still.' And then, after a few rustling seconds, a sequence of quiet, smothered whimpers.

Jason looked down at his feet, biting his lip. He didn't need to be told what was going on, not now. That was a girl having, having sex . . .

Or *two* girls having sex? That was Kathy and Julie's tent. Had they made some arrangement that one of them wouldn't be there, so that a man could visit the other one and have sex with her? But he hadn't seen either of them hanging around the mess tent.

And it had been a woman's voice issuing that quiet command. A woman talking, another woman moaning.

Jesus Christ. There was no getting away from it. Kathy and Julie were having sex in the tent next door to him.

Rick looked at him, head a little on one side. 'So,' he said, 'are you clear what is going on there?'

Jason swallowed and nodded.

'And I have to tell you,' Rick said, 'that all the noises you've been hearing at night have been the same sort of noise. Nobody on this trip is prone to nightmares, Jason.'

Sex! All around him, people having sex! He'd known that Greg and Sandy had been having sex right from the start, of course, but that was because they were married – that was obvious. But the other noises . . . That first night it had been Priss or Diva, he was sure he remembered that it was their tent the noise had come from. God, another pair of girls having sex together! All these people at it like rabbits! Were all of these trekking holidays like this? It was like a blue movie or a wet dream. It was unbelievable. He hastily pulled his sweatshirt on to his lap to conceal the fact that his boxers were beginning to turn into a tiny tent of their own.

Rick was watching him with a calm curiosity that Jason found extremely unnerving. After a little while Rick said, 'I find your level of disbelief remarkable, Jason. Just how naïve are you?'

'I don't know what you're suggesting,' Jason blustered, though he knew perfectly well that Rick was insinuating that he, Jason, was a virgin at 22. 'I have had girlfriends, you know.' Absolutely true: he had. More than one. Three, in fact. He didn't happen to have one at the moment, but that was just by the way, just a gap. Because there had been three. And he had had sex with two of them. So there.

'Ah.' Rick nodded, smiling gravely. What a smug twat he was! Jason would have liked to leave the tent and the entire conversation. But he didn't dare emerge from under his sweatshirt, because the noises were still happening next door, and now that his willy knew what they were it was reacting strongly, and he had a stiffy like a milk bottle and he did *not* want to show it to Rick, who would probably make some snide comment.

'Well, anyway,' Jason said, 'I bet this kind of thing doesn't usually happen. I mean, it wasn't what I was expecting. I bet it's unusual.'

'Well, that's true,' Rick said. 'I've been on several trips like this, and I have to say that this is the first time that anything like this has happened. So I suppose it's understandable.'

'Exactly.' Whenever there was a pause in the conversation he could hear what was happening next door, and now it was as if his ears were sensitised, attuned to it, so he could make out the liquid moans, even a little slurpy sound as if someone was – as if Kathy, or was it Julie, was –

Rick's sombre face lightened slightly. 'Of course,' he said, 'it isn't just women who can make their own entertainment.'

What had he just said? What had it meant? Jason would have taken it lightly, but in this mad new world he didn't think he could, and all the meanings that he could possibly think of were both strange and unwelcome. He said hesitantly, 'I beg your pardon?'

'I mean,' said Rick, leaning a little closer and smiling, 'that if rather than sitting here listening to two women bringing each other to orgasm you would rather do something to relieve the tension, there are plenty of possibilities.'

Jason's mouth dropped open. For a moment he just gaped in horror. Say something! Say something cool and chilled that indicated that you understood exactly what this kinky bastard actually meant and that it really wasn't your scene, OK? Come on, come on –

In fact, what came out of his mouth was a strangled sort of squeak. 'Possibilities?'

Rick's smile widened. It was like watching an approaching piranha. 'Well,' he said, 'it's a bit warm for two in a sleeping bag, but anything else –'

Jesus, he was trapped in a tent with a raving homosexual! How could he have thought that there might have been something going on between Rick and Kathy? For a moment he sat staring like a rabbit in front of a snake, clutching his sweatshirt across his groin as if it was some kind of armour. Then Rick moved, leaning slightly towards him, and he catapulted to his feet and muttered something about needing a slash and hurled himself through the flap of the tent and feverishly, fumblingly zipped it up behind him, as if the flimsy zip could protect him from the ravening pervert inside.

In the porch of the tent he rammed his feet into his Speedos and then lurched out into the camp, zipping up the second flap as well, just to be safe. He started off towards the mess tent, then stopped after a couple of steps and looked down at himself.

He was wearing just his boxer shorts and Speedo mules and he had a stiffy, bouncing in front of him like a flagpole. If there was anyone in the mess tent, would they really welcome him in his current state? Probably not.

So now what the hell was he going to do? He wasn't going back into his tent, that was for damn sure as mustard. Was he supposed to sleep under a tree for the duration of the trek? That was going to be fun, wasn't it? Besides, everywhere was soaking wet after the storm. He'd get pneumonia and die and then they would all be sorry.

He looked around the camp, woebegone. Noises

were still coming from Kathy and Julie's tent, damn them. It was all their fault. Where would he find a haven?

There was a tent on the other side of the camp, outer and inner flaps open, a light faintly glowing inside. Perhaps it was Steve. Steve had a tent to himself, as befitted the leader of the trip. He could always go to Steve for refuge, couldn't he? Hah, that would be quite a problem to lay on their leader; what would he do about that one, eh?

Feeling a little better, he made his way carefully across the dark expanse between the tents towards the little light.

He had to be out of luck though; it couldn't be Steve's tent because he thought he could make out more than one person moving inside. Well, maybe it was a couple of the guys, Josh and TJ shared, didn't they? Anything would be better than going back. He took a couple of steps closer and lowered his head slightly to peer inside.

And peered. And stared. And felt his drooping flag-pole stiffen again until it stood up against his belly.

It wasn't a guy's tent. It was Priss and Diva's tent. And they were inside it. And they were naked. And they were having sex, right before his eyes.

Had he walked into a wet dream? That's what it felt like. What he could see was Diva's long opulent brown thighs, widely parted, her perfect, full, high arse split like a peach, dark fur fringing the puckered mouth of her arse, the lips of her fanny pouting downwards all flushed and gleaming, and Priss's blonde head between her legs, white fingers denting the soft thighs, pink tongue reaching upwards, burying itself between the swollen lips, Priss's eyes closed, moaning as she licked.

He took a step closer, unable to tear his eyes away. For a while he just stared at Priss licking Diva, and then he focused a little further beyond the flickering tongue and saw Diva's firm breasts hanging down, dark nipples swollen and taut, swaying slightly as her body moved, and Diva's fountain of dark hair hanging over her face, which was dipped down between Priss's spread thighs.

Priss's head tilted backwards, her eyes closed. She was still moaning, making words. He took another step and heard her. 'Yes, yes, I'm coming, I'm –' And then Priss's closed eyes tightened in ecstasy and she let out a long, heartfelt sigh of delight and her fingers tightened on Diva's thighs, gripping hard while her body twitched and jerked.

Fascinated, he stared. And as Priss's body relaxed, she smiled and opened her eyes and saw him.

He wanted to run, but he couldn't move. And then, to his amazement, she didn't scream or jump. Her upside-down face smiled at him, and she freed one hand from Diva's thighs and crooked her finger and beckoned him.

Hardly able to believe it, he took a step towards her. She smiled encouragingly, and then she opened her mouth and ran her tongue around her lips in a way that was so sexy that he'd come to the entrance of the tent almost before he'd thought about it.

'Diva,' Priss said in a low, husky voice, 'we've got company.'

Diva's long body arched as she turned to look over her shoulder. She saw Jason and her dark eyes flashed. 'If he can keep it up,' she said, 'get him stuck in.'

Priss smiled up at him, seemingly unfazed by her inverted position. She licked her lips again and crooked her finger and he felt himself drawn closer, as if by wires. He ducked under the outer flap of the tent, came in, closed it behind him, kneeled down in the little confined space between the outer and inner doors. He was surrounded by their clothes, their packs. He could smell them. They smelled hot and female, intoxicating. He didn't know whether to look at Priss's face, at her moving hands, or at Diva's exposed body, her tight arsehole, the curves of her bottom, the gleam and shine of her pussy. He could actually see the hole of her cunt, dark, tiny, enticing. He could see up inside her. He'd never looked at a girl from this position. When he looked at that little dark hole all he could think about was how much he wanted to push himself up it, and when he thought about that the spunk churned and swelled in his balls and his cock twitched and jerked as if it was buried there already.

Priss smiled again, encouragingly, and her hands reached out for his boxers. He swallowed, hardly knowing if he was excited or afraid. His stiff cock was aching, ripe. Would he burst as soon as she touched him? Probably. A worm of anxiety gnawed at his insides. That wasn't what Diva wanted, for sure.

Priss's hands touched his belly. They were warm, and he shuddered. She said softly, 'Come a little closer, I can't reach you.'

She could reach him; her hands were pushing inside his underpants. But he didn't question her, just shuffled a little closer. She pushed the boxers down and his cock bounced free and she smiled and put one hand under his balls and wrapped the other around the shaft of his cock and he began to pant and whimper because he was so excited that he was going to come very soon.

'Hang on, Diva,' Priss said softly. 'We've got a loaded gun here.'

'I bet he reloads quickly,' Diva said, still looking over her shoulder at him.

'He'd better,' Priss said. Jason hardly understood and he didn't care that they were talking about him as if he was some kind of object, because Priss's wet red mouth was reaching up for him and she was sticking out her long pink tongue and it was touching him; there was a long cool stripe along the shaft of his aching cock, and then her tongue curled around the head and he closed his eyes and gasped and she took him into her mouth and it was wet and warm and gorgeous and her lips closed around him and squeezed and she sucked and he came at once, instantly, shooting into her with such energy that he shuddered and wavered on his knees and had to put his hand to the ground to steady himself while the spots danced in front of his closed eyes.

It was over so quickly and for a moment he felt disappointment, but then he realised that he didn't need to be disappointed. Priss was swallowing his come, another thing that made him blink in amazement, and now her mouth was closing on him again and she was sucking gently, persistently, and her hands were cupping and stroking his balls and caressing the tender place between his legs and he stretched his eyes and gasped because he was getting hard again straight away, as hard as he had been before, as hard as he had ever been.

Priss lifted her lips for a moment and whispered, 'Very good.' She smiled at him and said, 'Nice cock, Jason. Lovely and thick.' He'd always suspected that, but when someone like Priss said it he really believed it, which made him feel very good indeed. He preened, and Priss held the shaft of his cock in one hand and with the other she stretched down towards Diva and hissed, 'Durex.'

Then she was tearing the little packet open, pulling the rubber out, smoothing it on to the swollen head of his cock. She looked up at him, seriously now, and said, 'Jason, you're going to fuck Diva first, and then you're going to fuck me. You're not going to disappoint us, are you?'

He'd never felt like this, as if his balls were full of liquid fire. This must be what the master of a harem felt like, knowing he had all those willing women, knowing he had to service them all. He'd never felt so strong. He licked his dry lips and managed to husk, 'No problem.'

'Start with me then,' Diva said, wriggling her backside, drawing his attention back to the tempting, gleaming darkness of her cunt. 'Come on.'

Priss's hands were on his thighs, pulling him a little closer, and he reached out and stroked the perfect full hemispheres of Diva's arse, and it was warm, and now Priss was guiding the head of his cock to that little dark hole, and any moment now he was going to penetrate her. For a second he wondered if he ought to wait, if he ought to hang on for a while and savour it, but he couldn't. He wanted to get stuck in there, and the moment he felt the slight give that meant that there was somewhere for him to go he lunged and she was so wet that his cock slid straight up her, all the way up to the hilt in one smooth stroke, and he gasped with amazement and clutched her hips and thrust and thrust in desperate eagerness until suddenly there was a shaft of pain and he stopped dead.

Priss was holding his balls, not hard, but firmly, so that if he moved it would hurt. Her voice said from between his spread legs, 'What are you, a woodpecker?

Slowly, Jason. There's me as well, you know. Take it slow.'

How could he go slowly when all his body wanted to thrash in and out as fast as it could, racing to another come? But he didn't have any choice: she was holding his bollocks hostage, and so he moved very slowly, sliding himself deep into Diva, pulling out, sliding in again.

And it was wonderful, so much better than rushing, sending sensations flooding through his cock from the root to the tip, making his fingers and toes tingle, burning in the pit of his belly. He thrust again and this time Diva moaned and he felt a surge of pride and withdrew slowly, slowly, thrust again.

There was a rhythm, a magic rhythm, which filled his cock with delicious tension and made Diva groan. Priss let go of his balls and he felt her fingers around the base of his cock, probing, stroking. She was touching Diva, because now Diva was moaning fast and her body was quivering, the orbs of her backside shuddering. Should he fuck her faster, in time with her moans? But if he did he'd risk coming again, and that would be too soon, because he was enjoying himself: he wanted to spin it out; he wanted to make it last. So he kept up the long, slow thrusts, eyes cast down, watching the darkened swollen shaft of his cock coming and going between those coffee-brown cheeks, watching the gleam of Diva's juices on his cock and pubes and belly, noticing how her arsehole clenched whenever her body twitched, how when her arsehole clenched her fanny tightened around his cock, making his breath hiss and his body tense.

'Oh,' Diva was moaning. 'Oh, oh, God.' And then she had slumped forward, her face hidden between Priss's legs, her body shaking, and he actually felt her coming, felt the pulses moving through the warm wet flesh surrounding him. He'd never felt that before, and it was wonderful. He tried to thrust again, but Priss's hand was back on his balls, restraining him, and so he waited patiently for Diva's body to stop quivering around him.

After a moment Diva sighed and drew her body gradually away from him. He watched, hypnotised, as the lips of her cunt clung and sucked at his cock as it withdrew. Then she was gone, and he knelt there, panting, gleaming cock sticking straight out in front of him, waiting for someone to tell him what to do.

Diva and Priss seemed to know what they had in mind. They both got up and drew him into the tent, pushing him down to the mess of mattresses and sleeping bags. He lay down obediently, wondering what would happen next.

Diva stooped over him and lowered her lips to his. He thought that she was going to kiss him, but she didn't. She stopped short of his mouth and instead whispered, 'Now you're going to fuck Priss. She's going to sit on your cock. And I'm going to sit on your face.'

It sounded almost frightening, but he wasn't about to object. He managed a brief nod.

'How good are you at giving head?' Diva hissed, her face still very close to his.

Based on his experience to date he was very much afraid that the answer was *crap*, but he wasn't going to say so. He licked his lips and shrugged, as much as he could while lying flat on his back.

'OK.' Diva pushed one hand through his hair, a perfunctory caress that left him vaguely disorientated. 'Well, listen. Go slow, don't gobble. Take your time.

And pay attention to me. Don't worry about you – Priss'll look after you.'

Her face moved away from his and he closed his eyes. He was on trial, obviously. They were testing him out. Perhaps if he did well he'd be able to do this every night. Perhaps he wouldn't even have to go back into his own tent, where fearful Rick was waiting with his alligator smile. Perhaps he could spend every night in Priss and Diva's tent, rolling around in a tangle of flesh, shagging to his heart's content. Wildest dreams come true. Well, he would do well. He would show them.

They had turned to face each other, both straddling his prone body, and as he looked up through Diva's thighs he saw them lean towards each other, cling, kiss, hands on breasts, fingers pinching nipples, bodies rippling like moonlight on water. His cock jerked, protesting at being abandoned, but he didn't dare reach up for them. He watched and bit his lip as Diva reached down for him, took hold of him, held him pointing upwards for Priss to impale herself.

Slowly Priss sank towards him. Her thighs were tanned and muscled, softer than Diva's but appetising all the same, and her bush was full and fair and the lips of her cunt were fatter than Diva's, paler, softer-looking. The head of his cock brushed against her pubes and he could hardly feel it through the condom and for a moment he wished that he was properly naked, and then Priss was poised and sliding down and he was inside her and he could feel that, he really could. She was tighter than Diva. The muscles of her belly were moving as she clutched him. It felt like a hand tightening on him – it was wonderful. He lurched up towards her and Diva's hands flattened on his stomach, holding him down. 'No,' she hissed, 'let Priss do it.'

So he lay still, resisting the urge to thrust. Priss leaned forward and she and Diva kissed, a long, languid kiss, and the velvet grasp of Priss on his cock tightened and relaxed, tightened and relaxed. He gasped, and then Diva straddled his face and lowered herself and he remembered what he had seen Priss doing and stuck his tongue out to lap at her.

He was supposed to find her clit, he knew that, find it and concentrate on it, and he knew it was sort of at the front, and he moved his tongue very, very slowly as she had told him, easing it through the folds of flesh, seeking.

And there it was. Why had it never been so obvious before, when he had been trying this with girlfriends? He knew he had it right because it was a little hard nugget of flesh and when he touched it Diva moaned, so now he curled his tongue around it and then began to lap, over and over, and she moaned again and again, like music.

He really concentrated and the delicious sensations of Priss sliding up and down on his cock receded, becoming almost like background to the task of making Diva come. It wasn't a bad task either. He was enjoying it. He lapped harder, she moaned louder, and when it was too hard she moved fractionally away from him and then he knew she wanted it softer. It was easy, so easy to give her pleasure. He reached up to put the flats of his hands against the soft skin of her inner thighs, spreading her legs even further apart so that he could reach right up for her, burying his nose into her neat trimmed pubes, squeezing with his thumbs in the delectable crease where her thighs joined her body, touching with his fingertips the soft slit where not long before he had fucked her.

It seemed hardly any time before she was moaning, 'Oh, that's good, yes, yes –' and then arching above him, pressing herself down on to his face so that he was deliciously smothered, shuddering and gasping as she came. He kept still, realising that she wouldn't want to be touched while she was coming, and after a second she lifted herself away from him and whispered, 'Priss, come on.'

And now he could really feel Priss, her tight tunnel squeezing him as she rose and fell. Diva moved to squat beside him and he reached down and grabbed Priss's arse because he had to do something now, he had to. He held her arse and lifted her a little so that he could thrust up into her, gritting his teeth because he could feel his spunk rising now, his own come not far away. Priss flung her head back and humped furiously and Diva pinched her nipples and reached between her thighs to touch her, and it was going to be close; he needed her to come now because he wasn't going to be able to wait much longer and, thank God, her head fell back and her mouth went slack and she stopped moving so he could hold her still and fuck upwards into her sagging body, four fast hard thrusts and then he exploded, shooting stars in front of his eyes, body arched up from the ground, pulsing everything into her.

After not very long Priss lifted herself off him and both of them kneeled looking down at him while he panted and wondered what on earth to say.

Eventually Diva said, 'So what were you doing wandering about the camp with nothing except a hard-on?'

It all came flooding back. He shuddered and sat up,

drawing his knees in unconscious reaction. 'God,' he said, 'I can't believe it, Rick, he actually suggested that we, well, you know.'

Priss looked as if this was very funny. 'What, and you fled?'

He was affronted. 'Of course I bloody fled. Wouldn't you?'

Diva cocked her head. 'He's a smart one. He promised us he would get you out of the tent, but he didn't tell us how.'

Jason's mouth dropped open while the implications of this sank in. 'You mean – you mean he was doing it because he told you he would?'

Priss opened her hands and shrugged. 'Difficult to say with Rick. He might have meant it, you never know.'

He wrapped his hands around his knees. 'Well, I'm not bloody going back there.'

'You can't stay here,' Diva said unkindly. 'These tents are absolutely not big enough for three.'

'No,' said Priss, to his surprise. 'No, let him stay. I'll go and barge in on Kathy and Julie.'

Diva smiled, as if she appreciated something. 'Oh ho, and ask Julie to move elsewhere, eh?'

If they were hoping to get Kathy too, they would be disappointed. 'I wouldn't bother,' he said, trying to sound cool. 'They were at it before I left. I heard them.'

'Sure,' Diva said casually. 'Kathy said she was going to target Julie tonight. We inducted her into the relay team today. I think what Priss has in mind is moving Julie on to someone else.'

'The relay team?' he said, totally lost.

'I'll just grab this torch and move out,' said Priss, pulling a crumpled big T-shirt from under Diva's knees and wrestling it over her head. 'You can stay here, Jase. And Diva will explain the relay team to you.'

He wasn't sure if his head could cope with any more new information. But if it meant he got to stay the night with Diva, he would bloody well pay attention.

Chapter Eight
Julie

It still felt like a dream, as if it couldn't be happening. They were lying naked on the top of the sleeping bags, Kathy's hand cupped possessively over her breast. Julie heard the footsteps outside the tent and saw the light of the torch, and she started to sit up and reach for her clothes, but Kathy said, 'No, don't move,' so she didn't. She didn't move even when whoever it was unzipped the flap of the tent and came in.

It was Priss, wearing just a T-shirt and knickers. She said, 'We're going to have to move around a bit.'

Kathy sat up, but Julie stayed where she had been told. Her whole body felt sensitised, as if tiny moths were fluttering their wings over her skin. Priss's appearance must mean that something else amazing was going to happen, and she waited to find out what it was.

Priss looked directly at her and said, 'Julie, I'm going to have to ask you to move to another tent.'

Julie sat up now. She had been happy with Kathy, who had made such wonderful demands of her. It was the first time she had had sex with another woman, and it had been sublime, and she would have quite liked to stay where she was. Also, she wondered if this meant that Priss and Kathy had something going, and if she should be jealous. She said, 'Move? To your tent?'

'Not my tent. Jason's in there. I need you to move to Rick's tent.'

Julie felt cold, icy cold, as if she had been dunked in a freezing stream. Rick's tent! How had Priss known that she thought Rick looked like the Prince of Darkness, that she could imagine him doing all sorts of unspeakable things to her? And now Priss was telling her to move to his tent? She said faintly, 'I couldn't.'

'No choice, I'm afraid,' said Priss, coming further in.

Kathy turned and looked at her and said, 'Julie, I want you to go to Rick's tent.'

Julie's body strained to obey, but her mind objected. 'But,' she said faintly, desperately aware that Rick's tent was only next door, that he might be awake and listening to them. 'But if people see me coming out, they might think –' She could not finish.

Priss laughed. 'Julie, do you know one reason why Jason came to our tent? Because he overheard what you and Kathy were doing. Would you really worry about what people might think if they saw you with Rick?'

But they would think I was dirty. They would think I was a whore. She knew what she ought to say. And yet, somehow, she couldn't. Kathy's expectant look was like a hand in the small of her back, pushing her to her knees.

She pulled her sleep-shirt back on, looking at the ground. Should she say something, in some way signal that she was going to do what she had been asked?

No, there was no need, better just to go. Priss nodded at her and handed her the little torch she had been carrying, and she ducked her head to go out of the tent, leaving them in darkness.

Outside it was very dark, cloudy, and still warm and humid, with no breeze. She couldn't stand around in the open, the insects would bite her to pieces. And she didn't feel she knew anybody else well enough to trespass on their privacy. The only possible choice would be Zoe and Sarah and to explain to Sarah . . . Well, it was easier just to do as she had been told.

So she unzipped the outer flap of Rick's tent, hesitated, and then ducked her head inside.

The inner flap was open. She didn't shine the torch straight in – that felt rude. She said very quietly, 'Rick?'

And straight away his dark voice replied, 'Come in.'

She swallowed hard, then shone the torch in just enough to see that Jason's abandoned bed was on the left-hand side of the tent. Switching the torch off, she scrambled in in the dark and said, 'I'm sorry, but Priss and Kathy –'

'It's fine,' he said.

There was a silence. She was hugely conscious of him beside her in the dark. He'd been lying on his sleeping bag, not in it, wearing just a pair of close-fitting trunks. And now he was lying next to her, wearing them, and at any moment he might reach over and touch her. She trembled at the prospect.

Eventually he said, 'So what do you want?'

'Nothing!' she squeaked.

'You've just come to sleep?' he insisted.

He couldn't expect her to say anything else, could he? She whispered, 'Yes.'

'Well then, good-night,' he said. And she heard a rustle and imagined him turning away from her as he got ready to sleep. After what seemed like only a few moments, she heard his breathing change.

She ought to be relieved. Why did she feel cheated?

After a night of fitful sleep she woke very early. Rick had not stirred, and in the half-light she wondered what she should do. In the end she decided to make her escape while she could and she climbed stealthily out and heaved a sigh of relief as she looked up at the dawn. Kathy had been far enough, after all. Rick as well would be, well, too much.

She covered up for herself by going to the stream for a good wash and by the time she came back the camp was stirring and she thought she had got away with it. Forget the sense of disappointment, it was better this way.

So why, when she saw that Rick had decided to do the optional climb that day, did she suddenly change her mind and decide that she would do it too, rather than taking the chance for a rest in camp? She hadn't meant to do it. It just – happened.

And when she said, 'I'll go,' he looked at her, a dark, significant look. She tried to avoid his eyes, but as he came towards her she found herself quivering with anticipation. If only he wouldn't ask her what she wanted this time!

He was standing in front of her, looking down at her. People were passing by on either side of them, coming and going, but she knew that that wouldn't stop him saying whatever he wanted to say. She swallowed, staring at her boots.

'You were disappointed last night,' he said.

Her head jerked back with surprise, and she stared at him. How had he known?

'Don't worry,' he said. 'Since you're climbing today,

I'll settle scores with you tonight. You won't get away with it so easily.'

She stammered, 'I don't understand.'

His face lightened slightly, a little smile. 'Oh yes, you do.'

And of course she did. She didn't know how he had guessed, but he had guessed how she felt. And tonight, tonight he would be in charge.

She had felt tired on waking, but the walk that day seemed to pass in a haze of delicious fantasy. She didn't talk to anyone else, just strode onwards wearing her personal CD player, concentrating on herself. She relived the previous night, where Kathy had been demanding and insistent and seemed to know exactly what would give the most pleasure. And she walked with Madonna playing in her ears and dreamed of the coming night, of Rick, of what he would do to her, of what he would make her do to him.

Julie's ex-husband and most of her boyfriends before and since had never really made demands of her, not sexually. If they had expected something, they hadn't said so. Sometimes they'd made suggestions, and when she sounded shocked and rejected them they'd accepted it and gone on in the same old boring way. They'd never insisted. They hadn't realised that she needed someone to insist. And Julie had had straightforward boring sex with them, and mostly she hadn't come, and when she had it was because she had been thinking about a man who would know instinctively what she dreamed of and what her shame kept her from doing, and who would insist that she do it. A man who would make her expose herself in lewd and inventive ways, who would make her display her body like the whore she was under the skin, not the nice quiet girl her surface showed, who would compel her to take his cock in her mouth – and in other places – and who would show her all the outer limits of pleasure. She had thought of those things, and then, sometimes, she would come.

And now, perhaps, she had found a man who would do those things in real life. The rocks passed beneath her feet unnoticed; she hardly saw the magnificent vistas that unfolded all around her, because she was thinking about the night, about what Rick would do to her, what he would make her do. Occasionally, very occasionally, she caught him looking at her, and each time she was launched into a fresh flight of fantasy.

It was only when they had stood on the peak and watched the sun set and then started down the slope towards their bivouac for the night that she began to think that she had deceived herself. After all, it was not as if they were sleeping in tents tonight. They were in a hut, and from what they had been told it was a pretty rudimentary one. Would this really be a suitable venue for her fantasy? Her mind had always located events of this kind in faceless but lush surroundings, where there were beds and sheets and silk scarves and all other necessary props.

And looking at the sky it didn't seem likely that they would be able to go outside for privacy, either. The humidity had built up once again to thunderheads and people were hurrying downhill now, eager to get to the shelter of the hut before the heavens opened. Julie hurried too, and there was the hut in front of them, nestling in the shelter of a rock face and overhung by a couple of tall pine trees, and all her dreams evaporated.

It was cosy enough, with a sturdy roof and a chimney and a heap of firewood piled on the sheltered side of the building, quite like an Alpine chalet. But inside there was just one big room, with mattresses for people to sleep on, and nothing else. No privacy, no luxury, just one big room and an open fire.

Josh and TJ had come with them, but everyone mucked in to prepare some food. They all felt that they deserved it, having carried it all the way up the mountain. Julie sat plastering peanut butter on to chunks of bread and trying to manage her disappointment. The others were eating and laughing and chatting, and she simply didn't feel able to join in.

And then Rick was at her shoulder, murmuring into her ear, 'I hope you don't think that you're off the hook.'

What? She glanced up at him in horror, but he had taken a chunk of bread and gone. She handed more out to the others, still gaping with shock, hardly able to grasp the implications.

It was dark outside already and big drops of rain were beginning to slam against the roof shingles. Inside there was not much light, just the flicker of the fire and the glow of two or three upturned torches. It was warm and strange, and suddenly she felt a surge of paranoia. She was sure that the others all knew what was going on, that something was planned, that she was the likely victim. And now the rain was hurling itself against the windows and there was no escape.

Her appetite deserted her. She sat a little way back from the fire, in the shadows, watching the others eating. Priss and Diva, laughing with Kathy and Zoe, TJ and Josh hanging around them. Had Kathy betrayed her? How had this happened? Jason talking to Sandy and Greg, who looked as if they were laughing at him. And Rick, standing rather than sitting on the floor, leaning against the fireplace, watching her.

Impossibly soon people had finished eating, and

Diva said in a loud voice, a voice which Julie could tell was staged, 'OK, TJ, what happens now?'

TJ stretched and grinned. 'Well, usually at this point we tell ghost stories, but I get the feeling that there might be something more interesting to do on this trip. Priss?'

Everyone fell silent and looked at Priss. She smiled too. 'Well, amazingly, everyone who's in the relay team is here. Seems a shame not to do something, doesn't it?'

People murmured in agreement, and Greg said in his brash voice, 'How about an orgy?'

Priss laughed. 'Great idea, Greg. But in fact I think Rick has some entertainment planned for us.' She arched her head over her shoulder, smiling up at him. 'Rick?'

Julie found herself breathing as if she was still climbing, breathing like a trapped animal. She fastened her eyes on Rick, begging him in silence to be merciful, to say something other than what she dreaded.

Rick lowered his head, gesturing at Julie. 'There's the entertainment,' he said.

Everybody swivelled to stare at her. She felt her cheeks burning; she didn't know where to look. Their faces were hungry, excited, amazed, all focused on her, all expecting she didn't know what.

'What, you mean Julie's the entertainment?' That was Jason. 'What, is she going to dance or something?'

Everybody groaned, 'No, Jason!' and Rick said with a shake of his head, 'Not quite. I have here –' he opened his fist '– a die. We're all going to roll the die. The first person to get a six can tell Julie to do anything he, or she, wants. And Julie will do it.'

Goosebumps sprang up on Julie's arms and down her spine. She looked around at the eager faces staring at her, at Jason's look of disbelief and incomprehension, and wanted to shout, 'No, that wasn't the deal!' and to Rick, 'But it was supposed to be just me and you!'

But he was frowning at her, and she didn't dare protest, and when he said, 'That's right, Julie, isn't it?' she looked down and whispered, 'Yes.'

'So it's like forfeits,' Jason said. 'But Julie gets to do them all.'

Sandy leaned over and touched Jason's arm and whispered in his ear. Julie watched his face change and knew what Sandy was saying. She was telling him that these forfeits were to be of a particular kind.

'Well,' said Rick, 'let's start. Julie, come and stand in the middle.'

When he spoke like that, with such quiet assurance, somehow she just couldn't disobey him. She got to her feet and walked closer to the fire, feeling its warmth through her clothes, and stood quiet, looking into his face.

'Take off your fleece,' he said, and she obeyed, tossing it into a corner. Now she was wearing just her trekking trousers and a T-shirt, and she was standing and Rick was standing and the others were all sitting there, sitting around her in a circle, gazing up at her, and her legs felt like jelly.

'We'll start,' he said, and he tossed the die to Diva. She caught it, rolled it, peered in the dim light, said, 'Damn, a three,' and passed it on.

Sandy rolled, Greg rolled, and Julie watched the little skittering cube with dazed disbelief. Why was she not refusing to do this, objecting, denying? Why was she standing with her head hanging meekly, her hands folded, her belly wrenching with excitement?

Jason rolled the die and yelled with delight. 'Six! I win!'

'Then it's your choice,' said Rick. 'What do you want her to do?'

Jason glanced at the others as if he were startled to find himself with so much power. He frowned, seeming to strain his brain, and said after a few minutes, 'Anything?'

People sighed and rolled their eyes, but Rick said patiently, 'Anything.'

Licking his lips, Jason said after another fractional hesitation. 'OK. Julie, I want you to – to take all your clothes off. Please.'

Her hand crept up to her throat. She looked across at Rick, as if he would countermand the request, as if he would save her. But he just lifted his dark brows and gestured that she should begin.

Slowly she unfastened her trousers, pulled her T-shirt over her head, all the time keeping her eyes on Rick. While he was looking at her, she felt safe, as if he would keep her secure, somehow. She stooped to untie her boots, pushed off trousers and boots and socks, and stood up in the firelight naked except for bra and panties.

Rick smiled slightly. 'Jason, I think you said all her clothes?'

Jason swallowed hard. He was staring, everyone was staring. 'Yes,' he said.

'All your clothes,' Rick said quietly.

She couldn't do it. She couldn't be naked in front of all these people, these strangers. But then what would Rick say? She glanced around the circle and saw the men quiet and intent, Sandy openly aroused, Priss and Diva looking thoughtful, almost as if they were marking her, and Kathy –

Kathy blew her a kiss. And then she knew she could do it.

She closed her eyes, unfastened her bra and let it fall, then delicately pushed down her panties, keeping her legs modestly together. She let them lie where they fell and stood with one hand across her breasts, the other in front of her triangle, the classic posture.

There was silence. Then Rick said, 'Next,' and the die rolled again.

Julie tried not to watch, tried to stand still like a statue, but she couldn't help it. Would it be Greg? TJ? What would they want her to do? What would Kathy ask for? She wanted it to be Kathy.

But it was Sandy who rolled the next six, and she sat back with a smile, running her tongue over her teeth and trickling her fingers down over her nipples, which were showing through her shirt. 'OK,' she said silkily. 'Julie, I want you to open your legs. Stand there and open 'em wide, wide apart. Wide as you can. Hands behind your head, too.'

Bitch! How could she have asked for something so embarrassing? Julie was standing, the others were sitting; her crotch would be right at their eye level. God, they might even be able to *smell* her – smell that she was already turned-on. She said, 'I –'

'Julie,' said Rick, 'I think you should do as you're told.'

She felt the atmosphere in the room shift and change. Before she might have seemed scared, but she hadn't protested. Now she had protested, and Rick had commanded, and she could sense that everybody knew the nature of this game. This was not about exhibitionism. Oh no, the opposite. Sandy had been clever, subtle. This was about slow torture. It was about humiliation.

Rick said, 'Julie,' and his voice was warning and stern.

Slowly, reluctantly, she slipped her feet apart on the wooden floor. As they moved she lifted her hands and clasped them behind her head. Her small breasts lifted and tautened, her slender belly stretched. She closed her eyes in desperation, knowing that these movements made her look sexy and also made her look as if she wanted sex. Her legs parted further and air stirred against the shifting petals of her pussy, feeling cool against the dampness. They would be able to see her flesh shining. They would know.

'Good,' said Rick, and she closed her eyes more tightly as she heard the die rolling again.

Who would it be? What would they demand? If only it would be something big, something final, so that everyone would join in and she would no longer be the centre of attention. Perhaps it would be Greg – he had asked for an orgy, perhaps he would do that again and then it wouldn't be just her.

Kathy's voice said, 'It's me.'

Kathy! Julie opened her eyes and gazed at Kathy, silently begging.

'You look lovely, Julie,' Kathy said. 'It's a shame to move you. But I'm going to ask you to masturbate.'

Masturbate! Julie almost wept with desperation. How could Kathy ask it of her? She said, 'Kathy,' but there was no mercy in Kathy's face. She dropped her eyes and said, 'I don't think I can, like this.'

There was a pause. Then Kathy said, 'You can sit on one of the mattresses then.'

It felt like a victory to be able to sit down, no longer poised above the others, exposed and shamed. She lay back on the mattress, closing her eyes. She could sense that people were moving round so that they could watch her, but it didn't seem to matter so much. Lying like this she could pretend that she was alone, in her own bed, bringing herself to a solitary orgasm as she so often did. And as she slipped her finger between her legs, keeping her thighs modestly clasped, she knew that in future when she masturbated like this she would imagine herself back here, her naked body warmed by the firelight, surrounded by people watching her stroke herself, watching her clasp her breast in one hand and tease the hard nipple.

It wasn't even very exposed, masturbating like this. She would look lovely, artistic, not crude. She touched her clit and sighed with pleasure and thought of ten people listening to her sigh and shuddered with delight.

The tinkle of the rolling die almost made her jump. Were they not going to wait until she had an orgasm? Obviously not, but she didn't care, because she was shielded behind her closed eyes, touching herself, imagining Rick's stern gaze resting on her naked body, compelling her to obey.

Priss's voice said, 'I win. Julie, stop. Look at me.'

Now that she had started, Julie really quite wanted to finish. But she knew she had to do as she was told, so she stopped and propped herself on one arm and opened her eyes.

Priss was smiling at her, and she was holding something up. It was a vibrator, a big one, eight or nine inches long and thick. Julie's pussy clenched hard.

'Now,' said Priss, 'I want you to go on, but I want you to have your legs wide apart, and I want to watch this going into your cunt.'

Julie flinched at the use of the c-word. Priss cocked her head, looked thoughtful, and then said, 'Repeat those instructions, Julie.'

No, that was too much. Julie said, 'You want me to go on, but you want me to – to use the vibrator.'

'That's not what I said,' Priss chided her. 'Repeat after me, Julie. I want to watch this –' she hefted the vibrator '– going into your cunt.'

Julie glanced hopelessly at Rick, but there was no help there. Miserably she murmured, 'You want to watch – it – going into my –' she swallowed hard and finished in a tiny voice '– into my cunt.'

'Very good.' Priss leaned forward and handed her the vibrator, flicking the switch as she did so. It buzzed into life, cold and hard. Julie thought for a moment that she was going to burst into tears, but it wouldn't achieve anything and it would make her look silly. So she lay back and took a deep breath and parted her legs and slipped the vibrator between them.

The first touch of the cool plastic on her clit made her start and gasp with the intensity of the pleasure. She'd never used one of these before, and now she could see why people did. The pulses seemed to travel right through her, stiffening her nipples, arching her spine, making her gasp and moan. She massaged her clit gently for a moment then let the tip of the vibrator slip downwards, touched her clit with one finger instead as the smooth shaft eased into the hollow of her vagina, her cunt, and began to enter her.

Someone took hold of her ankles and moved them gently apart. She didn't jump, didn't struggle, because now the vibrator was buzzing inside her and her finger was on her clit and she was beginning to pant. She cried out and then there were other hands touching her, caressing her shoulders, pinching her nipples, and now someone had taken the vibrator from her and was pushing it into her hard, really fucking her with it, and even as she felt her orgasm building she knew it was

Kathy doing that to her and it felt so good that she gave a great groan of pleasure and came, twisting under the caressing hands, and sagged back to the mattress with the vibrator still humming and fizzing deep inside her, making the aftershocks last for ever.

Presently someone pulled the vibrator out and she rolled over on to her front, hiding her face in her folded arms. She had just climaxed in front of all these people, and now she wanted to die, or at least to be taken instantly a very long way away, somewhere where nobody would know her shame.

But there was to be no respite. The hands that had touched her withdrew, and she heard the rattle of the die. When an Australian voice exclaimed 'Yes!' she felt almost relieved. It was Greg. He would maybe just ask to fuck her, and then everybody would fuck everybody else, and soon it would be over.

'Julie,' said Greg's voice, and she reluctantly pushed herself up and turned to face him.

He was watching her with a face of extraordinary hunger and delight. 'Right,' he said. 'Get on your hands and knees. I want you to suck my dick.' He grinned at the group around him. 'Suck it good, babe. And while she sucks it, guys, you touch her. Touch her all over. But I don't care what they do to you, baby, you keep on giving me head, yeah? Give it your best shot.'

Slowly, she got to her hands and knees. She didn't find this particularly exciting, compared to what had come before. It was what she would have expected from Greg, who had struck her so far as basically self-centred. But she was prepared to obey because Rick was watching and because, secretly, she knew that after her orgasm it would be bliss to have a cock in her mouth.

She crawled forward and Greg pulled off his top and whizzed his fly open. 'Jesus,' he said, 'let's get naked, what the hell,' and he pulled off his trousers too. Then he kneeled down in front of her, stiff cock bobbing before her face, and said, 'Get busy, babe.'

Closing her eyes, she let her face just brush against the head of his cock. He smelled rank and hot, sweaty. Normally she would find that a turn-off, but now it just added to her excitement. If she did this well, if she served Greg to his satisfaction, perhaps Rick would notice and allow her later to do the same for him.

She licked the shaft of Greg's cock, then gently took the head into her mouth and listened to Greg sigh and say, 'Yeah, baby.' She began to suck him, moving her head gently so that her lips slid smoothly over him and, as she did so, hands began to touch her, stroking her bottom and thighs, caressing her dangling breasts. They felt like male hands. But they couldn't be Rick's because out of the corner of her eye she could see him standing there, still watching her, presiding over the ceremonies.

Suddenly, with a shock, she realised that Rick wasn't trying to do anything to her. He wasn't even rolling the die, just standing there controlling what everybody else was doing. Why? Didn't he want her? Did it amuse him to have her just used by everybody else?

She couldn't bear to think that. Better to believe that he was just waiting, biding his time, knowing that it didn't need the roll of a die for him to possess her, that he could have her just at a word.

Greg's hands were resting on her head, his fingers probing the roots of her hair, and his hips were thrusting towards her face. She carried on servicing him, but she wasn't enjoying it as much as she had thought she would. Realising that Rick wasn't involving himself had cast a damper over her pleasure. She could hardly feel the hands touching her, the fingers pinching her nipples, insinuating themselves into her pussy and bumhole. It was Rick she wanted.

'Oh, baby, that's good,' Greg said. He was holding her head firmly now and she couldn't move, even by the small distance it would need to see Rick, to notice how he was looking as he watched her. She closed her eyes and sucked hard, wanting it to be over soon, and she flickered her tongue under Greg's cock head, over the little supersensitive spot just under the ridge, and he gasped and dug his fingers into her scalp and came, his cock pulsing in her mouth, his breath shuddering.

She swallowed hard and then pushed herself away from Greg's limp hands, turning to Rick, imploring him with her eyes.

And he met her gaze, and he smiled. Not much, just the shadow of a smile, but it told her that he understood; it reassured her that he did want her, that all of this was just play, just the preamble, the appetiser before the main course.

The die was rolling again, and this time it was Zoe who shrieked with glee. Josh grunted in disappointment and Zoe wrapped her arms around herself and hugged herself with delight and said, 'I know, I know! Julie, I want you to sit on Jason's face.'

Jason gaped, and everybody else laughed, and Diva said, 'Hey, Julie, good one, you'll enjoy it – he's really hot.'

Was she joking, or was she trying to make Jason feel better? Neither thing mattered, because Julie could hardly imagine how she would obey, how she would straddle the face of a young stranger and invite him to kiss her there, in the most intimate part of her, with all these other people looking on. Zoe might have noticed her shock and hesitation because she added, 'Hey, and no getting off him until the next person rolls, OK?'

'Bloody hell, it had better be my chance soon,' Josh said. 'You guys have fixed the bloody dice.'

'Come on, Jason, get down on the floor where you belong,' Zoe called.

'But –' Jason said, and everybody shouted, a chorus of disapproval and encouragement that made him shake his head and slowly settle down on to the mattress where Julie had been lying. He looked at Julie and grinned, and his young face was full of simple eagerness. 'OK,' he said, 'I'm game. And I just want to say that I shall be expecting someone to reciprocate for me later.' He cast a hunted look in Rick's direction and added, 'Some *woman*.'

Julie looked at Rick, and he was smiling, and she thought suddenly that while she did as she had been told she could watch him, and while she watched him she could imagine that it was him doing this to her. So, holding his eyes, she stepped forward and stood above Jason and drew in a deep breath. Then, very slowly, she placed one foot on either side of Jason's grinning face and lowered herself down. As she descended Rick watched her, and in his eyes she could see a strange sort of proprietorial pride. The feeling that he owned her surrounded her with confidence, and when she felt the first touch of Jason's tongue she flung back her head and cried out with delight.

Whether or not Diva had been serious, she had been correct. Jason licked her beautifully, his tongue and lips slow and intense and searching and, safe in the knowledge of Rick's eyes on her, she held her breasts in her hands and pushed herself against Jason's face, taking her pleasure with an abandonment that she would not have believed she could show.

Behind her the die rolled again and both TJ and Josh cried out with dismay. 'It's me,' Diva shouted.

Julie hoped that Diva wouldn't stop her from enjoying Jason's attentions. She was vaguely aware of whispering and low voices, and then she felt bodies close to her on either side. She opened her eyes and found that Josh and TJ were standing by her, both of them naked, Josh's lean sinewy blondness contrasting splendidly with TJ's heavy physique and inky skin.

'We got our instructions,' Josh said, and he stepped around behind her and put his hands below her arms and lifted her away from Jason. Before she could protest TJ was in front of her, and his hot erect cock was pressing against her belly. She barely had time to notice that he already had a condom on when he slipped the head of his cock between her legs and found the slit and thrust and he was inside her. She moaned with shock and delight, and then moaned again in disbelief and fear as she felt Josh behind her, the head of his cock probing and slipping. For a moment she was afraid that he was trying to enter her anus, but instead he pushed and nudged until his cock tip was lodged beside TJ's slippery shaft. He grunted and tensed against her and slowly, slowly, stretching her wide, he entered her. She cried out and her head fell back as she felt herself filled, filled to the brim with two eager thrusting cocks.

'Very good,' Diva's voice whispered, 'very good.' And Diva was there beside her, her hand easing itself between Julie's body and TJ's and then, as well as the cocks that filled her, there was a finger on her clit and her whole body felt ready to explode with the overwhelming sensation.

'Say it,' whispered a voice in her ear. It was a man's voice: it was Rick's voice. 'Say what you're feeling.'

She closed her eyes and whimpered, and he said again, 'Say it. Say it, Julie.'

'Oh,' she moaned, 'oh, I'm full, Rick. I'm full.'

'What's filling you?'

Her head rolled. 'Two – two cocks. Two cocks.'

'Where are they?'

She was coming now, the pulses were starting, her body was beginning to shake. 'In my cunt,' she said, and then she cried out, 'They're in my cunt and I'm coming, I'm coming!'

The waves rolled over her. She would have fallen if she had not been held so tight, held up by the two strong thrusting bodies. Hard hands caught her arms, caught her buttocks, held her as the speed of their movements increased until they were lunging against her, slapping their bellies against her body, driving themselves to their own grunting orgasms and then standing shuddering, their flanks heaving like exhausted animals.

Julie didn't even attempt to stand and, as the men withdrew, they let her fall to the mattress. She moved weakly, opened her eyes and saw Rick kneeling beside her.

She reached out and touched his arm and whispered, 'Rick. Please.'

He shook his head gently. 'Not tonight,' he said. 'Not here. There's something else you have to do for me first.'

Her face crumpled in disappointment. She felt as if she would burst into tears. He stroked her cheek and whispered, 'Only one more thing, Julie. Only one more thing.'

'What?' she whimpered, sounding like a child. 'What?'

'Folks,' he said, raising his voice, 'Julie has volunteered to induct a couple more of our friends into the relay team. She's going to pick off Steve and Alan tomorrow. So paws off them, ladies.'

A babble of voices surrounded her, but only snatches of what they said entered her ears. 'Who's going to take Jan?' 'Me!' 'No, I will.' 'Well, what about both of you?' 'What about Sarah?' 'Oh, forget Sarah, what about John?'

She looked up into Rick's eyes and he said softly, 'You were very good. You were very obedient. But now you have to do something, hmm, proactive. And then –' He leaned forward and she realised that he was going to kiss her and closed her eyes, waiting, waiting. For a second his lips touched hers, firm and gentle, soft and strong, promising everything. And then he drew back and said, 'Alan and Steve. And then you will have earned it.'

Chapter Nine
Alan

It was shamefully pleasant to have a couple of days without walking, and Alan and Jan made the most of it. Experienced travellers as they were, they never missed an opportunity to do some washing, and when the others left to climb the peak they bashed their shirts and underwear on rocks in the nearby stream and then strung them out to dry, hoping that the storms would hold off long enough. Then there was a chance to walk up and down the stream to find a waterfall and pool for a swim and a thorough wash, all over, hair too, and then time just to relax, lie in the sun when it was out, read books, enjoy the landscape.

For most of the day Steve sat on a rock near the camp doing his paperwork, and Alan was quite prepared to leave him be. Privately he thought that trek leaders had a very hard time, with everybody turning to them whenever anything went wrong and hardly a moment to themselves. Sarah had hung around Steve for a while, complaining as usual. But during the afternoon she had vanished, as had John, and there had been perfect peace and the sound of the birds.

Eventually Alan suggested a cup of tea and set the kettle to boil over the camp fire, and Steve came from his rock to join them.

'All going well?' Alan said.

Steve wagged his head, making his hair flop, and said, 'Yeah, sure.'

'I wonder how the others are getting on,' Jan said musingly.

Alan caught her eye. They had had some earnest discussions about the more and more obvious goings-on between the younger members of the group, and some pretty hot and carefully silenced sex too. Just because they were more than ten years older than everybody else didn't mean that they didn't notice what was happening. It didn't mean that they didn't get turned on by it either.

Steve didn't reply, but he looked anxious. Alan said, 'What was Sarah having a go at you about this time?'

Now Steve looked positively hunted. 'Well,' he said, 'she was saying that she would have liked to climb the mountain too, and she didn't feel she could, and she thought I should have done something about it.'

'So you've sent her off with John instead.'

Steve nodded. 'I thought if she had a guided walk of her very own she might cut me a bit of slack.'

Jan glanced again at Alan and said, 'She must have been pretty sure that she wouldn't have enjoyed the climb.'

'No,' Steve said, miserably. 'She was sure she would have enjoyed the climb. It was everything else that she wasn't looking forward to.'

After a short silence, Jan said curiously, 'So does this sort of thing often happen on your trips, Steve?'

It was funny how they were talking about the subject even though they hadn't made it clear exactly what they were talking about. Circumlocution, an Anglo-Saxon speciality. Steve looked up and asked anxiously, 'You don't mind, do you?'

Jan laughed, and Alan said ruefully, 'We just feel a bit left out, to be honest.'

Steve looked amazed, and Jan explained, 'Al and me were the original free love exponents, once upon a time. I'm sure this crowd think they invented sex, but they really didn't, you know.'

'I mean, we're heavily out of practice,' Alan added. 'It's not the kind of thing you tend to get up to when you've got a family. And you sort of lose the urge anyway. But –'

'But with all this going on around you, it does sort of turn your mind to it,' Jan said, looking at him sidelong. That smouldering look of hers hadn't changed since he first met her, when she had looked a bit like Liz Taylor in *Cleopatra* and dressed like sex on legs. He hadn't seen it much in recent years, and he welcomed it.

'Well,' Steve said, not sounding very convinced, 'I'm glad it doesn't bother you.'

'Sounds as if it bothers you,' Jan said.

Steve wrinkled his nose. 'Well, not exactly, no. I mean, nobody's asked me yet, so in one way I'm feeling a bit left out, if you get my meaning.'

'Absolutely,' said Alan, who felt just the same.

'And on the other hand, I'm supposed to make sure that everyone has a good time. And OK, lots of people are, but one person for sure isn't, and I could get in trouble if she makes a complaint when we get back to Nelson.'

'Sarah,' Jan said flatly.

'Jesus, she's uptight. Says she doesn't want to share with Zoe now. At least that's not a problem, our last night there's a big hut.'

'Think that'll stop them?' Alan queried. 'I don't think so!'

'Oh, Lord,' said Steve, looking even more miserable.

'Cheer up,' Jan said. 'Maybe she'll hit it off with John.'

Steve rolled his eyes. 'Doubt it. John hardly ever says a word. Can't see anyone hitting it off with him, really.'

'Well,' Alan suggested, 'we could always tell your company that it wasn't your fault.'

'Thanks,' Steve said, mournfully.

Later that night, they lay in their tent and listened to the rain pattering on the canvas and talked in low voices about what the others would be doing, cloistered up the mountain in their hut. Speculation became shared fantasy and they made love with an eagerness that Alan could have believed they would have lost after so many years together.

Afterwards Jan rolled back on top of him and kissed him and said, 'Sarah looked happier this evening.'

'Yes, I thought so.'

'She's hitting it off with John – I told you they would. I'm never wrong.'

'Well, that should make it easier for everyone else to have a good time.'

There was a little silence. Then Jan said, 'Al, if they ask you to play and not me, I'll kill you.'

He squeezed her slender waist. 'Are you serious, sweetheart? I don't mean, will you kill me? I mean, do you really want to join in?'

'I wouldn't have said so when we came,' she said, laying her head on his shoulder. 'But now I can't help thinking, what's the risk? And I can't really see that there is one.'

'As long as it's safe sex, you mean.'

She laughed. 'Well, yes, I ought to remember about that, oughtn't I? The pill isn't enough for safety these days. But seriously, why shouldn't we? It's not as if the kids will find out, or anyone who knows us.'

'They'd certainly be shocked in the village,' Al said, thinking of the typical conversations in their local pub on the Welsh Marches.

'They certainly would. But they won't know, will they? It's just here and now. It doesn't mean anything other than fun, and then we'll be back in the real world being a married couple and grandparents and nobody would believe it of us anyway.'

He was silent for a moment, marvelling at how much he wanted it to happen. To balance his hope he said, 'Maybe they won't ask us. They'll think we're too old.'

Jan sighed. 'Maybe. But you never know your luck.'

Next day the storm clouds had gone and the sun was bright and hot in a fresh sky. Sarah and John disappeared again with hardly a word of explanation, though Jan thought she had heard Sarah muttering something about 'Fascinating geological outcrops'. Steve found a moss-covered rock in the shade and fell asleep on it, boneless as a warm cat. The horses, picketed in a grassy spot, stamped and tore at the grass and switched at flies and nibbled the backs of each other's necks. Jan and Alan sunbathed for a while, then moved under one of the broad trees and looked up the mountain path, wondering who would be the first down.

'You know,' Jan said tentatively, 'we don't have to wait to be invited. We could ask to join in.'

Alan took a deep breath. 'Well, I suppose we could,' he said. 'But I'd really hate it if I thought that they were, well, just putting up with us. You know, they might be too polite to say they didn't want us.'

Jan looked unconvinced. 'I think it would be worth a try.'

'You ask then. Who would you ask?'

She hesitated. 'It would have to be Priss. Or Diva. I could see myself asking them.'

'All right,' he challenged. 'You ask. I'll wait and see if anything happens.'

'No, Al, you toe-rag, it doesn't work like that, you have to ask with me!'

He laughed, shaking his head. 'Oh, let's play it by ear. Come on, let's pretend it's all going to go well. Tell me who you want it to be. Which one of those red-blooded young men would you go for?'

Jan threw back her head, smiling, her heavy hair swinging. 'Oh, Lord, I don't know. I bet all the girls fancy TJ. I think I might prefer Josh, myself.' She leaned across and gave him a quick, affectionate kiss. 'I like 'em tall and skinny. How about you?'

He whistled. 'Tricky one. So many to choose from. Not sure, really, but I think . . . Well, I think Julie's more my type than the others. Though any red-blooded male would like to get Diva with her knickers down.'

'I think they've hardly been up throughout,' Jan said. 'If she has any knickers.'

'Mee-ow!'

'No, I'm just jealous.'

They dozed a little, and then Alan stirred and opened his eyes and saw movement on the path. He touched Jan's shoulder and they both sat up and watched.

'How many people?' Jan didn't bother with her glasses much when trekking and she was getting more and more short-sighted. 'Three or four?'

'Looks like –' Alan pulled his sunglasses on against the glare. 'It's Julie, and a couple of guys . . . Looks like Josh and Jason.'

Jan raised her eyebrows. 'Our dreamboats. What d'you think they're doing coming back early – they don't have the stamina of the others?'

'Let's go and find out.' Alan stood up and stuck his hand out to help Jan to her feet. Leaving Steve snoring quietly on his rock, they headed up the track.

In a few minutes they saw the others coming down towards them. Josh waved, and Jason jumped up and down like a mad thing, swinging his arms. Julie just smiled, a small secret smile like the Mona Lisa. She really was very attractive. 'You know,' Alan said, finding Jan's hand and squeezing it, 'Julie reminds me of you. Her hair, and that look . . .'

'Flatterer,' Jan said. 'I love it. Don't stop.'

'You might say that Josh reminds you of me.'

'No, love, he's better looking than you ever were.' Jan stopped, pulling him to a stop too, and swivelled to face him. 'Look, this is our chance. Why don't we try it? It could be simple. You offer to show Julie the waterfall; I'll look after Josh.'

He looked at her in admiration tempered with a touch of anxiety. He knew she was feisty, he knew that she was cool, he knew that very little fazed her, but this was above and beyond his expectation. 'What about Jason?' he asked, because he couldn't think of anything else to say on the spur of the moment.

'Leave him to me.' She sounded so confident! That was all very well. What about him, left alone with the slender silent Julie? What if she told him to take a running jump? He had to be nearly twenty years older than her, and she knew he was married, and besides, he was pretty sure that she was sweet on Rick. She'd jumped at climbing the mountain the moment Rick had announced his intention to go. If she'd been clasped in his strong arms all the previous night she probably wouldn't have anything whatsoever to say to a bearded fifty-something husband.

'Well?' Jan insisted. 'Are you game?'

He couldn't say no to her, not when she looked at him with her face all lit up with excitement like that. 'Yes, OK,' he said, and then swallowed hard.

Jason was running down towards them. 'Wow,' he shouted, 'that was so excellent up there, you wouldn't believe it!' He looked beyond, at the camp. 'Where's the others?'

'Steve's asleep,' Jan said. 'And John and Sarah went to look at an interesting geological outcrop, apparently.'

Jason blinked. 'Right. Well, you know, Jan, you like flowers, there's some amazing flowers just back up the path, if you want to come and have a look. Josh found them.'

Josh and Julie joined them. Alan felt a bit swept along by Jason's enthusiasm, but all the same he managed to say, 'Flowers are OK, but I was going to offer to show you a waterfall we found, not far from the camp. If you're up to another walk.' He felt like a teenager asking a girl out: terrified, and sure that if it went wrong everybody would laugh at him.

Julie rested her big dark eyes on him and smiled. 'I'd like to see the waterfall,' she said calmly.

'Well, I'd like to see the flowers.' Jan wasn't actually grinning, but he could tell that beneath the surface she was one enormous smirk. 'Show me the way, guys.'

'Great!' exclaimed Jason, and Josh held out his hand to help Jan over a rock and said, 'This way.'

Julie didn't say anything, just stood there regarding him gravely with those liquid eyes. She did remind him of Jan; it was her slenderness and the way her hair was cut long and with a square fringe à la Cleopatra, but Jan had always been vivacious, without Julie's elusive stillness. To be honest, it perturbed him rather. He said slightly awkwardly, 'I don't know if you want to take a breather, I mean, it's not far to the waterfall, but, if you're tired –'

She smiled at him. 'All I've done is walk downhill for a couple of hours. I'd like to see it, while this lovely weather lasts.'

'Fine.' He led the way down to the camp, past where Steve still slumbered on his rock, and on down to the stream. After a while he said, 'So what was the climb like? Did you have a good time?'

'To be honest,' Julie said, 'I was a bit preoccupied on the way up. And it was cloudy too. The views coming down were amazing though, really fabulous. And the hut was fun. There was an open fire and everything, and just one big room.'

His fantasies about how they had spent the evening revived, fuelled by the thought of an open fire. 'Sounds lovely,' he said weakly. 'Did you have rain? It poured down here.'

'Yes,' Julie said, her voice strangely distant. 'There was such a storm, rain in torrents, thunder, lightning, everything. It was cosy in the hut. I . . . had a good time.'

'I wish I'd come,' he said wistfully.

'I'm sure there will be compensations,' she said, and her voice held such shades of meaning that he turned to look at her. But her face was opaque, he couldn't tell what she might have meant. If anything.

They turned up the stream and presently he said, 'You can hear the waterfall now. It sounds louder than yesterday. That'll be all that rain.'

'I like waterfalls,' she said. 'And the more water, the better.'

They turned a corner and he fell back to let her go first. She ducked under an overhanging branch and he was pleased to hear her gasp.

'It's beautiful!' she exclaimed.

He knew it was beautiful but, even so, seeing it again in the glorious sunshine took his breath away. A perfect spot. The water leaped down a cliff thirty or forty feet high, bathed in sunlight, spray glittering like flung diamonds, and tumbled and roared into a broad, deep pool. One side of the pool was bounded by rock. The other had a few big boulders and an expanse of fine pebbles, more sand than shingle, before the grass began and ran back to the ferns and moss of the forest undergrowth.

Julie ran forward to the edge of the pool and looked up at him, face glowing. 'It's perfect,' she said. 'Have you swum here?'

He nodded. 'Jan and I found it yesterday. It was so sticky, we thought we'd take a dip. It's damn cold.'

She glanced up at the sky. 'But the sun's so warm. And I'm hot from the walk. I just have to.' She stooped and began to untie her boots, then looked up at him again. 'Would you mind not looking? Just while I get in?'

That seemed a strangely modest request, and it was exactly not what he wanted to do, but he couldn't really say no. So he said, 'Well, sure,' and turned his back straining to listen to the little noises of her clothes coming off. Her trousers unzipped, her shirt rustled. He was sure he could hear the tiny click of her bra fastening.

'Here goes,' she said, and then she gave a little shriek and gasped, 'Oh, God, it really is cold!'

'I warned you,' he said.

'Don't turn round!' she said, and he heard her wading deeper into the pool. 'Oh, oh, oh, there's nothing for it.' And a splash.

He turned and saw her surface, dark hair sleek as a seal's, naked shoulders just visible as she bobbed in the deep centre of the pool. Foam from the waterfall swirled round her and he could not see her naked body. She smiled at him and shook her head. 'It's cold, but it's lovely!'

Just because she had asked him to turn his back didn't mean that he stood no chance at all. Steeling himself, he said, 'D'you mind if I join you?'

'Feel free.' She took a quick deep breath and dived, and for a moment he saw her slim back, glossy with water, and the rising orbs of her buttocks.

Quickly, in case she changed her mind, he pulled his clothes off. He had the beginnings of an erection, but the moment he waded into the icy water his prick thought better of it and shrank until it resembled a small acorn. Probably just as well, while he didn't know how she was going to react.

The water wasn't any warmer, but the sunshine was very brilliant and, although he shivered, it was still pleasant to swim. Julie was over at the other side of the pool, clinging to the rock wall, and he took a few powerful strokes to join her. But when he lifted his head she had gone. He shook the water out of his eyes and looked around and suddenly she popped up in front of him, laughed, splashed him, and dived away.

She wanted to play! With a roar he plunged after her. He swam faster than her, but she was as supple as an otter, quick to dive, quick to change direction. Once or twice he managed to touch her, and her skin was as cold and smooth and pale as the pearly inside of a shell, and so slippery that she squirmed away from him without any apparent effort. He changed tack and began to cut her off whenever she tried to swim towards the beach, herding her towards the waterfall. She saw what he was trying to do and swam faster, but he was too tall and his reach was too great – she couldn't get past him. Eventually he had her trapped, the only way to retreat blocked by the cascade of water from the rock lip above.

She surfaced, panting, and met his eyes. Then she turned and dived and he saw her pale body sliding beneath the tumbling water and emerge again beyond it, the other side of the waterfall.

He didn't fancy diving through that turbulence. But as he hesitated she caught hold of the rocks and pulled herself out. He could barely see her through the curtain of falling water, but the pale blur of her naked body drew him despite his caution. He took a deep breath and dived.

The water battered him and he had to kick as hard as he could. For a moment he thought he would be tumbled, spun, spat out ignominiously where he had started. But then he was through, swimming up, breaking the surface in the glittering moving sunlight beyond the fall.

Now he could see her. She was sitting on the rock, in a patch of almost unbroken sunlight, naked as a mermaid, her feet dangling in the water, her long body glistening. She looked down at him and reached up behind her head, twisting her dark hair into a rope to squeeze the water from it. Her arms were pale and slender and they arced elegantly to form a frame for her serene face, and the plane of her belly from ribcage to the dark shadow of her pubic hair was smooth and flat and glistening with pearls of sunlit water.

At that moment he would have done anything to have her. He swam to her feet, but there was no room on her little ledge for him. Reaching up, he caught hold of her calf. 'Julie,' he said.

She looked down at him, calm as a goddess, her breasts lifted, nipples tight with the chill, seemingly unmoved. She said nothing.

'You are lovely,' he said, his voice almost choked.

She leaned forward, small breasts dangling, and now she was smiling. 'There's no room here,' she said.

Tease! He pulled himself closer to the wall, rubbed his face against her leg, kissed her ankle. 'Come down,' he begged. 'Come back to the beach.'

Her brows arched. 'After you took so much trouble to get me here?'

'I just wanted to catch you.'

'And you caught me.' She leaned back, weight on her arms, back arched, trickles of water outlining her breasts and belly. 'And now what?'

If he pulled her, would she fall into his arms? But he didn't dare. The water was deep, and if he hurt her on the sharp rock he wouldn't forgive himself. 'Come back to the land,' he said again. 'It's warm there, there's sun, it's soft. Come back.'

Slowly she leaned forward. The muscle in her leg tensed and he let her go. She looked into his face for a moment, then said, 'Catch me, then,' and dived through the water and into the sunlit pool beyond.

Wrong-footed, he turned as fast as he could and dived after her. She had a head start and, although he swam as hard as he could, she was out of the pool before he was. But she hesitated on the pebbly beach and he took two long strides and reached out and caught her arm and pulled her towards him, cold skin against wet skin, and wrapped his arms around her and kissed her upturned mouth and felt himself warm and harden against her belly.

For a moment she kissed him back, passionately, and he was infinitely relieved that she didn't mind about the beard. But then she pushed him away with the flats of her hands. He hesitated, panting, not wanting to force her or make her do something against her will.

'Alan,' she said, her voice low and teasing, 'what are you doing?'

What was he supposed to say to that? In the end he smiled and said, 'If you haven't noticed, I'm not doing it enough.' His prick was fully hard now, and he moved his hips, nudging them against her so that she could feel his hot readiness. That was one part of his body he wasn't ashamed of anyway. Jan had always reassured him that he was on the splendid side, at least when he was at the right operating temperature.

'Oh,' Julie said, as if she had only just noticed. She pushed herself a little further away from him and looked down and said 'Oh' again, her voice betraying pleased surprise. She glanced up at him, looking naughty now, and licked her lips.

When she began to lower herself to her knees he wanted more than anything just to stand there and enjoy it. But he felt as if to let her service him like that would be wrong, unchivalrous, ungrateful. So he kneeled down too, catching her by the shoulders to kiss her again. 'Not just me,' he said. 'Let me do you too.'

She looked taken aback, but then she said, 'All right.' And he lay down on the soft grass and she straddled his face with her beautiful long thighs, and he laid his cheek against the cold smooth flesh and stroked it with his beard and she said in a voice of surprise, 'Oh, that's *nice.*'

'You're beautiful,' he said, looking up at her pussy. There were diamonds of water drops glittering in her dark abundant pubic hair, and he knew that she would taste fresh and sweet. As her mouth stooped towards his straining cock he reached up to touch her with his tongue and was gratified to hear her moan.

She was good with her mouth and once or twice her deft licks nearly brought him to the point of no return. But he was determined to be a good guy and finish last, and he concentrated on what he was doing to her and did not allow himself to feel the full pleasure of her squeezing lips and swirling tongue. After a while he found her rhythm and she began to moan and, as he licked her harder, more directly, she cried out louder and slumped forward a little and her lips went slack. He thrust his straining cock up into her mouth, excited by the sudden soft wetness, sucking and nibbling at her clit as she groaned and shuddered and came.

Then he rolled out from underneath her and stretched himself over her, shading her from the strong hot sun. 'I want you,' he said.

She put her arm across her eyes and sighed, 'That was lovely.'

If only the world hadn't changed and he could just push her legs apart and penetrate her, shove his cock up her and hold her shallow breasts and start moving. But it was different now, and he didn't know how to raise the subject. In the end he stammered, 'But, but it's not safe.'

She said from under her arm, 'Condom in the cargo pocket of my trousers.'

She had come prepared! Thank God someone knew what they were doing. He sprang across and rifled the pockets, found the packet, opened it. It was a long time since he had worn one of the damned things, but fortunately he hadn't lost the knack of putting one on. Sheathed, he leaped back to her and poised himself.

'I'll get cold like this,' she said, wriggling out from underneath him. 'I want the sun.'

So he lay on his back and let her spread her thighs around his body and impale herself on him. The sun was directly behind her, spilling through the tendrils of her drying hair, blazing around the edges of her body like an eclipse. She sighed and leaned back and rubbed herself as she rose and fell, and he reached up in wonder to tease and tug the tight nipples of her shifting breasts.

She seemed still very excited and soon she was rubbing herself hard and crying out as she humped him, driving herself fast and furiously to another orgasm. He held on, held on, and then, when she arched and wailed, he grabbed her hips and pumped upwards into her, hard and fast, shafting her shuddering body as her pussy spasmed around him. He had done it: he had taken her, and he groaned as his spunk boiled and spurted and left him shaking and full of a confidence he hadn't felt since he was a young man.

After a little while Julie lifted herself off his softening prick and sat down beside him, stretching like a cat in the sunshine and running her fingers delicately through the greying hairs on his chest and belly. Her hair was drying, settling into its long dark tresses. He reached up and curled one around his finger and said, 'That was amazing.'

She smiled at him and said nothing. He thought of his wife and hoped that she had had as good a time as he had. To Julie he said, 'I hope Jan liked the flowers.'

'Oh,' Julie said, stretching her slender arms in the sunshine, 'I think I can promise you that.'

Chapter Ten

Jan

What Jan wanted to say as they climbed up the path through the beeches was, 'So, what orgies did you get up to last night then?'

But she was reluctant to be so direct so quickly. Not because it wasn't her style. Being direct was very much her style. But experience told her that young people were very much more easily shocked than they liked to believe, and that the younger they were the greater the shock was likely to be. Jason and Josh were the youngest people on the tour and she thought that someone more than old enough to be their mother might well shock them almost beyond repair by asking them straight out about orgies.

Instead she said blandly, 'It sounds as if you had a good time on the climb.'

'Oh,' Jason exclaimed, 'it was awesome!' and Josh muttered something about 'Really cool.'

'Which was the best bit?' she asked, and repressed a smile when Jason gaped and hesitated.

'Well,' he stumbled, 'it was, it was –'

'The storm,' Josh suggested.

Jason's face cleared with relief. 'Yes, the storm! That was it.' He grinned significantly at Josh. 'Yes, the storm was great.'

They were so young, they seemed to think that she wouldn't notice that they were talking in what they believed was some impenetrable private code. She was finding it really, really difficult to resist puncturing their bubble, either by confronting them or by smiling the sort of smile that indicated that she understood.

But for now, she resisted. It seemed very likely that these two had been chosen to, well, involve her in whatever was happening. The way the group had split into Julie with Alan and her with the boys was too slick to be a coincidence. But if she scared them, would they back off? Or would they find their tasks easier?

She couldn't help but wonder what they had in mind, if it was their job to seduce her. How would a couple of callow youths go about seducing a woman in her fifties? And were they volunteers or conscripts? She hoped that they had volunteered, but she was by no means certain. All right, for her age she was both well preserved and attractive, but that didn't mean that men in their early twenties were falling at her feet on a daily basis. In fact, so far the tally of men in their early twenties falling at her feet hovered dangerously close to zero. So what would these two do? She decided to let things flow for a little while just to see what happened, because it would be amusing. If they fouled up too badly, she could always come to their rescue. So she said, 'What were these flowers then?'

There was a moment of silence. Jason stared at Josh with an expression that said *save me* and Josh stared back as if he didn't have a clue. After a moment he said wildly, 'Gentians. Yeah, they were gentians.'

They'd seen gentians in every single Alpine grassland that they had passed through, but never mind. If flowers were their excuse, well, they would have to do. She said placidly, 'Gentians are really pretty.'

'And rock lilies,' Josh added, getting into his stride now. 'That's right. Rock lilies. You don't see so many of those.'

'Well, that's true.'

She followed them up the path, which grew gradually steeper. Eventually they came to the treeline, where the beech trees grew more and more infrequent and the spiny clumps of alpine grass began. She looked up the path ahead of them and said, 'I thought we'd have seen the others coming down by now.'

'Oh, TJ said he'd bring them back by a different route,' Josh said. 'They'll be coming down by the stream.'

'And frolicking in the rock pools on the way down, no doubt.' She couldn't resist it, and the sharp exchange of glances between Josh and Jason left her in no doubt that she was not mistaken. Her mind moved of its own accord to hypothesise on the sort of frolicking that might be going on in those rock pools, who with whom, what exactly. How many men were left in the party, without these two? TJ, Rick and Greg. Three men to, let's see, five women. Well, that should allow for some imaginative frolicking.

She wondered, too, what Alan was getting up to with Julie right now. The poor darling had looked hideously nervous, but then he'd always been a little lacking in self-confidence, at least when it came to women. He'd taken a long time to believe that Jan thought he was the sexiest man she had ever met, and no doubt he was similarly uncertain about whether Julie would want to be with him. Well, if Julie didn't, she didn't realise what she was missing. Jan was looking forward eagerly to whatever the day brought her, but she knew that her excitement was underpinned and actually made possible by a rock-solid certainty that Alan was the man she loved, and that nothing that happened would change that.

They had been walking for nearly twenty minutes now and, apart from exchanges of glances, the boys had shown no instinct for action whatsoever. She was still very curious about what had gone on the previous night, and suddenly she didn't see the point in hanging on any more. So she said, 'Hey, guys.'

They stopped and looked at her.

'You have to tell me,' she said, 'I'm really curious. How is Greg reacting to someone else running the show?'

They both looked puzzled, and she realised that she hadn't picked the best couple of people to ask. These two would both be so astonished by everything that was happening to them that they really wouldn't notice an awful lot of what was going on with anybody else. After a moment Josh said, 'Ah, I don't quite get your drift.'

Now it was time to shock them, if they were going to be shocked. 'Well,' she said, 'you must have noticed that Greg and Sandy are at it like knives every night.'

They stared.

'And if you talk to Greg, he really is quite an unpleasant specimen. He's disparaging about Sandy, and you'd think that nobody else in the world but him had ever had an idea. And I imagine that it wasn't exactly his show last night, right?'

Silence. Eventually Josh said faintly, 'Right.'

'So how did he react?' She put her hands on her hips

and her head on one side, challenging. 'Did he get the sulks?'

They were still staring. Josh said after a long pause, 'Well, no, no he didn't, but then –'

'Then what?' she asked impatiently.

Josh swallowed hard. 'Then Julie was, ah –'

She couldn't help but laugh. 'Spit it out, Josh, for God's sake. What, d'you think I'll die of shock? Julie was what? Fucking him? Going down on him? What?'

Two pairs of enormous eyes regarded her with total astonishment. She stared back for a moment, then flung back her head in abandon. 'Blimey, look at the pair of you! You'd think I'd grown horns and a tail. Is someone my age not supposed to use rude words? Or not supposed to have guessed what was going on?'

Jason appeared to be incapable of speech. Josh looked at him, realised that he was on his own, and looked as if he was coming to terms with the situation. After a moment he began to smile, a slow, lopsided smile that spread gradually over his lean tanned face. 'Well,' he said, 'guess that might make our lives a bit easier, eh, Jase?' Jason gaped at him, and he explained, 'If she's on to us, yeah? Means she's probably up for it.'

Now it was Jan's turn to feel shocked, although she made sure that she didn't show it. Hearing Josh talk about her in those terms gave her qualms. Was she up for it, really? Did she know what she was doing?

Well, no, she didn't, in that she hadn't previously had sex with two young men at once. And did that mean that she didn't want to, now that the chance appeared to be coming her way?

For a moment she found herself wondering what her children would say if they knew what she was doing. But she dismissed that thought. Her children were grown up, and so was she, and she didn't interfere in their lives and she expected them not to interfere in hers. And she'd already done her best to convince Alan that what anybody else might think was the last thing that ought to influence them. The only other person who mattered was Alan, and he had agreed to give it a go. So was she going to change her mind now?

She looked at the two of them appraisingly. Josh looked back at her as if he understood exactly what she was doing. Jason was out to lunch, as usual. Josh really was a dreamboat, just her type, long and lean, hardened and sunbleached, like the Marlboro cowboy. And Jason was a nice-looking enough lad, public-school type, with dark curly hair that had grown rather too long. He probably wouldn't have a clue about sex, but what good was an older woman if she couldn't teach?

'So,' she said measuringly, still trying to decide if she really wanted to do this. 'You two got the job of involving me, did you? How did that happen?'

They glanced at each other. Jason said, 'I volunteered,' and she felt a glow of delight in her stomach, warming her. He volunteered!

'Two seconds before me,' Josh said. 'I –' he hesitated, lowered his voice, and finished confidentially '– I have this thing about older women, you know what I mean?'

Oh, the confidence! She smiled, the smouldering sidelong smile which Alan had always found irresistible. 'Well,' she said, 'I'll do my best not to disappoint you.'

And then they all three stood there looking at each other. After a second Jan laughed. 'We're not really going to go and look for these damn flowers, are we? Come on, let's go back to the glade back there, the grass looked really soft.'

'Good plan,' said Josh, and Jason jiggled about and then shouted, 'Come on, I'll race you!'

So they hared over the rocks back towards the trees, and Jan gasped and in the end slowed down so that she didn't break her ankle. When she reached the glade they were waiting for her, arms outstretched to form a finish line, and she speeded up again and broke through them and Josh reached out to snag her and pull her towards him. Pressed against him she stood quite still, and he looked down at her, hesitating. For a moment she felt as apprehensive as a girl before her first kiss. He was so young, young enough to be her child, almost young enough to be her grandchild.

And then she thought of Alan with Julie by the waterfall and she smiled and reached up to bury her fingers in Josh's fair short hair and pull his lips down on to hers.

It was so, so strange to be kissed by a different man after so long, after thirty years. It was extraordinary. At first she found it hard to accept it, hard to enjoy it. But after a moment she opened to the newness of the sensation and relaxed against Josh's long hard body, sighing as his tongue entered her mouth. Everything was different from Alan, the pressure of his lips, the shape of his teeth, the way he held her, the smell of him. Eyes closed, she allowed herself to experience fully the sensations of touch, his hands on her back, his body pressed against her, his mouth on hers. She tasted him, savoured him, and shivered.

Then there were hands stroking through her hair, making her jump. Jason was standing close behind her, touching her hair, her neck, her shoulders, her buttocks. She gasped with surprise and pleasure, detached herself from Josh's kiss and leaned her head back on to Jason's chest. He pressed his mouth on to hers and kissed her hard. Compared to Josh he was inept, but his sheer enthusiasm was a delight. He thrust his tongue into her mouth and gasped, and Josh pushed harder against her and began to stroke her breasts with his long strong hands, and she couldn't believe her luck.

She really wanted to see her two young prizes naked, and quickly. She reached for Josh's shirt, began to fumble with the buttons. As she unfastened it she felt Jason behind her get the picture and start to struggle with his own clothes. Pulling herself free of his mouth she muttered, 'Please take your clothes off, both of you; let me see you.'

They hurried to do as she asked and she stepped away from them a little to watch. She stood with her arms wrapped tightly across her breasts and belly, struggling to hold in her increasing excitement, feeling her heart thumping and her diaphragm heaving as she breathed.

It was warm in the glade and brilliant sunlight streamed down through the pine needles and the beech leaves. There was a breeze, so the patches and powders of sunshine shifted constantly, throwing moving shadows over the dappled arching ferns and the moss and the pale clear grass. Even though she was intensely focused on watching Josh and Jason, she was still aware of the beauty of the glade, the clearness of the sky, the quality of the light, the looming bulk of the mountains behind her. There was a stream at the side of the glade and its chattering fall mingled with the sound of the birds singing in the trees and the wind in the topmost branches and the rustle of clothing being dropped to the ground. Beneath her feet the moss was starred with tiny white and yellow flowers, a little like

English celandines. She was never going to forget one detail.

Josh was naked now, and Jason stripped to his boxers. She realised that he was hesitating, and that he might be uncomfortable being naked next to Josh without her close physical presence as an excuse, as a buffer zone. The thought of being a buffer zone between these two young men made her smile and made her stomach tighten at the same time. She went closer to them, smiled at Jason and pushed at the waistband of his boxers, and he looked at her with mingled apprehension and excitement as he began to pull them off.

She looked at them with frank admiration and hunger. Josh still reminded her of Al when they had met, but she had to admit that Al, although lean, had never been as tough and strong-looking as Josh. His body was deeply tanned, the paleness of the skin covered by his shorts was startling, and his muscles were like whipcord, fine-drawn and hard, tendons visible like cords under the golden surface of his skin. He made her think of an animal, a dun-coloured desert animal built for endurance. A dingo, perhaps, trotting indefatigably along its trail, sprinting for the kill. Except, of course, that a dingo on the trail wouldn't be sporting a hard-on. He had a nice cock, not as big as Alan's, but a good size and bouncing against his belly with hardness. She reached out to touch his thigh, felt the skin hot with sun and rough with fine blond hairs and beneath it the muscle like wood. Her hand slid upwards and stroked along the length of his shaft and his cock jerked, begging her to hold it. She smiled and looked at Jason.

So different, this body. Jason really was the English type, with his dark hair on the nape of his neck and skin that even after a week in the sun was pale and starred with freckles on his nose and shoulders. He was broad-chested and perhaps he would be hairy when he was older, but for now his skin was as smooth as a boy's. He looked fit and strong, but the edges of his body were blurred with softness. He looked like a house dog next to Josh's hunting dog.

All the same, he was appealing, and his taut eager cock was luscious, thick and fat, with a slight upward curve that gave it a jaunty air. She stood for a moment marvelling at her luck, admiring the instruments of her pleasure, and the young men looked at her as if they were wondering what was going to happen next.

Oh, great seducers! She couldn't help but smile at the fact that she was going to have to take the lead but, after all, she wasn't surprised. And she was going to enjoy it too. She would be able to do, to take, exactly what she liked.

And what she wanted right now was to taste them. She said, 'Don't move, now,' and slowly kneeled down on the soft starry moss. Blond head and dark head drooped to watch her, and she sensed that each of them was hoping that she would start with him.

And where would she start? She held Josh in her left hand and Jason in her right and said, 'A little closer, please,' because she wanted to be able to reach both of them with just a turn of her head, with no ungainly shuffling. They stepped closer together like people having their photograph taken, and she caught a whiff of their scent, the smell of sun-warmed male, hot and musky. It filled her throat, and she closed her eyes and relished it.

Slowly, luxuriantly, she slipped her hands up and down the stiff shafts of the two cocks. She didn't mean to compare and contrast, but she couldn't help it. Josh's harder, like a bar of iron, but not so thick. Jason's still firm and rigid, but palpable beneath her fingers, and yet so broad that her fingers didn't quite meet around its swollen stem. The head of Josh's was scarlet, of Jason's purple. They were both magnificent.

Unable to wait a moment longer, she leaned forward and took Jason's cock into her mouth. He tasted of salt, of sweat, of soap, fabulous. Still gently rubbing at Josh with her left hand, she dipped her head, letting Jason slide right into her mouth.

God, he was big. He was thicker than Al, much thicker. The thought of that wide, strong shaft penetrating her made her shiver, made her press her thighs together. She'd never seen a thicker cock than this one. Whatever else happened, she wanted to feel it inside her.

Conscious that Josh might feel left out, she released Jason, not without regret, and turned her head to lick the shaft of Josh's cock. It lunged towards her mouth. He smelled different from Jason, wilder, more sweaty, and he tasted wonderful, sharp and piquant, Thai curry to Jason's steak au poivre. Jason had stood still while she sucked him, but Josh groaned and pushed his hips towards her and buried his hands in her hair to hold her head still. The feel of his long hard fingers against her scalp, his cock surging in her mouth, rippled right through her.

She wanted to go on sucking. She was hungry for the taste of come, but suddenly she felt that it was wrong that they were both naked and she wasn't. The thought of stripping before them made her anxious. There were stretch marks on her belly from three children, her breasts had seen better days, and her skin was soft and lined compared to the taut smoothness that they would have seen and tasted on the younger women. She was afraid that she would put them off, that they wouldn't want her.

But to be clothed when they were naked in this Eden seemed wrong. After another moment's hesitation she let go of Josh, sat back and pulled off her T-shirt. As if this was a signal the boys both kneeled beside her and began to help, unfastening her trousers, untying her laces, seemingly desperate for her to get naked as they were. When her trousers came off, when her bra was unclipped, she held her breath in silent apprehension. But they didn't wince, they didn't recoil. Josh was in front of her and he stooped his blond head to suckle at her breasts. His stubble scratched her and she flung back her head and gasped with gratitude and delight.

'Let me,' Jason began, hesitated, and finally stammered, 'let me go down on you, Jan, let me.'

She said nothing, just let herself subside backwards into Josh's lean strong arms. Her shoulders rested against his hard naked belly and his hands enfolded her, cupping and caressing her breasts. His blond hair shut out the sky, his lips brushed her face, her hair, then settled on her mouth. She closed her eyes and sighed with delight as he pinched her nipples and she felt Jason's face nuzzling between her legs, felt his warm tongue searching, searching, and finally finding.

He was surprisingly good, surprisingly good. Al hadn't got as practised, as sensitive as this until they had been together for years. Jason's lips caressed her entire pussy, his fingers brushed her perineum, his tongue encircled her clitoris, pressed it, lapped it until she could not keep silent and her body began to arch and sway with the rhythm of Jason's licking. He didn't rush, that was the miracle. So young, and he wasn't rushing. He took his time, licking her slowly, sometimes leaving her clit to run the point of his tongue down to her entrance, move back, return, and whenever that happened she moaned with delicious impatience, longing for him to resume his unhurried, skilful caresses.

'That's it, Jase,' Josh said in a low, tight voice. 'Make her come, mate.'

'Yes,' she said, pressing her head into Josh's lap and lifting her breasts towards his hands, 'yes, Jason, make me come. Yes, that's it, yes.'

Josh cupped her breasts and stroked the nipples in time to her groans and as she felt her orgasm rising he leaned forward and kissed her, thrusting his tongue into her mouth even as she trembled and shuddered and cried out, and her climax was full of bursting sunshine and green leaves and fragments of blue glittering sky.

It took a few moments for her to come to herself. She lay in bliss, cheek cushioned against Josh's hard belly, Jason's head resting on her thigh, panting and digging her fingers into the soft moss underneath her. Josh's cock twitched below her neck and she caught a whiff of its delectable scent and wanted to turn over and take it into her mouth. But then she had a terrible thought and said in a slurred voice, 'I do hope one of you two has got one of those vile condoms.'

'No worries,' said Jason, mimicking a Kiwi accent.

'Good,' she said, lifting her head and rather reluctantly drawing away from Josh's lap. 'I hope you know what to do with them too. I honestly don't think I've ever used one.'

Jason looked half-mournful, half-disbelieving. 'Really?' He frowned. 'Have you always been with Alan then?'

Little innocent. 'No, Jase.' He looked almost shocked. Did he really think that everybody his parents' age was a virgin until they got married? 'But before I met Alan I was on the pill. We didn't need Durex in those days.'

His eyes widened. 'Before AIDS. Wow.'

'Don't you wish you had lived then?' Josh asked.

'Absolutely,' said Jason. 'I hate them.'

'Well, Jason,' she said, 'I'm sorry to say that I'm going to ask you to put one on now. Because I want you to fuck me.'

Amazing, how easy it was to say those words. Because she really did want him to fuck her. She hoped that Alan was having a good time. She hoped that even at that moment his lovely cock was buried deep in Julie's slender tender body, but even if he had made a mess of it, even if he had been disappointed, she still wanted to feel Jason's big cock inside her. And she wanted it now.

'Josh,' she said, turning on to her side, 'let me suck you.'

'Yeah!' Josh said eagerly, and he straddled his knees on the soft moss and thrust his cock up to her face and she knew what she wanted. She had seen a porno movie once, one of those that somebody's friend brings back from Amsterdam or the States or wherever, and in it an air hostess went into the cockpit of the airliner and ended up naked on the pilot's seat with the pilot fucking her from behind and the copilot taking her in her mouth. She'd found that scene a hell of a turn-on and fantasised about it for years and now she was damn well going to live it.

She turned on to her front and came to all fours and reached out with her mouth for Josh's cock. He pushed it towards her face and she knew that this was the right way round, that her pleasure would be the greatest when she could taste this wild animal and at the same time feel Jason's big cock inside her. Holding Josh's cock, she licked the head, one long wet ice cream cone slurp, and then said, 'Jason, I want you to fuck me.'

'Absolutely,' Jason said. She half expected him to enter her straight away, but there was movement and rustling behind her and she realised that he was looking for a condom. She half laughed and smiled up at Josh and then slowly, lovingly, took his cock into her mouth and began to suck.

'God,' Josh moaned, 'that's good.' His hands returned to her hair and she sighed with delight because she loved the sensation of being held, the feeling that she wouldn't be able to stop sucking him even if she wanted to, that he was going to fuck her mouth just as he might have fucked her cunt. She let her lips slide right up to the tip of his shaft, flickered her tongue around the head, explored the rim, teased him and, as she had hoped, he moaned and tightened his hands on her hair and thrust his hips forward, forcing his cock back into her mouth, driving it between her lips until the head touched the back of her throat, until she had to close her gullet against the gag reaction. God, it was good. All she needed now was to feel Jason inside her.

As if he had heard her thought he kneeled down behind her, his hands on her naked buttocks, thighs brushing hers, and his cock was ramrod-stiff between her legs, flattened against her pussy, the tip banging against her belly. She'd expected to have felt the rubber, but in fact she hardly could. Obviously it was going to make less difference to her than to him. She wanted to speak to him, to tell him out loud to fuck her, but her mouth was full of Josh's cock and there was no escape. She just moaned, and as she moaned

Jason positioned the tip of his cock against her entrance and thrust and she cried out helplessly as she felt herself penetrated by that fat, fat shaft.

Oh, it was lovely, it was like being fucked for the first time, it was better than the first time, because now she knew how to enjoy herself. Bracing her left hand on the mossy ground she reached backwards with her right, felt between her legs, let her fingers explore the place where she was impaled on him, cupped and teased his taut bollocks, felt the wet slither of his cock sliding out, the slippery lunge as he filled her again. Then she put her forefinger on her clit and began to move it in tiny circles, one revolution for each thrust of Jason's cock, and her body seemed to leap straight back to the plateau of pleasure that comes before orgasm. She undulated her backside, drawing Jason into her rhythm, shuddering with delight as she felt him grabbing her thighs tight to hold her still so that he could fuck her harder.

'Yes,' she tried to say, but nothing came out past the gag of Josh's cock except a slurred and blurry groan. Josh growled and dug his fingers harder into her hair and fucked her mouth vigorously, lean hips arching. It was as if she was in that blue movie, positioned so that the camera could see both orifices at once, both scenes of penetration revealed in all their glory. She could have come instantly, and she wanted it to last, so for a moment she stopped touching herself and just luxuriated in the sensation of being held, penetrated, fucked, consumed by two strong young men, two hot eager cocks, four greedy grasping hands. It was like nothing she had ever known, like rebirth; it was magnificent.

Jason's movements were becoming jerky, desperate, and she didn't want him to feel that he had failed, so she touched herself again and cried out against Josh's surging cock as she began to reach her peak. Behind her Jason sobbed, 'Yes, Jan, please come, I'm coming, please, please,' and even as she crested the ridge and tumbled into orgasm she hoped that he would realise that she was there because she couldn't say anything, and he must have done because as the first ripples fled from her spasming cunt to her toes and her fingers he shouted and bruised her hips with his grip and lurched to a shuddering standstill. She let the weight of her head fall into Josh's hands and he grunted and gave a couple of odd jerking thrusts and then he was there too and her mouth was filled with that delicious salt taste. Everything she wanted, perfection.

She swallowed, swallowed again and gave a long, satisfied sigh. Josh let go of her head, Jason her arse, and she restrained a laugh because their hands were so gentle, so hesitant, so different from their greedy determined grasping of only a few moments ago. After a second Jason withdrew, and she let herself sink to the soft moss, stretching and rolling like a lioness after mating.

'That,' she said with decision, 'was wonderful.'

They looked as if they didn't quite know what to say. Then Josh squared his shoulders boldly and said, 'You give good head, y'know, Jan.'

'Why, thank you, sir,' she said, and smiled down at Jason, who was still panting. 'I could say the same for you, Jason.'

He brightened visibly. 'Really? Thanks! I'm learning anyway.'

'I'd say you'd learned a lot,' she said, stretching again, gazing up at the blue sky beyond the canopy. 'I'd imagine you've learned quite a lot altogether, on this trip.'

'You could say that,' Jason said.

This was bliss, but it couldn't last for ever. She rolled upright and reached for her bra and shirt. 'I suppose we ought to get back to camp,' she said. 'We are supposed to walk down to another hut tonight, aren't we?'

'It's not too far,' Josh said reassuringly. 'It's only a couple of hours' walk. No sweat. We'll be there for tonight.' He grinned, a wide, toothy, wolf's grin. 'Another night in a hut. We're going to have fun.'

'Got something planned, have we?' She wasn't a bit surprised to hear it. 'What's on the menu?'

'Well,' Jason said, 'I'm not sure, but I think a few people are getting pretty fed up with Greg. I think he might be in for a bit of, well, let's call it correction.'

'Excellent choice,' Jan said, picking up her trousers. 'He really is a prize arsehole.' A thought crossed her mind, and she added, 'Has anyone thought about Sarah? I can't see her welcoming this at all. And what about Steve?'

'Well,' Josh said, looking a little awkward, 'Julie was told to see to Steve as well as, as well as Alan.'

'Oh, I see. Big jobs.' Would Al be disappointed by that? Probably not, that would be taking this whole thing rather too seriously.

'And Sarah, I think we hoped that John might take care of her.'

Thinking about it, Jan still wasn't sure. 'Might work. They certainly spent a lot of time together yesterday and today. But she really is set against this kind of thing, you know. I think she could make herself difficult.'

Josh and Jason exchanged glances, then shrugged. It looked as if they didn't care two hoots about what Sarah might think. Which meant, if others were similarly determined, that they were in for an orgy. How would Sarah react? Jan had been enjoying herself on the basis that nobody would ever know, and she didn't fancy Sarah running off to the tour company and spilling the beans. Besides which, she wasn't sure what part she wanted to play for herself. At the moment, especially with the uncertainty about Sarah, she didn't feel that she really wanted to be in the thick of it. It would depend, of course, on what Al thought.

Suddenly she wanted to get back to camp. She wanted to see Al, to talk to him. They could get a bit of peace and quiet on the walk. She wanted to hear what had happened to him, tell him what had happened to her, get his views. She wanted to hold his hand.

She smiled up at her two young stallions. They had been fun, she had really enjoyed herself, and she didn't at all mind that it was over. 'Let's go,' she said.

Chapter Eleven
Greg

He absolutely did not know what the hell was the matter with Sandy.

They were almost at their last night's camp now, making good time along a wide, soft track. He should have been looking forward to the exciting possibilities offered by another night in a hut, but in fact he was distinctly unhappy. Nobody had seemed to want to talk to him and he was walking along towards the end of the group, ignoring the landscape. Up front TJ was telling them something about how significant this place was to the Aborigines, something about *tapu*, sacred places. He didn't give a shit whatever holy crap they believed about this particular bit of hill. He kicked viciously at the smaller pathside rocks, hands jammed in the pockets of his Stubbies, thinking about his wife.

Normally she was only too keen to hear his ideas on anything, never mind sex. She loved his suggestions for stuff they might try with other swingers, the more ingenious the better, and he was proud of how gorgeous she was and how obedient and how all the other men that they met just couldn't wait to touch her. Every time he saw another man with his cock in her he wanted to say, That's my wife you're fucking, mate, isn't she a beauty?

But now she seemed to have lost the plot. Last night, on the top of that mountain, he'd played along with Sicko Rick's weird *Story of O* plans for Julie, but after they'd gone round once he'd thought it was time to get things moving on more normal lines and he'd made a few suggestions and really expected Sandy to back him up. And she hadn't! At first she'd ignored him, the cheeky mare, and then when he'd absolutely demanded her attention she'd said – he almost gagged to remember it – she'd said that she preferred Priss's idea. Which was, needless to say, to leave things up to Sicko Rick. He didn't put anything beyond that man, it was incredible the things he thought of. OK, having Josh and TJ both fuck Julie at the same time had been pretty cool, pretty horny, he had to be honest. He wouldn't have liked to have done it himself, fuck a woman with another man's cock in beside his, but if Josh and TJ were cool with it, fair enough. But that had been Diva's idea, hadn't it? And later, when Rick had persuaded TJ to have her up the arse, well, that was going a bit too far. Greg had never had any woman up the arse, not even Sandy, and he didn't intend to start. Filthy shitty habit.

What he couldn't get over was the sense of betrayal. Sandy hadn't backed him up! Didn't she know that that was what she was supposed to do? Had she forgotten what she was for? He had the ideas, she did them. That was the way it worked. They were a team. What the hell had got into her?

And there was something else, something even worse than Sandy's behaviour. If he hadn't been feeling so bad he'd have avoided thinking about it, but he was feeling bad and he couldn't stop himself. He wouldn't have believed it, except that he had definitely seen it.

When TJ had been about to arse-fuck Julie, Sicko Rick had got close to them, to have a good close-up look, weirdo shitbag. And he'd actually got hold of TJ's cock and steered it between Julie's butt cheeks and helped it in, and then – God, it was enough to make you sick just remembering it – then he'd kind of stroked TJ's shaft as it went in and fondled his balls, and TJ hadn't even seemed to mind. It made Greg want to puke.

Greg practically barged into the person ahead of him and realised that everyone had stopped and clustered around TJ, looking expectant. Here came another bloody lecture on Abo culture and history, as if there was any worth having. The walking was all right, but why did they have to insist on all this poxy cultural stuff? Waste of time. Greg stood in the back row, checking out Zoe's gorgeous high black arse in her tight shorts and barely listening to what TJ was saying.

But having caught a few words he thought it was more interesting than usual, and listened with attention. TJ was talking about his *moko,* his tattoos. There was a lot of guff about the cultural significance of the *moko,* old sayings like, 'They can take everything away from you, but they cannot take your *moko.*' That was pretty dull, but then he got on to how the tattoos were made. The designs on TJ's thighs and arse, which Greg had seen last night, were apparently made by some pretty standard method, a comb or whatever which punctured the skin. Not much worse than a proper tattoo, really. But the facial tattoos, the curving parallel lines which followed the shape of TJ's bones, well, when Greg heard how they were made, he had to swallow hard to keep his lunch.

They were bleeding *chiselled* into the skin, using a big hollow chisel, and the grooves got filled up with the shit mixture they used for dye afterwards. *Chiselled!* He could hardly believe it. And the bloke who was having it done had to take it in complete silence, not a single sound, while the tattoo artist chiselled grooves in his face. Jesus! You had to respect them for putting up with the pain, but why the fuck would you want to? And if that made TJ pretty bloody hard, how the hell had he put up with Sicko Rick mauling him like that? It was a bloody mystery.

The lecture was over and people set off again. There was apparently only half a mile or so to the hut, and then they would make a campfire outside and some food. Greg fell once more to the back of the group, frowning as he thought about Sandy's treachery.

He couldn't just take this lying down. He needed to get her back on his side. What could he do to impress her, to remind her how much fun she had when she did what he suggested?

That was a tricky one. So much had already gone on that he was really straining his brain to come up with something different. Who could do what, to whom, that would have a good starring role for Sandy?

Frowning, he stared at the person in front of him and barely noticed who it was. And then he did notice.

In front of him was Sarah. Skinny, serious Sarah, who he was sure had not been involved in anything that had happened so far. That could be how he could shine. He could be the one who got Sarah involved.

Well, it was a good idea. But he looked at her thin legs and bony back and his heart sank. If ever there was a type of bird that he did not fancy, Sarah was it.

She was like the opposite of Sandy, whose opulent body and rich hair never failed to please him. Sarah was meagre, anxious, tense-looking. She didn't look the sort of girl to have an uncomplicated good time. And she obviously wasn't interested in joining in because her tentmate Zoe was already in the thick of it and Sarah must have had the excuse, and she had chosen to avoid it.

He didn't really think that he could get up the urge to fuck her himself. She just wasn't his type. But perhaps –

Yes, that was it! He stunned himself with his own brilliance sometimes. Another thing he'd noticed about Sandy on this trip was that she seemed to be really enjoying being with other women, even though in the past he was sure that she'd been kind of reluctant about lesbianism, had really only done it to indulge him. Well, he was cool with it, and perhaps it presented an opportunity. Maybe Sandy would like to try out her new cunt-sucking skills on Sarah.

It sounded good to him and, since Sarah obviously didn't really like blokes or she'd already have got busy, he suspected that it might be a good idea by her too. The man whose idea thawed the Ice Girl! That would get him some marks with Sandy, for sure.

He thought of how everyone would admire him for doing what they couldn't, and perked up. Walking a little faster, he came up beside Sarah and gave her his best, most boyish grin. Might as well start by getting into her good books.

'Interesting, wasn't it?' he said, because he knew that she was the sort of girl that liked that kind of cultural shit.

'I didn't realise that you were listening,' she said waspishly.

He hadn't expected quite that much hostility, but that was OK, he could handle it. 'Oh no, I was,' he said, and then with what he hoped was disarming frankness continued, 'Well, actually, you were right, to begin with I wasn't listening. But then I heard some bits of it and it kind of gripped me, y'know? I thought it was really amazing, how they make the tattoos on their faces and all.'

She looked at least a little mollified. 'Well,' she said, 'it is quite amazing, yes.'

'I'll be sorry when this trip is over, won't you?' he said.

She seemed to think a moment before replying. 'Yesterday I would have said that the sooner it was over, the better. But today, I think, yes, I agree with you. I will be sorry.'

Hey, that was good news! She must be coming round to the idea of getting herself a good time. 'Glad to hear it,' he said. 'Roll on tonight, eh?'

She gave him what his mother would have called an old-fashioned look and didn't reply, just speeded up so that she didn't have to walk next to him any more. What had he said now? Talk about touchy!

Well, not to worry. She was such an uptight girl, he'd probably just gone a bit too fast for her. He'd catch up with her later. It was great that she was moving on to his kind of thinking; it would make things much easier. He'd talk to her at dinner, in front of everyone else. They'd be really amazed when he brought her round.

There just ahead of them was the hut. Feeling excellent as he did, he couldn't help but notice that this one was in a really nice location, at the edge of the forest where the trees thinned and gave way to the tussocky grass that grew on the lower mountain slopes. Not far away from the hut there was a little stream, with a small waterfall tumbling down into a wide pool, which would make washing and watering the horses much easier. There was a mountain above the hut, or if not exactly a mountain in any case a damn big hill. He seemed to remember from what TJ had been saying that this was one of the sacred places and, to be honest, this time he could understand it. The mountain brooded and the sun's rays hit it sort of slantwise as the sun sloped downwards. Towards nightfall it would look really impressive, if there was a decent sunset. The last few days the sunsets had been magnificent, when there hadn't been storms, and this looked like another good one coming up.

Sandy was standing next to Sicko Rick, in a little group with Priss and Diva and Jan, pointing up at the mountain and exclaiming happily. She looked bright and vivacious and gorgeous and suddenly he was shot through with jealousy. It hurt him like a boot in the gut, and he went quickly over to re-establish himself.

'You OK, babe?' he said as he came up to them. Honestly, he didn't know what kind of weird stuff Sicko might have been saying to her.

'Sure,' she said, looking at him, he thought, without her usual welcoming smile. 'I'm fine, Greg.'

She sounded bloody cold! He couldn't put up with this. Time to make his play. 'Listen,' he said, 'I've got this great idea for tonight.'

The others all looked at him now, eyebrows raised. Rick particularly looked supercilious. Bloody Pom poofter, what did he know? 'I think you'll be impressed,' Greg said, looking at Sandy.

'Go on, Greg,' said Diva. 'Amaze us.'

And she was a bitch as well. No need to show that he was needled though. 'I thought,' he said, crossing his arms and standing aggressively, 'that we'd get Sarah involved tonight. I think she's been missing out, y'know?'

There was a long silence, while the others exchanged looks. They looked surprised. Yes, they looked bloody amazed! That had done it all right. Sandy looked interested too. She had something of her old expression, admiration, surprise. He felt much better.

'Well,' Priss said after a minute, 'that's certainly an interesting idea, Greg. Got any thoughts on how we might achieve that?'

'Oh,' he said lightly, 'I've already spoken to her. I'll sort it for you. I thought I'd talk to her over dinner.'

Rick snorted scornfully. 'Not a chance.'

Who the hell did he think he was? Greg turned on Rick, keeping his distance in case he tried anything on, and said, 'What the fuck do you know, you Pommy faggot?'

If Rick was insulted he didn't show it. Typical of those queers, they were even proud of being the way they were. He just said calmly, 'I know that you will never manage it.'

'Bet you a hundred dollars I will,' Greg said. For a moment he regretted the impulsiveness, but then he saw Sandy's wide eyes and didn't. That was the right thing to do, get Sicko to put his money where his mouth was.

'A hundred dollars? I tell you what,' Rick said, 'let's make it five.'

'Five hundred dollars?' Bastard! Greg didn't want to look small, but five hundred dollars was much more than they could afford, and he knew that Sandy knew it, and she was looking anxious.

'Not both ways,' Rick continued smoothly. 'Five hundred dollars to a forfeit.'

'Huh?'

'If you win, I pay you five hundred dollars. If I win, you pay a forfeit.'

A forfeit? He'd had a taste last night of the sort of sick forfeits that this pervert could come up with, and he didn't fancy it. Not one bit. He frowned, then said, 'Only if Sandy gets to name the forfeit.'

Priss and Diva and Jan exclaimed in protest. 'No way,' Diva said. 'She's your wife, Greg, that's cheating!'

'That's the bet,' Greg insisted. Sandy was looking at him spellbound, as if she couldn't believe it, and he felt great. She would give him something tasty to do, maybe even ask him to name his own forfeit. 'Five hundred dollars against Sandy's forfeit. You think that's OK, babe?'

Sandy hesitated, then said, 'Yeah, Greg, that would be fine.'

Rick looked as if he was thinking about it, then said, 'All right.' The women went on making a fuss, but Rick shook his head and ignored them and said, 'I accept, Greg.' He stuck his hand out.

Greg didn't want to shake, but it would look bad not to, so he did. Rick's grip was surprisingly strong. Greg was glad when it was over and he could preen in front of Sandy's admiring look. He spirited her away from the others and said, 'Five hundred dollars in the bank, babe! No sweat!'

Sandy frowned. 'What on earth did you say to her, Greg? How did you talk her into it?'

He tapped his nose and grinned. 'Can't give away trade secrets, babe.'

'Well,' Sandy said, shaking her head, 'I'll be really impressed if you pull it off.'

'Hey, don't doubt me!'

* * *

At dinner he managed to sit himself down next to Sarah at the end of the long wooden bench in the hut's living area, between her and the miserable Chinese git John. She didn't look too happy about it, and he wasn't that surprised, because he didn't think that he was her ideal company any more than she was his. But he wanted to be sure that when the time came she was right to hand, so to speak, ready for his suggestions.

'So,' he said, trying to be polite, 'what are you planning to do when we get back to civilisation?'

She looked at him with a completely unreadable expression. He waited, and after a really very long silence she said, 'I think I'll come back here.'

He blinked. 'Come again?'

'Or somewhere like it. In a smaller group.'

'Ah, I get it. You've really enjoyed it, huh?'

'It would seem so,' she said. 'Pass the bread, please.'

He was surprised she ate at all, she was so skinny. But at least she was being civil. He returned to his own meal, biding his time. There was no point in trying to talk to John, he never said anything to anybody. If Greg hadn't heard him answer Steve a couple of times, when directly addressed, he might have believed that the bloke was actually dumb.

Everyone except for John and Sarah was noisy and cheerful, just what you would expect on their last night. A few beers wouldn't have gone amiss, but even without them a good time was being had by all. Sandy was sitting a bit further down, next to Josh, and she looked as if she was having a suspiciously good time. Greg would rather she had cast a few longing looks in his direction. Up at the top of the table Steve was making coffee out of instant and milk powder and sugar with a considerable amount of ceremony, passing it round solemnly, like it was holy water or something. There was one packet of biscuits left, and as everyone took their coffee they took one biscuit and passed on the packet.

By the time it reached Greg and Sarah at the end of the table it was nearly empty. He held it out to her. 'Ladies first.'

Her face was unreadable. 'No thanks.'

At the far end Steve said, 'Well, ladies and gents, this is it, the last coffee of the tramp. I'd just like to say that this has been the most unusual tramp I have ever led, and I've been doing this for years.' People laughed and clapped and said Hear! Hear! and when Steve went on, 'I can't tell you how much I'll miss you,' they cheered.

This was, without doubt, the right time. Greg tinged his knife against his plate and every face turned his way.

'Well, ladies and gents,' he said, 'I think we've all had a really good time, and I'd like to thank Steve for his great route, and TJ and Josh and John for their hard work.' Everybody murmured and cheered and said Hear! Hear! again, and then looked expectant. He hadn't quite thought about how he was going to do this, but now he knew that the only way was just to plunge in there. She'd be up for it, she'd practically said as much. 'And I'm very pleased to say,' he went on, looking Sarah's way, 'that the one person who hasn't had a good time will be joining us tonight. Isn't that right, Sarah?'

Sarah stared at him. Her face was tanned, but he could have sworn she went pale. There was total silence and he got the sudden horrible feeling that he might have made a mistake.

After long seconds Sarah squeezed out from behind the bench and stood up. Her hands were shaking. She said, 'I,' and then, without warning, she slapped him hard. 'I have never,' she said, 'never met anyone as utterly crass as you!' And she stalked to the door of the hut and out into the night.

She had hit him really hard, and for a moment he sat with his cheek on fire and his ears ringing, hardly knowing what was going on. Then he came to himself and his first thought was one of absolute relief and satisfaction that he had had the sense to get Sandy to own his forfeit. It was bad enough to have failed. It would have been unbearable now to be at the whim of Sicko Rick.

Everybody was looking at him. After a silence Diva said, 'Ooh, Greg. That was hardly subtle.'

'Looks like you lost your bet,' said Jason. How did he know? Greg might have guessed that the story of the bet would have gone around like wildfire.

'Well, bollocks to it, eh?' Greg said, proud of the fact that his voice sounded light and cheerful. He grinned at Sandy. 'Over to you, babe.'

She smiled at him. 'Oh yes, it is, isn't it? OK, Greg. Let's just finish up the coffee and then I'll, well, I'll let you know.'

Why was she being so coy? Greg finished his coffee in silence, looking warily up the table at his wife. She met his eyes a couple of times, but she looked – different, somehow. He was beginning to be afraid that she had been nobbled. Nobody else seemed to be taking much notice of him either. He didn't like this situation one bit.

'Let's push back the table, shall we?' Sandy said once everyone had finished. 'Make a bit of space.'

Everyone jumped to do as she suggested and presently the room was clear, tables and benches stacked against one wall. Greg found himself standing in the centre of the circle, opposite Sandy. What would she ask him to do? She looked as if she might be pissed off with him. He didn't know what exactly he'd done to annoy her, but if she was pissed off maybe she'd choose something embarrassing. If only he knew! It hadn't struck him before that he didn't really know that much about what she would choose under any circumstances. Normally it was him that did the choosing.

'Well, babe,' he said, with a grin that he hoped didn't show his nerves. 'Here I am. Give it your best shot.'

'Oh,' she said, 'I'm not sure.' She put her finger to her lips in what had to be a pretence of looking like a bimbo. What was all this about?

'Come on, babe,' he said. 'D'you want me to make some suggestions, babe? How about if I give you a hand-fuck, yeah? You know you like that.'

'Mmm,' she said, 'I'm not sure. Let me think.' What was she playing at? The tension was killing him! And he was sure that he sensed something unpleasant, something around the circle of watching eyes that made him feel as if they already knew what Sandy was going to say.

'Oh, I don't know,' she said, and her smile looked malicious now. 'I'm just so not used to thinking for myself; I think I'll just have to pass it on.'

'Pass?' he gasped, hardly believing his luck. 'Hey, thanks, babe! Now –'

'Not *pass*,' she said, cutting across him. 'Pass it on. My forfeit, Greg, is that for the next hour you do everything that Rick says.'

He felt slightly sick, and cold. 'No,' he said, 'no, you can't do that.'

'Oh, yes, she can.' It was a chorus from around the circle, and he glanced from face to face like a hunted animal. Everyone was staring, everyone was grinning at him; they all wanted to see him tormented and abused by that fucking pervert, and he wasn't going to stand for it!

'No way,' he said, and then louder, 'no fucking way!' If escape was OK for Sarah, it was OK for him. He headed for the door and when Josh reached out to grab him he smacked him one. But instead of letting him go Josh just pulled harder and suddenly the men were all around him, Josh and Al and Jason and TJ, grabbing his arms and holding him so, although he struggled, he had to stand there, arms pinioned like a prisoner, waiting while Rick approached him.

'Jesus!' he exclaimed, still fighting. 'Keep away from me, Sicko!'

'Sticks and stones,' said Rick. His Pommy voice sounded so fucking self-satisfied. 'Listen, Greg, what are you so worried about? All I'm going to do to start with is get someone to suck you off. Pick a girl, any girl.'

Greg stopped struggling, although he was still panting. He looked at Rick warily, not trusting him one inch. 'You're going to get a girl to suck me off?' he clarified carefully. He certainly did not want Sicko's gob anywhere near him.

'Absolutely,' Rick said. 'Any girl you like.'

What was his game? Greg tried to read his intentions in his face, but it was bland and English and inscrutable. So what should he do? He'd still like to get out of it, but he wasn't going to be able to get away, that much was clear. So it seemed like the sensible thing to sort of go along with it for now, while it suited him, and then later, if things got uncomfortable or out of hand, he would stop.

'OK,' he said. 'I want –' Now who to choose? Which

of those girls? It had to be between Zoe and Diva. Zoe was the more gorgeous, that lovely black skin. But Diva had scorned him and made fun of him. Much more satisfying to have her on her knees. 'Diva,' he said.

'Diva it shall be,' Rick said. 'Take off your clothes, Greg, if you wouldn't mind. Diva?'

If Diva was still scornful, she didn't show it. She stepped out of the circle and came forward smiling, walking with a model-girl wiggle that made her lovely tits stick out. She touched TJ and he stood back, and the others all let go of Greg and retreated. 'Hey, Greg,' she said, and she smiled, and her white teeth were gorgeous in her coffee-and-cream face. 'Better get naked, man.'

Now this he could handle! Let them all see him stark bollock naked, getting head from this gorgeous Indian-princess girl. That was what he deserved. He pulled his clothes off quickly and stood there bare, head up, defying them. There was his bitch wife looking at him as if butter wouldn't melt. He would settle up with her later, that was bloody certain. Handing him over to Sicko! Jesus, she was in trouble. She'd be sorry.

Despite the shock he'd so recently had he still managed to will himself into erection before Diva even kneeled down. He set his jaw and closed his eyes and waited for her mouth, and when he felt it he let out the breath between his teeth in a long hiss of satisfaction. She was good, as he had known she would be. He wanted to make sure she did it right and he put his hands in her hair, holding her still.

'That's not the deal,' Rick said, and then people were taking his arms, pulling his hands away. He opened his eyes and saw that it was TJ and Josh holding him and for a moment he wanted to fight them, but then

Diva flickered her tongue over his cock head so exquisitely that he relaxed and stopped caring about the restraint and just gave himself up to the delicious warm wetness of her mouth.

'Diva,' he heard a whisper. It was Rick's voice. 'Diva, don't let him come, whatever you do.'

That sounded so scary that for a moment he thought he might lose his hard-on. But he couldn't do that, not in front of everyone. They had to see that he wasn't threatened by sicko arseholes like Rick. He concentrated on the feel of Diva's tongue and lips and imagined himself pushing her down, holding her hands together above her head, tearing her clothes off her body, forcing her legs apart, thrusting his cock right up her cunt and making her squeal.

God, she was good. From being afraid that he would lose it, now he was trying hard to stay in control, but still could feel it getting away from him. His hips started to move of their own accord, pushing towards her working mouth, eager to hump him to a climax. He heard himself grunt as she gave a swift, hard suck, and then moan as she pulled her mouth away and pinched the tip of his cock hard, really hard, forcing back the rising spunk.

A whisper, and he opened his eyes and saw Rick stooping over Diva, murmuring into her ear. What the fuck? What was he playing at? But he couldn't pull away or fight, not when Diva's mouth was hovering in front of his cock, just waiting to suck him again.

She looked up at him, long dark eyes glowing. 'You taste good, Greg,' she said, and kept her eyes on his as she opened her mouth and slipped her lips around his cock head, slurping and sucking as if he was a delicious ice-cream. She was using her hands now, cradling them around the shaft, nursing his balls, fondling him between his legs. He closed his eyes and moaned as she sucked harder and one finger caressed the smooth skin between balls and arsehole, making him gasp.

Her finger slipped further back, rimmed his arsehole. He stiffened, reluctant to let her touch him there, and she stopped sucking. Opening his eyes, he looked down at her and she said, 'Listen, Greg, I just want to touch your prostate, yeah? Like your G-spot. You'll like it, trust me.'

He didn't really like the idea, but he couldn't say no to her, not when she might stop sucking him. He muttered, 'OK' and closed his eyes again, sighing as she began once more. Her hand reached between his legs, she was touching his arse. He tried not to tense up, tried to relax, and her finger was actually going inside him. It felt weird, really strange, and not as unpleasant as he had imagined it would. He groaned and then she sort of felt inside him and suddenly it was as if the top of his head came off; there was such an extraordinary, incredible sensation radiating out from between his legs and up his cock and all the way up his backbone to the top of his head and the ends of his fingers, so powerful that he flung back his head and cried out. He was amazed that he didn't come instantly, spurting his come into her mouth, but she had stopped sucking; she was applying pressure again. He felt like a bottle of champagne in the hands of a Grand Prix winner, full of potential, full of froth, shaken to the point of bursting, shaken and shaken and fizzing and bubbling and still stoppered, held in, no way out.

'Please,' he whimpered, not caring who heard him begging as long as she took pity on him. 'Please, please, come on, Diva, he said you would suck me off, please.'

She took her finger out and he moaned with disappointment, because it was like a light was being switched off. But she caressed his balls and began to suck him again, with a strong, steady rhythm now, and he thanked God that she was going to let him come this time. He relaxed into it, grunting with each slither of her warm lips down his wet shaft, and at first he didn't notice that there were hands on his arse again, and when he did notice that someone was parting his cheeks Diva was sucking really hard and he couldn't tell them to stop straight away. And anyway, maybe it was one of the other girls, come to help out, maybe it was Zoe, easing one long dark finger inside him –

And then he noticed, he realised, he understood, this was not a finger pushing at his arsehole, it was too thick, it was different, and he knew what it was just as his sphincter gave in to the pressure and began to open.

'No!' he screamed, but it came out just as a scream and then it merged into a cry that was half-scream, half-sob, because the thing was a cock and it was already a little way inside him and it didn't feel bad, it didn't feel bad at all; it felt good. It felt shamefully wonderful, and Diva's lips were still clasped around his throbbing, aching cock, and he knew that if he protested she would stop.

'Please,' he sobbed, tugging feebly at the hands that still held him, 'please.'

'Please what?' said Rick's voice from behind him. 'Please stop? Or,' he murmured, 'please go on?'

Everything was stillness, nothing was moving, and Diva's mouth was warm around the head of his cock and he wanted to fuck her. The sensation in his arse was warm and stretched and delicious and he didn't know what to do. He wanted to get away and he wanted it not to stop. He sobbed again, 'Please.'

'Please what,' Rick insisted softly.

And as he spoke he shifted slightly and his cock just stirred in the entrance to Greg's arse, and that little movement sent a feeling like flame going through him, and it was so good he couldn't, he couldn't resist it. 'Please,' he gasped, and he couldn't say it, but he had to have it, and at last the words came out. 'Please. Please go on.'

'Yes,' Rick hissed, and there was more pressure and a feeling of fullness and pain, but it was good pain – it felt good – and Diva's lips were on his cock but that hardly seemed to matter any more. Greg moaned and arched his back and twisted because he didn't know what to do – he wanted to push himself towards Diva's mouth and also towards this brutal delicious invader and in the end he just writhed, impaled on Rick's cock, his own cock throbbing and surging in Diva's mouth. When Rick withdrew and thrust again harder he lost it and began to come, helplessly, shamefully, in great spurts and jolts, and then he could barely stand and he was glad of the hands that held him up so that Rick could hold his backside and thrust into him hard and fast, four, five times, and then it was over. Rick withdrew and TJ and Josh let him go and he folded slowly to the floor, huddled, whimpering, sated and ashamed.

He'd been buggered. Sodomised. And all of these people had seen him beg for it, gasp with pleasure, jerk in feverish climax.

It was unbearable. He curled into a ball, hands over his head.

'See?' It was Sandy's voice at his shoulder. 'You should trust me, Greg. I knew you'd like it.'

Chapter Twelve

Sarah

She managed to stay angry until she got outside. Only once the door had slammed behind her did the tears come, as she had known they would. She pressed her hands to her face to keep in the gulping sobs while she was still close to the open windows of the hut. If anybody heard her she would be totally mortified. Not that they were going to be listening to anything going on outside, or remotely interested in her, since she didn't want to play their sordid game.

After a while the first storm of sobs passed off and she wiped her face with a tissue and blew her nose. It was always like that when she got angry. Generally she managed to control herself for long enough to put whoever it was who had angered her in their place. But that really took it out of her and so, after the anger, the tears would come, and the more angry she was, the worse the tears were. This time hadn't been too bad, comparatively. Greg was such an appalling person that she hadn't really expected anything more from him. It wasn't as if she had been shocked, although it was always a shock to discover that someone who could walk and talk could be that stupid.

It wasn't dark yet outside, but still a long southern twilight. The first fat planets hung on the horizon, just visible between the trunks of the tall trees, glowing like lamps. She went over to the stream and sat beside it on a handy rock so that she could splash her face with the cool water, washing away the tracks of her tears. Then she drew a deep breath and looked up.

There was a window of sky visible between the surrounding trunks. It was perfect, translucent blue, dark in the east, in the west shading to clear paleness and then almost to green, brilliantly dotted with the planets. Near where the sun had set there were three little clouds, puffy in the centre and wispy at the edges, and they were all different colours. One was baby pink, one was scarlet, and the third was the rich pinky-orange of the inside of a conch shell.

There was surprisingly little noise from inside the hut and she could hear all around her the birds of daytime finishing up their business and putting themselves to bed, the birds of the night-time wakening. Not far from where she sat a songbird let out a call of such piercing sweetness that it almost made her cry again. She listened attentively to the song, wondering which of the birds that John had told her about it might be, but she couldn't identify it.

This was why she had come, to experience the sounds and silence of an unspoilt land. Not completely unspoilt, of course, with native species hunted to extinction or driven out by introduced competitors, and with the inhabitants' skins threatened by the thinning of the ozone layer, but still, compared to where she lived in the Midlands, Paradise found. She had not come to enjoy herself at other people's expense, and she was both angry and disappointed that the same did not apply to her fellow travellers.

The bird called again and she frowned, trying to remember its name. It was a common bird, those that were listening had heard lots of them, and it was frustrating that the name had slipped her mind.

'It's a tui,' said a soft voice near her.

She jumped and turned, prepared to lacerate whoever had broken in on her. But when she saw who it was, she relaxed. 'John,' she said. 'I am glad it's you.'

That was absolutely true. John seemed to be the only other person on the trip who wasn't interested in the goings-on begun by Priss and Diva. She and he had been thrown together a fair bit over the last couple of days, since Steve had also fallen to some woman's blandishments, and she had found him excellent and interesting company. She didn't understand why the others said he was odd, or silent, or stand-offish. He was quiet, certainly, and reserved, but then so was she. Most of the people on this trip only seemed to like you if you were as in your face as they were. They didn't understand depth or subtlety. She and John had spent a very pleasant day yesterday looking at rocks, and he had also told her about the plants they had passed on their way. He seemed to know almost as much about the island and its wildlife as TJ, although he hadn't even been born a Kiwi.

She also had to agree with Zoe that he was a most attractive man. She had actually been tempted to follow him one morning and watch him doing his exercises because Zoe's description of them had been fascinating and she thought she might learn something from him to help her own yoga practice. But she hadn't done it because it had felt improper and intrusive. He obviously valued being alone and she absolutely understood that.

He was silent for a time, listening to the tui singing. After a while it stopped and didn't start again. He sighed, then said, 'I hope you're wearing some bite protection. Sitting out at this time of night, the sandflies will get you.'

'Oh, lord.' She looked helplessly down at herself. 'My repellent's inside. I can't possibly go back for it.'

'No,' he agreed hastily, 'don't go in there.' When had he come out? Did he know what was going on? Well, she wasn't going to ask because she really didn't care. 'Look, I've got mine,' he said, extracting a small spray from one pocket of his shorts. 'Give yourself a dose. Don't forget your ankles.'

She took the spray and began to apply it. 'Thank you,' she said, handing it back at last. 'I've managed to escape the little wretches up to now. It would be sad to start on the last night.'

'And such a beautiful night,' he said.

Following his gaze, she tilted her head up to the sky. In between the branches of the pines and beeches the stars were coming out and she scanned the unfamiliar constellations in wonder. So many stars, so many patterns. 'At home,' she mused, 'I can show you all the signs of the zodiac and lots of other constellations too. Here I hardly know any.'

There was a silence. Then he said, 'I was going to go up the hill to finish my exercise. I didn't get a chance earlier. If you want to come, I could show you some constellations later.' He glanced over his shoulder at the hut. 'I imagine they're going to be busy in there for a while. You might want to spend the night out.' Looking judiciously at the sky, he added, 'I know it can rain any time, but I think I've hardly ever seen a sky that looks so fair. I think it'll be safe.'

She frowned anxiously. 'I'd like to, but all my stuff's in there. I mean, it's not as if I need much, but it'll get cold later, won't it? I don't even have a sleeping bag with me.'

'I've got blankets,' he said. 'Over by the horses. I often sleep out. It's nicer than inside in a hut, with everybody snoring.'

'Oh yes, I agree. The noise, and the smell of all those people.' She snorted. 'Imagine what it'll be like in there tonight!'

He rolled his eyes and she felt a huge sense of relief that at least there was someone who understood. 'John,' she said impulsively, 'I really want to say how pleased I am that you see this the same way that I do. I think I would have gone mad if it had been just me.'

He nodded slowly, then said, 'It's their right to do what they want. But I think you came here for something else.'

'Yes,' she said, 'I did.'

There was a silence. Then he said, 'I'll get the stuff and then I'll take you up.'

'I can carry something,' she said, hurrying after him.

'All right.' She liked that about him, that he wasn't burdened with any stupid ideas about men doing the carrying. She was thin, but she was strong, and she hated any implication that she might be feminine and therefore feeble. He handed her a fleece blanket tied up with straps, a water bottle buried within it, and she figured out quickly that the straps could slip over her shoulders and not obstruct her as she walked.

'All set,' she announced, and he nodded and led the way across the stream and then up towards the hillside.

She followed him at a little distance, watching where he set his feet. In the long mountain twilight it was still light enough to see, and she knew that the moon would soon rise. The thought of climbing this hill in the moonlight filled her with joy.

He glanced back occasionally, but did not ask her how she was or burden her with concern. He walked on at a moderate, steady pace, one she could follow without complaint. Gradually it became darker, but soon they were out from among the trees and the glow from the sky showed her the path. Presently the moon appeared on the horizon, first a sliver, then a rind, then a segment, and finally the whole disc, golden as it lifted, smudged with craters. It was only a couple of days off full and even the slightly dark portion of its surface was gleaming with Earthlight.

A beautiful night, a perfect night. There was a very slight breeze now, just enough to move the warm air, and insects chirring in the brush beside them. Sarah felt excited and young, thrilled with the prospect of sleeping out, like the times when she was little and her mother let her put up the tent in the garden and spend the night out there, awake and listening to the traffic and the urban foxes.

It wasn't a very big hill, and all too soon the climb was over and they were on the summit. Behind them the forest sussurated in the breeze, and all around them taller peaks glowed in the moonlight. She couldn't tell what the vegetation was, but it was low and soft. It reminded her of the hollow, cropped turf of the Downs, except that here there weren't any sheep to crop it and so it grew in soft tussocks. Sweet smells rose up when she moved her feet; it must be a carpet of herbs.

'Oh,' she said, moved almost beyond expression by

the beauty around her. She took off the blanket and unfurled it, spread it on the ground, took off her boots and socks and sat down, drawing the fragrance of the herbs into her nostrils, bathing her eyes in the blue moonlight, listening to the tiny sounds of the insects and small birds. Her whole body was electric, intensely alive, and yet she felt none of the tension and stress that she normally associated with climbing. She just felt – whole.

'This is the most beautiful place I have ever seen,' she said softly.

John looked at her for a moment in silence. Then he said, 'I entirely agree with you.'

'Thank you for bringing me,' she said, like a polite child.

'It is my pleasure,' John said, rather formally. He had spread out his blanket and removed his own boots. He glanced at her, then announced, 'I'll practise now.'

How calm he was! He wasn't asking her permission, and it didn't seem to matter to him whether she was there or not. She admired him and felt very flattered that he was allowing her to be present. She said timidly, 'If you're going to do the *Suryanamaskara*, I will too, if you don't mind.'

'As you wish,' he said, and then added, 'I'm not a guru, Sarah. I don't teach.'

Did he think she was asking for something? 'Oh, no,' she said quickly. 'No, no, I know. I'll go at my own pace. It's just – companionable, to work with someone else.'

He nodded. 'Perhaps,' he said, 'later, we could try some joint postures.'

'Oh.' She didn't quite know what to say. 'Well, perhaps, but I've never actually done any postures with anyone else. I'm not sure I'd know where to start.'

'Let's play it by ear,' he said. 'Now, I must begin.'

He stood in Tadasana, the Mountain, and closed his eyes. She could almost feel the thread of his breathing, filling his core with energy, grounding him, connecting him to the earth. He seemed to have all the strength and solidity that she sought in yoga and rarely found. But tonight, she felt it. It was as if there was a current of power running up from the mountain, through the soles of her bare feet, through her spine and into the centre of her. She took deep breaths one after the other, and felt herself calm.

She wanted to concentrate on her own practice, on the smoothness and strength of the movements, on her breathing. It was bad to be distracted – it meant that the world had a hold on her. But somehow she just couldn't let go of the fact that John was practising so close to her, body flowing through the postures with a speed and suppleness and strength that she couldn't match. He finished the first Suryanamaskara and stopped, took two deep breaths, and pulled off his shirt. His bare torso gleamed in the moonlight, and she couldn't help looking. Then, without so much as a glance at her, he unfastened his shorts and kicked them away.

She was afraid that beneath the shorts he would be naked, but he wasn't. He was wearing trunks, close-fitting smooth fabric from just below his waist to the tops of his thighs. She glanced at him, looked away, and felt her eyes drawn back again.

Zoe had said that he was beautiful, and he was. He moved into the second Suryanamaskara and she couldn't stop herself from watching him move. The moonlight highlighted every curve and plane of his smooth bare skin; he shone as if he were made of white marble or etched from glass. She tried to go back into her own movements, but she couldn't. Her body would not obey her. After a while she gave in to it and sat down on the blanket, lifting her feet into the lotus position on her thighs, resting the backs of her hands on her knees, contemplating him as if he were an object of meditation.

He moved into the Warrior sequence, and watching him she felt herself lifted out of her life, out of her body, as if she floated in the clear warm air. He was made for these postures. As he stretched and turned, each muscle on his arms and shoulders and torso delineated by the moonlight as if with silverpoint, she could practically see the spear balanced at his shoulder, his enemies quailing before him as he prepared to smite.

She realised now that she had never really looked at a man before, not like this. This must be what it was like to be an artist, to encompass the whole of a man with your eyes, to know him completely, to possess him. And this man was so magnificent. Once or twice in her vet practice she'd treated eventing horses, great powerful beasts whose muscles rippled and bunched beneath their satiny skins, and that was what this man was like. Power, strength, control, grace. Watching him made her heart ache.

He completed the Warrior postures and moved on to the seated poses. His strength was matched by his flexibility; he seemed perfectly supple, as if each limb were connected to his body not by bones, but by strong cords. He stretched himself out and began to move into the Bow pose, and she had not seen anyone bend themselves backwards into a hoop so supply since she was at school. He said he was not a teacher, but he was better than her teacher, that was for sure.

From the bow he moved into a headstand, slowly, steadily lifting both legs, then extending them until his body was straight as an arrow, toes pointed, belly flat as a wall, breathing steady and slow. There seemed to be no effort, no trouble in doing these things, from which she knew how very skilled he was.

He moved slowly into a full handstand, poised on both hands, head lifted from the ground, body totally still, apparently at rest. She gazed at him, and as she did so she became aware that her own feelings were changing.

From a sense of detachment, of floating, she now felt a sense of emptiness. Her heart was no longer full, but hollow. She did not recognise the sensation, hardly knew how to give a name to it. It felt like – yearning.

She had been satisfied just with watching. Now, filled with this strange new hungriness, she no longer wanted to be only a spectator. She wanted – she hardly dared say it, even to herself – she wanted to touch that body, to feel its firmness, its texture, its warmth. She wanted it to touch her.

John lowered himself from the handstand and returned into the Bow posture, hands and feet on the ground, body arched into a high curve. Sarah found that she was breathing more quickly, and that her eyes were moving along his shining torso to the bulge of his genitals, thrown into stark relief by the backwards curve of his supple spine.

She looked away hastily, blaming herself. How could she fall into this trap; how could she become so crass, so like Greg? This was a contemplative, a meditative thing that he was doing. He was not inviting her to lust after him; he was probably not even aware that she was watching. He understood the importance of focus, of concentration, even if she didn't. He ought to be an inspiration to her, not an object of desire.

Slowly John subsided into the Corpse, flat on the

ground, hands at his sides. His chest and abdomen lifted and fell very slowly with his breathing, and again she looked away, horrified by how strong the desire to touch him was. She felt hot across her throat and cheeks and her heart was beating fast. It was absurd.

He had finished, and slowly he sat up. For a long time he didn't look at her, and she was suddenly afraid that he had noticed her watching, that he hadn't liked it, that he was angry with her.

But eventually he looked across at her and she thought he was smiling, although it was hard to tell because of the way the blue moonlight slanted down across his face, catching in his black brows. He said, 'You stopped.'

'I –' What could she say? She felt tongue-tied. At last she managed, 'I was so enjoying watching you. You are, well, you are a master.'

He looked serious now. 'This is what I am good at.'

'I am so impressed,' she said sincerely. 'I wish I could do it.'

He smiled again, she was sure this time. 'Sarah, you are a healer. You cure sick beasts. What can I do to compare with that? You should like yourself.'

Like herself! His words struck her right through, like the shadowy spear the Warrior held. She stared at him, then looked quickly away, unable to bear it. She knew she should like herself. But it was hard, so hard, when everything she did was flawed, when nothing was perfect. If only she was like him, able to attain perfection.

He did not speak for a long time and she was afraid that he would have seen how much effect his words had had and perhaps was regretting saying them. But at last he said, 'Would you like to share some postures?'

'Well –' Her body clamoured for her to say Yes! Yes! It was an excuse to touch him!

What she said was, 'I don't think you would enjoy it. I would hold you back.'

'I may not be a teacher,' he said, 'but I am not so selfish as all that. Let's try it.' He got to his feet and gestured that she should join him. 'Come.'

She hesitated. Her heart was pounding. She felt terrified, appalled. But she was used to terror – her days were filled with it – and after only a few gasping breaths she got quickly to her feet and joined him on his blanket.

He looked down at her, at her cumbersome trekking trousers and long-sleeved shirt. 'Your clothes will restrict you,' he said practically. 'You might be more comfortable in less.'

She could have reached out now and touched him, he was so close to her. She could actually feel the heat radiating from his smooth silvered body. The thought of having her bare skin close to his was almost more than she could bear. But he was right, she couldn't do postures dressed as she was, and she knew that her underwear was sensible, Dry-Flo racer-back crop top and briefs. He would see her in less at a swimming pool. She nodded quickly and unfastened her trousers, stepped out of them, stripped off her shirt and tossed them all off the blanket.

She was so thin. She nerved herself to look up at him, sure that he would scorn her. He was so strong, so muscular, every bone with its covering of strong flesh, and she was skinny, like four pipecleaners, with no more breast than a boy. Of course it didn't matter whether he found her attractive or not; it didn't matter in the slightest. But it would have been so nice to have a body like Diva's, or like Zoe's, strength and slimness combined, not this look of a starving martyr.

'So,' he said. He didn't look as if he minded her body, but then again he didn't look as if he particularly liked it either. Of course he didn't! He wasn't carnally inclined; if he had been she wouldn't have taken her clothes off, would she? He was pure, and she was the one at fault for finding him so beautiful, for wanting to touch him. 'Are you warm?'

'I'll stretch into it,' she said.

'All right. If you do the first Sun Salutation and stop at the Downward-facing Dog, I'll show you how you can add to the stretch.'

'All right.' She chewed her lip self-consciously, then drew in a deep breath and began the sequence.

She tried to concentrate, to focus on herself as she knew she should, but she couldn't. She was so intensely aware of his body close to hers, his movements mirroring hers, of the rhythm of his breathing. Only half-consciously she found herself synchronising her breathing with his, easing into a deep, steady pattern. He breathed so slowly, so evenly. In following his breath, she felt a whisper of his strength and steadiness passing into her nervous body.

'Now,' he said softly, and she breathed out and dropped into the Downward-facing Dog, reaching her head low between her arms, dropping her heels, lifting her tail bone to the starry sky.

And then she felt his hands on her lower back, his body weight slowly coming on to her. He was in front of her, body extended, propped on her hips, and slowly his weight was straightening her spine, deepening the stretch. His hands were just on the border of her briefs, fingers on the fabric, the heels of his hands on her bare skin. His palms were warm and dry and where he touched her she tingled.

After a long moment he straightened, and she stepped her feet between her hands and lifted herself into Mountain pose. He was standing now with his hands outstretched, and she knew without being told that he wanted her to place her hands in his and, with less hesitation now, she did so.

He didn't speak, but slowly, slowly leaned back, away from her, his dry grip secure and strong. Mirroring his movements, she kept herself straight, tightened her abdomen, leaned back and back until they were poised, their straight tight bodies and joined arms making a perfect triangle, their eyes meeting, waiting for the moment when the balance would be concluded and they would return to their own bodies.

It was time, and she let herself return slowly to upright position, expecting that he would let go of her hands. She didn't want him to let go because it felt as if she was drawing strength from him. And to her pleasure he didn't. He held her hands still and stepped away from her, and she matched him, and then he slowly sank down and straightened his legs and they formed another geometric figure, backs low and straight, torsos exactly bent. The stretch in her hamstrings was delicious. She sensed him breathe in and out, and she also breathed out, and the stretch deepened until she knew she had never gone so far before. Normally when she extended herself she felt afraid, but now, with him, she didn't. She felt strong and flexible, and even as she sensed it she knew that he would know, without being told, exactly what she was feeling.

This was what she had meant when she had talked to Kathy about a union that was as much spiritual as it was physical. This delicate, poised collaboration, this understanding of each other's body, this conversation without speech. Kathy hadn't grasped it, and most people probably wouldn't, but she had known that it was possible, and here it was. This was what she had dreamed of.

Slowly they lifted out of the stretch and looked at each other. There was a silence like a note of music. And then, to her surprise, John looked away, as if he were anxious or embarrassed. At once she blamed herself. What had she done that had made him uncomfortable?

She couldn't think of what to say, and in the end he broke the silence. 'Your back is very flexible,' he said. 'That's good. How about your front? Can you do the Bow?'

With a self-deprecating laugh she said, 'Only the beginners' version, the pelvic lift. I think my arms just aren't strong enough.'

He shook his head. 'No, you are strong. Perhaps you have never properly felt it. Show me.'

Now she was the one to feel self-conscious, anxious and embarrassed. She was afraid that she would look stupid, afraid that he would think her stupid, afraid that she would make a mistake. But he had said that she was strong, and she didn't feel that she should let him down, so she lay down and positioned herself, her heels planted against her buttocks, hands by her shoulders. She took a deep breath and raised her hips, felt the familiar panic rising.

'Rest your head,' he said, and he reached quickly under her body and guided the crown of her head to the blanket. To her surprise, this position felt quite secure, and she couldn't stop herself smiling.

'Good!' he said. 'Now breathe, and when you are ready, lift on the thread of the breath.'

She felt fear returning. Drawing in her breath deeply, she tried to lift her chest into the arch and thought she would slip, but then he caught her waist with his strong hands and lifted her, only very slightly, and she was there, bent backwards in an arch, and his hands were on the bare skin of her waist and she could think of nothing else. She didn't know how she was going to get down. Nothing made sense. She heard herself whimpering, and then she felt him lift her, lift her right off the ground, and her head came up and the world surged around her. She reached for him and her arms found his neck and she was standing, so close to him, her arms resting on his shoulders, his hands on her waist, and his black eyes were blacker than ever in the clear moonlight. The waves of giddiness receded and replacing it came another surge of empty yearning, rushing through her so strongly that it was all she could do to prevent herself from reaching up and kissing him.

His breath, which had been so steady, seemed strangely ragged now. Had he been afraid that he would drop her? Surely not. He stared at her, and his fingers tightened on the bare skin of her waist, and the emptiness inside her increased until she found herself gasping.

He said, 'Sarah.' She couldn't reply, but her hands on his shoulders moved, slid to the nape of his neck, under the curtain of his strong straight black hair. She took one tiny step, and with that step her body touched his, pressed against him, all the way down the length of his strong hard torso. The moonlight flooded down over them and she slid her fingers into the tumble of his hair and slowly, slowly his head stooped down and she lifted her lips to his.

Oh, that kiss, like nothing that had ever befallen her, so tender, so searching, open mouth to open mouth, breathing together, and as they kissed his strong arms wrapped around her, tighter and tighter, until she could barely breathe at all and thought that she would die from the sheer bliss of it.

Then suddenly he let her go, stepped back, his hand stretched out as if to keep her away, and she knew that she had tempted him, that she was wicked, a slut, no better than all those other girls, and he would never forgive her.

But he was saying, 'I'm sorry, I'm so sorry, I couldn't help it, please forgive me.'

As she realised what he meant, that he wanted her as much as she wanted him, she felt that, until that moment, she had never known the meaning of real happiness. Joy flooded through her, as if the moonlight had turned to liquid gold and filled her whole body. She laughed, and when he stared she said, 'John, I almost said the same thing.'

He stepped one hesitant step towards her. 'But you hated all that. You said you thought it was wrong.'

'Yes.' She held out her hands to him and he came forward another step and took them. 'Sex as a sport, that's wrong. But not this. This is right. I've never felt anything so right in all my life.'

'Yes. That's it.' He came closer, and she realised that inside those tight trunks his penis was hard and erect, held flat against his flat belly by the tightness of the fabric. It should have scared her, but it didn't. Perhaps nothing would scare her now, not ever.

She could see that he still didn't quite believe her, and so she stepped back and caught the band of her bra and pulled it off, pushed off her briefs, and stood in front of him naked. His eyes flickered over her body and returned to her face and he came close to her and whispered, 'You're beautiful.'

Her cup ran over. She closed her eyes and tears leaked from under her lids and trickled down her cheeks, and his lips kissed them away. She put her arms around him again and pressed herself against him, feeling him warm and strong, and into his ear she whispered, 'Have me. Heal me.'

He tightened his arms, holding her close. Then she felt something change, felt tension enter him, and she drew back. 'What's the matter?'

He shook his head, lips tight. 'I haven't got, I haven't got one of those things. You know, a condom.'

She nodded gravely. 'Well,' she said, 'for my part, you don't need it.' He looked a little blank. It was strange, she had always believed that it would be excruciating to explain this. A twenty-seven-year-old virgin! But in fact, it felt easy. 'Sex with me will be perfectly safe,' she said steadily, 'because I'm a virgin.'

His face lit up, then clouded. 'But,' he said, 'that means you have to trust me, Sarah.'

Of course, she didn't expect him to be a virgin too. But she did trust him. 'If you tell me you're all right, John, I will trust you.'

He shook his head. 'I've hardly had any partners in the last five years . . . and always with condoms anyway, ever since I started.'

'Well then.' And if she got pregnant? Well, what then? Then she would be pregnant, and she couldn't think of anything that would make her happier than carrying this man's child.

And now she didn't want to talk any more. She reached for him again, and this time there was no hesitation. He held her and his mouth found hers and they kissed and this time he slipped his tongue between her open lips and she gasped, because the pleasure was so intense.

His hands found hers, drew them above her head, held her in the Mountain pose. She smiled and closed her eyes and breathed, and he kissed her again on her closed mouth, then on her cheeks, her forehead, her chin, her throat. Slowly his lips travelled down her body, resting in the hollows of her armpits, caressing the slight swells of her small breasts. He took one nipple into his mouth and her closed eyes tightened and she gasped, the sensation was so piercing, so annihilating.

He was whispering her name, murmuring into her skin between kisses. She tried to keep the pose, but her head wanted to turn, her neck ached to arch. He kissed her belly, explored her navel with his tongue, rested his hands on the hollows of her flanks, and the emptiness was back, filling her until she thought she would fall.

Lower and lower his lips travelled, and now she knew that she should be afraid, that she should be embarrassed, that his face was so close to the secret heart of her. But she wasn't afraid, she was full of joy. When he rested his cheek against her flank, then pressed his face to her pubic hair and kissed her there, her arms fell of themselves and she staggered. He held her tightly and thrust his tongue between her legs and she cried out and lost her footing, but he caught her and lowered her to the blanket and pushed her thighs apart with his strong broad shoulders and lay between them, licking her with aching, sweet slowness.

She had wondered sometimes, in her stolen masturbatory moments, if this caress really was as good as women cracked it up to be. Now, writhing under the touch of John's gentle tongue, she knew that it was better. Nothing that she had ever felt could compare to the delight, the slow, swelling sensations awoken by his soft movements. She cried out, and he didn't stop, and sooner than she had believed possible she felt her climax coming, burning in the heat between her legs, shivering its way up her spine, clenching her fingers, twisting her neck, making her utter strange noises and grasp helplessly at the tussocks beyond the blanket. Her eyes opened, staring up at the glittering sky and, as she came, she saw meteors flashing like brilliant streaks of flame and she did not even know if they were real.

Then he had stopped, and his broad strong body appeared between her and the stars, blotting them out, a male eclipse. He was poised over her in Plank position, and the shuddering sensitised flesh of her vulva responded with a desperate twitch to the touch of something hot and hard which could only be his penis.

With all her heart she wanted to feel him inside her. Why did he not move? She said his name, and he kissed her quickly on the lips. Then he said, 'Sarah, are you sure?'

'I've never been so sure of anything,' she said. Still he hesitated, and she smiled and ran her hands through his heavy, straight, coarse, foreign-feeling hair. 'John,' she said, 'I want it to be you.'

He said, 'Sarah,' and then he pressed his lips to hers and slipped his tongue once more into her mouth, and as he did so she felt him between her legs, pressing, thrusting. At first it didn't hurt, and then it did, a brief sharp pain that made her wince and turn her head. He drew in a quick anxious breath, but then the pain was gone, replaced by a delicious feeling of fullness, of contentment, a soothing of that terrible vacancy.

'John,' she said, and of themselves her hips lifted up towards him, asking for him to do it more, to do it again. He hesitated, then withdrew, and she let out a little moan of discontent before he thrust once more and she realised that this was the nature of it, this agonising withdrawal, this wondrous penetration.

'Did I hurt you?' he whispered, the words riding on the breath of another strong thrust.

'A little. It's gone,' she gasped, and then, 'Oh, that's so good, please don't stop.'

His body was shining now in the moonlight with a faint film of sweat. 'You'd think I should be able to keep this up all night,' he gasped, 'but I'm out of practice, Sarah, I'm sorry –'

His face contorted and she reached up for him, anxious, hardly understanding. He thrust into her twice, hard, and then he jerked himself away and she cried out with the shock of the cool air where his hot body had been and then felt warmth and wetness jetting over her belly and realised what he had done.

'Well,' she whispered, stroking his hair, 'that was sensible.'

He was panting, head hanging. 'I don't want you to regret it.'

'I think there's little chance of that,' she said.

He lowered himself down beside her, wiped her belly with his hand, cleaned it on the grass, then drew her close. 'We have all night,' he said.

All night, and then it was over. The bus was coming for them not long after dawn; it was going to drive right up the rocky track to the hut. She pressed herself against him, hardly able to believe that she had found this so soon before it was time to leave.

Unless, of course, she never left. For a moment she almost asked him whether he would like it if she would stay. But then she felt it was rushed, too soon.

But she wouldn't forget. Later, when they had lain together and named the constellations and watched the falling stars, later she would ask him. And he would reply.

Chapter Thirteen
Priss

One of Priss's favourite books was *Cold Comfort Farm*, and on her good days she fancied herself as a latter day Flora Poste, unerringly moulding the people around her to suit her preferences. And as she looked around the hut, she knew that this was definitely one of the good days.

She felt particularly proud that her fellow trampers had taken control of their own destinies, almost as if the whole thing had been their idea, not hers. She hadn't had to do anything at all to achieve Greg's humiliation – Rick and Sandy had cooked it up all by themselves. An excellent outcome, mind you! She couldn't have devised anything better herself. His face, when he realised that Sandy wasn't going to give him an easy way out! Worth coming to the other side of the world for.

People had needed a breather after that. It was getting very dark now and, as the hut had no electricity, they had brought in the gas lamps from the packs and hung them strategically around the room, illuminating its wide wood-walled space with a flattering, flickering white-gold glow. They had managed to persuade Steve to make a final ceremonial cup of coffee. They had dragged the mattresses in from the bunk rooms and spread them around on the floor, and now they were all lying around on them, drinking the coffee and talking and laughing.

All except for Greg. He was curled up on the bare boards in a corner of the room, hands clasped over his head, knees drawn in to his chest, practically a foetal position. Priss looked at his huddled form and felt a twinge of guilt. She scooted over to Sandy, who was sitting next to Kathy, and said in a low voice, 'Hey, Sandy, d'you think Greg's OK?'

Sandy glanced once over at her husband, then shook back her red-gold hair. 'Should I care?'

Priss was rather startled, and she must have shown it because Sandy said, 'Listen, Priss, I've learned something on this tramp. I've learned that my husband is a total dickhead. If he wants me to stay with him, there are going to have to be a few changes.'

'Changes?' asked Kathy, with interest. 'Like what?'

Sandy hesitated. 'Well, I'm not sure. But I'm not going to let him use me as some kind of shop-window model any more. I get to say what goes, as well as him.'

Priss nodded, and indeed she understood Sandy's viewpoint perfectly. However, it took two to have a relationship and, from the way she'd seen Greg look at Sandy when he'd been handed over to the tender mercies of Rick, she had serious doubts about whether he would want to persevere. If, indeed, he ever uncurled. She could have felt pretty bad about that, so she told herself that a marriage built on such shaky foundations would never have lasted anyway and it wasn't entirely her fault. In fact, it was an accident waiting to happen.

She looked over to where Jan and Alan were sitting, talking to Jason. Jan was nestled in Alan's lap, her head resting on his shoulder, and he was stroking her hair. Their pose wasn't lovey-dovey; they were both animated and engaged in conversation. It just revealed that they were deeply attached, now as much as when they arrived. So it wasn't just a question of cause and effect. Different starting points made for different end points.

'D'you want to hear a joke?' Jason yelped.

Everybody groaned, because Jason's jokes tended to the puerile. But of course he went ahead anyway. 'What's the difference between a cop with a speed camera and going down on a girl?'

More groans, and shaking of heads.

'At least when you're going down on a girl you can see the cunt in the bush!' he said, and howled.

'All right, all right,' Kathy shouted. 'Keep it clean, Jason. Did you hear about the two aerials who got married? The wedding was terrible but the reception was great!'

A chorus of 'No more, please,' amid the laughter.

After a moment Zoe said, 'Do you think John went after Sarah?'

People looked around, at each other, wondering if anybody knew. Steve, who was lying beside Zoe, stretched at his usual full boneless length on one of the mattresses, said after a moment, 'I should think so. He wouldn't want her to be out in the bush alone at night. Looking after the client, you get my drift.'

'If he's doing any more than just looking after a client,' Zoe said, 'I am going to be so pig sick.'

'Why, Zo?' Jason asked.

'It's such a damn waste!' Zoe exclaimed. 'That man has the fittest body I have ever seen. *Ever*, and believe me, boys and girls, I've seen a few in my day. I'm damn sure that he can't see anything in a skinny tight-ass like Sarah.'

'Not so sure about that,' Jan said. 'I thought they were getting on pretty well. I mean, John talked to her, and he never really talked to anyone else, did he?'

'Not bloody fair,' Zoe said, throwing herself backwards on her mattress with a pout.

'Never mind,' Steve said. He draped one long arm over her and pulled himself up, looking down at her. 'Never mind. We'll try to make it up to you.'

The next second he and Zoe were kissing, open-mouthed, devouring each other, and the atmosphere in the room seemed to change at once. Priss had wondered where it would start, and it looked as if this was it. She decided that unless anybody came directly to get her, she would just watch for a little while, observe the interactions, see what unfolded, and assess the success of her idea.

Steve and Zoe were snogging desperately now, lean bodies twisting together. Steve pulled off Zoe's top, revealing beautiful shallow breasts with long, dark nipples, and buried his face against them, licking and sucking. Zoe gasped, her hands burrowing in his shorts, looking for his cock. She found it and pulled it out and swung over Steve, pressing her cunt against his face and pulling his cock deep into her mouth. He clutched her hips and they rolled into a tight 69, moaning with their mouths full.

Around the room the others were starting to move. Priss could have watched any of them, but she looked for Julie because she was particularly interested in the dynamic between Julie and Rick. Julie obviously felt that she had found her master, but Priss had been quite surprised that on the previous night Rick hadn't bothered to take her personally. Was there a problem, or was that part of the game? She should have asked Diva, really. Diva admired Rick's game-playing propensities, whereas to Priss they didn't really have much appeal. Frankly, she thought they were a waste of time. If two grown people wanted to get it on, why didn't they just do it, rather than going through all those time-consuming ramifications? OK, a little bit of faked resistance now and again was fun, a bit of role-playing made a change, but people like Rick and Julie just seemed to take the whole thing so seriously. For Priss, sex was supposed to be recreational, not serious.

Right now, what Julie was doing was crawling. She was crawling over the mattresses to Rick, like a guilty dog fawning on its master. Priss could see from her face that she was aroused; there was a flush on her cheekbones and her eyes were as dark as pools. She reached Rick and practically squirmed against his feet, pressing her cheek to his leg, looking up at him with adoring eyes. Her lips were moving, and Priss guessed that she was begging.

There was something which Priss found vaguely distasteful about this, and she looked away. Nearby Steve and Zoe were still giving it to each other, their deep sighs and heaving bodies revealing that they were almost at the point of climax. As Priss looked at them Steve groaned and thrust himself up towards Zoe's face and she swallowed convulsively even as her hips ground down on his searching tongue. For a moment they hung poised, tense with orgasm, and then they subsided to the mattresses, faces still buried, nursing gently.

Well, they seemed happy, at least for now. Priss

looked beyond them and saw that Diva was catching hold of both TJ and Josh, drawing them close to her. Two at once? Greedy girl. But she had to be owed something for having so selflessly distracted Greg last night, even down to swallowing his come.

And how was Greg? Glancing over his way, Priss saw that he was still curled into his ball, naked, an adult embryo. She felt a little concerned and after a moment she got up and went over and sat down on the floor next to him. She touched his shoulder and said, 'Greg.'

No response. She shook a little harder. 'Greg. Are you all right?'

A faint voice from behind the shielding hands. 'Fuck off.'

Well, at least he was conscious. But he'd been punished enough for being a prat, and if he didn't sort himself out soon he was going to miss his last chance to participate. 'Greg, it's Priss. Listen, things are getting exciting out here. You going to join in?'

'No. Fuck off.'

Well, what could she do? She thought for a moment, then sat back beside Greg and said conversationally, 'Let me tell you what's up then, just so you know what you're missing. Zoe and Steve just did a great 69. They're resting right now. Diva looks as if she wants to get it on with TJ *and* Josh. She's got no restraint, that girl. Alan and Jan –' she looked over to their corner and saw them wrapped in each other's arms '– Alan and Jan are snogging like teenagers and I confidently predict that they will soon be at it like rabbits. Julie's begging Rick for something. Jason looks interested in Julie –'

Greg uncurled very slightly, like a cautious hedgehog. 'Shut up,' he said, in a low passionate voice. 'Just shut up and fuck *off* and leave me alone.'

'Please yourself,' Priss said, rather offended. She got up and walked a few steps away from Greg, found herself a spare mattress and arranged herself in a comfortable sitting position, ready to continue her observations.

Rick was whispering in Julie's ear, and her face brightened. She sat up and began to remove her clothes. Her body really was lovely, not fit like Zoe's or magnificently Lara-like like Diva's, just simple, slender, elegant, effortless. She couldn't make an ungraceful movement. Naked, she turned on to all fours and sidled across the spread mattresses to Jason, who watched her with his usual out-to-lunch expression. Couldn't he see, just from Julie's posture and the sensual parting of her delicate lips, that she was offering to go down on him? Apparently not, because he just sat there and stared at her. She licked her lips. Still no luck with Jason, who had learned a lot on this holiday but still didn't seem to have mastered the delicate art of sexual signalling. At last Julie actually said something, and Jason jumped, apparently amazed and delighted, and hurried to open his fly.

So was Rick finally going to oblige Julie, while she serviced Jason with her mouth? Priss was dying to know, and she wasn't the only one. On the other side of the room Kathy caught her eye. She was sitting beside Sandy, who was already naked, although Kathy was still fully clothed. Kathy had one arm around the pale voluptuous girl's shoulder, caressing her bare breast. The other hand was resting between Sandy's parted thighs, and it was holding the vibrator.

Now there was another person who seemed to have come a little closer to her sexual vocation on this trip. Kathy didn't seem to have had that adventurous a sex life, and now she had discovered a real liking for sex with other women and a distinct talent as a sexual predator. Sandy, too, seemed to be enjoying herself.

I did it with my little hatchet, Priss thought smugly. For a moment she watched Sandy and Kathy. They made a lovely picture, illuminated in the golden glow of the lamps. Kathy buried her hand in Sandy's tumbling hair and pulled back her head and Sandy arched her neck like an odalisque, opening her lips to receive the deep kiss which she knew would come. Kathy teased, touching her lips to Sandy's lightly, delicately, and only when the pale body twisted and sighed did she slip her tongue deep into the other girl's mouth and reach further between her legs, not using the vibrator yet, just touching. Sandy moaned and her thighs spread wider apart and Kathy let go of the vibrator and pushed her middle finger right up inside Sandy, up until it was all hidden and the other fingers splayed out over the gleaming pink petals of flesh.

Kathy began to finger-fuck Sandy, thrusting the finger deep inside her in a steady rhythm, and then she glanced over the room and said something and pulled Sandy's head up to watch. What had she seen? Priss returned her attention to Julie.

Julie was on all fours in front of Jason, slowly, lasciviously, lubriciously sucking his cock. Her mouth was opened wide, her lips tense around him, he was so thick. Jason kneeled with his hands resting on Julie's head and his own head thrown back, eyes closed, mouth open in a soundless gasp of pleasure. Her movements were so slow that he must have been in complete torment. Once, twice, three times she took him in to the very root, then released him and began to swirl her tongue up and down the length of his shaft, tease the tiny eye at the tip, the little bridge of flesh below the head. Jason moaned out loud and his buttocks clenched feverishly.

And behind Julie, Rick was poised, still fully clothed. He leaned forward over her and caught her dangling breasts in his hands, stroked and squeezed them, and her eyes closed tightly in ecstasy. Then he pulled back and kneeled behind her and extended his tongue to lick her pussy.

Priss had pretty much kept her cool up till now, but there was something really very rude and arousing about what Rick was doing. It wasn't like ordinary licking; there was something about his position, the way his nose was buried between the cheeks of Julie's arse, which was really dirty. He was licking her in a dirty way as well, long, wet strokes of his tongue, like a dog. It made Priss shiver to watch him, and she clenched her legs tightly together to put some pressure on her warm empty cunt.

She thought that she knew what Rick was planning to do. He was certainly an arse man, indeed he was a man who seemed to like arses no matter whom they belonged to, and she thoroughly expected him to take Julie up the jacksie then and there. But she was wrong. Having licked Julie until the whole of her pussy and perineum and bottom gleamed with his saliva, he straightened again and kneeled almost beside her, leaning forward so that he could see her face. Her expression was contorted with pleasure and with the effort of sucking Jason's thick cock. Rick slipped one hand under her belly and between her thighs to caress her clit, and with the other he started to push his fingers into her cunt. First one finger, then two, then three, then all of them together, all the time watching her face, watching the flinching and twitching of her closed eyes and her distended mouth as he piled sensation upon sensation until it was almost too much for her to bear. At last his fingers were thrumming on her clit and his whole hand was sliding in and out of her and she gave a frantic, stifled cry and began to come, her back and belly jerking up and down as the contractions raced through her. Jason groaned and dug his fingers into her hair and began to thrust into her slack mouth, hard. Once, twice, and then he was coming too, grunting and leaning forward over Julie's quivering head.

Priss licked her lips and swallowed hard, working on resisting the temptation to go out right now and get something for herself. Jason was young, his recovery rate was high, it would be easy to go over and grab him and enjoy that lovely thick cock. But she didn't want to, not straight away. She wanted to know what else was going on. She wanted to know if Rick had anything more in store for Julie.

Perhaps he did, but what he was doing now was holding her, dropping delicate kisses on to her face and throat as she lay sobbing in his arms. Allowing her a little time to recuperate, perhaps. Priss turned her attention to the others.

Diva seemed to be enjoying herself to the full with Josh and TJ. They were tangled together, Josh thrusting his cock into Diva's mouth, TJ lying with his arms around her thighs and his face buried between her legs, and even as Priss glanced at them they flowed into another arrangement, the men changing places so that now it was TJ getting head, Josh giving it, and Diva stretched between them with her smooth brown body quivering with delight. Well, she was as happy as a pig in muck. Priss watched for a moment, remembering her original reason for starting all this, before it developed a life and urgency of its own. Had Diva had such a good time that she would give up that marriage which to Priss seemed suspiciously arranged? Or would she see it just as a diversion, a final fling?

Time would tell. Priss turned her attention to the two girls. They had stopped watching the Julie–Jason–Rick triangle and now they were concentrating on their own pleasure. Sandy was arched back over Kathy's arm, moaning as the vibrator purred against her clit, slipped deep inside her, withdrew, circled her perineum, entered her again. Kathy's left hand was cupping one heavy breast and she had leaned forward to suckle at Sandy's other nipple. Delicious ripples stirred up and down Sandy's soft pale body as she whimpered and sighed.

Steve and Zoe were kissing again, and as Priss watched Zoe rolled on top of Steve and sat upright, lifting up his cock so that she could roll a condom on to it. Then, without a fuss, she kneeled over him and penetrated herself, rising up and down, balancing herself on her strong thighs to take her own pleasure. Steve just lay back, hands folded behind his head, eyes closed, smiling. Well, that was a suitable pairing! Zoe was as fit as a flea, and Boneless just liked to lie about whenever he had the opportunity.

What about Jan and Alan? They were still in their corner of the room. They had folded up a mattress to make a sort of chair against the wall. Alan was sitting on it, legs extended, and Jan was sitting in his lap, impaled, leaning back against his chest and barely moving. His hands were stroking up and down her body, caressing her breasts, smoothing her throat, touching her clit, and both of them were watching the goings-on with dark eager eyes. Jan caught Priss's glance and smiled at her, then closed her eyes and leaned her head back on her husband's shoulder as something he did made her sigh with pleasure.

Everybody happy then, everyone involved, except for Greg and Priss herself. She wasn't going to be able to hold out much longer without doing something, and now she felt so horny that she just had to take her clothes off. She sat down again naked, thighs parted, and slipped her hand between her legs as she returned her attention to Rick and Julie.

Rick was kneeling now, still fully clothed, but with his fly open and his erect cock sticking out of it, already sheathed in rubber. He had Julie face down in his lap, her body flat on the mattress, arms spread, her legs spread on either side of his, and he was stroking her arse with tender fingers. Her face was turned towards Priss, her eyes closed, lips parted, tongue quivering with pleasure as Rick teased her clit, her buttocks, her anus.

God, he was going to fuck her now. Priss gulped and slid one finger into her pussy, found it as wet as it had ever been. Her slippery finger eased out, moved forward, rested delicately on her clit. She increased the pressure, released it, increased it, released it, and felt orgasm only seconds away.

Rick positioned the head of his cock at the little tight mouth of Julie's arse. The tiny rose gleamed with moisture and when his cock touched it it opened and closed briefly, pulsing like a sea anemone. He put his hands on her buttocks and pulled them further apart and the tip of his cock lodged itself in that little hole and pushed forward.

Julie's closed eyes tightened as Rick began to penetrate her. Her slack lips opened wider and she moaned. Rick's hands tensed on her slender hips and pulled her towards him, pulling her on to his cock. She cried out and her hole pulsed again and then it opened to admit first the tip, then the head of Rick's cock. Her body undulated as if it were resting on the surface of the sea, pressing her breasts against the mattress. Again he pulled her towards him, again his cock entered her, another inch, another, another, and she began to moan continuously, writhing about the nail that fixed her to him. One more tug and he was fully inside her, the whole length of his cock crammed into her arse, pinning her to his lap.

Priss gasped, then shuddered as she came. Orgasm clutched at her, then slowly receded, leaving her hungry for more. Even as she watched Julie squirming on Rick's invading cock she knew that she couldn't observe any longer, that she simply had to participate.

But who with? Sandy and Kathy, Zoe and Steve were still deeply engaged, and when she looked over at Jan and Alan she saw that they had turned away from the rest of the room and rolled on to the mattress in the missionary position, Alan thrusting steadily into Jan and all the time looking down at her face with an expression that made Priss jealous, because she had never known a long steady love like that and she thought it must be wonderful.

There was always Jason, of course. He was sitting on the mattress a little way from Rick and Julie, gazing in drop-jawed amazement, and his cock was already as stiff and thick again as it had been while Julie was sucking him off. But even as Priss decided that he would do, he got up and staggered across the big room towards Sandy and Kathy. She opened her mouth to call him back, but he had already dropped down beside the two of them, speaking urgently to Kathy, clearly determined to get involved. Priss sighed with frustration as the two women parted like the petals of a flower, arms open to receive Jason among them. He disappeared at once between Kathy's legs, obviously eager to hone his newly perfected skills with his tongue. Shit, that tongue could have been hers!

Diva's voice said in her ear, 'Feeling frustrated, are we?'

'Dee!' Priss turned with relief and delight and held out her arms to her friend. Diva bent down and kissed her, then pulled back, smiling.

'I hope you're feeling proud of yourself. Look at this.' She waved one hand at the scene in the lamplit room. 'This is all down to you.'

Priss grinned. 'I just hope that Sarah and John have managed to achieve some sort of transcendental union of their own.'

'Wouldn't bet on it,' Diva said.

'I would,' said Priss, giddy with her own success. 'Everything else has gone right, I'm sure they will too. Twenty quid says they got it together.'

'Done.' Diva spat on her palm and stuck it out and Priss slapped it with hers and laughed.

'Now,' Diva said, 'come over here at once and join me and Josh and TJ. We've been waiting for you to get fed up.'

This suited her very well indeed. Josh had been her pipe opener for this whole thing, and TJ was the one man whom she was still waiting to try out. So she scrambled to her feet and staggered across the mattresses and fell down beside them and Josh and TJ dived on her, lean tanned body and dark muscled body tugging at her arms, her legs, her hair, mouths on her breasts, between her legs, two stiff eager cocks just waiting to get busy. She relaxed back on to the ground, letting out all her need and tension in a long sigh of delight, and for a while let them do exactly what they wanted.

Then Diva stroked her and caught hold of her hand and said, 'I've got an idea, quick, get up,' and she obeyed, because she couldn't be arsed to think of anything more to do.

Diva arranged the men lying on their backs, knees drawn up, heads facing away from each other so that their knees were almost touching. 'Now,' she said, 'if you ride TJ, and I ride Josh, we'll be able to see each other.'

'Cool,' said Priss, and she swung her leg over TJ and lowered herself towards his waiting cock. His hands stroked the curves of her arse and supported her as she began to impale herself, and she leaned a little forward, resting against his raised knees, bringing her supersensitive clit into contact with the soft hairy pouch of his updrawn balls. It felt very good, full and satisfying, and the constant movement of his hands and fingers around the cheeks of her arse felt gratifyingly dirty and reminded her of what she had watched Rick do to Julie. She watched Diva mount Josh and then reached out for her.

'Look,' Diva whispered, when their lips were almost touching.

Priss turned her head and saw that Jason and Sandy were now alone. Sandy was on her hands and knees and Jason was fucking her from behind, taking her with long, slow, juicy thrusts while she rubbed herself between her legs and let out guttural cries.

So where was Kathy? Not with Zoe and Steve, who were still engaged in their long, slow ride. Not with Alan and Jan, and certainly not with Rick, who was now pulling Julie hard back on to his buried cock. She was in the corner with Greg, and Priss realised that she wasn't asking him to join in, nor trying to comfort him. She was telling him what to do. She said, 'Greg, that's enough. Roll over,' and he obeyed her. She said, 'Uncurl,' and he opened up like an armadillo. Then she straddled his face and said, 'Suck me. Do a good job,' and Priss saw Greg's eyes close and his mouth open and his tongue reach obediently up to lap at Kathy's clit.

Well, if she could like a rest from having ideas, why shouldn't Greg? And she was pleased that Kathy had been able to get him to snap out of it. Turning back to Diva, she said, 'See? Another satisfied customer. I'll win that bet yet.'

And then she rose and fell on TJ's gorgeous cock and for a while thought only of taking her own pleasure. She leaned forward against his strong thighs and rubbed her clit against him and kissed Diva and squeezed her breasts and sighed as Diva responded in kind, and when TJ pushed one finger into her arse she moaned and came, and after her orgasm she hung on the plateau, waiting in delicious anticipation for the next one.

Her rhythmic movements took her back towards the peak and she looked again around the room, drawing in her success. Alan and Jan, asleep in each other's arms; Steve and Zoe, collapsed in a post-orgasmic pile; Jason, vigorously shafting Sandy; Julie sprawled lewdly in Rick's lap, his cock still sliding in and out of her arse; Kathy shouting her climax over Greg's working mouth; Diva with her head thrown back, her mane of hair swinging as she impaled herself on Josh. And somewhere distant, up some hill under the stars, John and Sarah in their secret world, doing whatever it was that they were doing. Priss climbed up to orgasm again, and as she slipped into it she hoped fervently that wherever John and Sarah were, they were having a good time.

She woke up very early, as thirsty as if she had been drinking, and slowly sat up. The rest of them were sprawled all around her, limbs touching or entangled, Diva's black hair mixed with Josh's bleached, even Greg in the middle of all the others. They looked like a heap of kittens.

She gently lifted TJ's arm from her waist. He stirred but did not wake, and she got slowly to her feet and went to the window of the hut and looked out.

It was a perfect dawn, pale and opalescent, and the sun which had set behind the mountain was rising over it, making a brilliant star as its edge just lifted over the blackness of the rock. She blinked, holding up her hand against the brightness.

Movement behind her and a hand on her hair. That was Diva. A voice whispered in her ear, 'You OK?'

'Thirsty,' she replied, speaking low. 'Want to come out and get a drink?'

Diva nodded and the two of them went naked to the door. As they opened it Priss turned and looked back into the room and let out a low chuckle.

'D'you remember the Musée D'Orsay in Paris?' she said softly. 'Those Victorian paintings? This looks like that *Decline of the Roman Empire*, you remember, all those scenes of debauch.'

'More like that one of the raft from the shipwreck, with all those bodies strewn about,' Diva whispered, and closed the door.

Outside it was cool and their skins tightened and puckered into gooseflesh, but neither of them wanted to put any clothes on. They walked over the grass and moss, past the dozing horses to the stream. All around them the birds were singing to the sun, and the water caught its first rays as it leaped over the little rocks and tumbled gurgling into the pool.

They cupped their hands and drank, then splashed themselves with the cool water, shivering. Priss said eventually, 'It'd be less chilly just going in,' and she walked into the pool and dunked her head, then emerged and began to wash properly, easing away the sweat and stickiness of last night's exertions.

Diva came in beside her, gasping with the chill of the water. They stood there in silence for a while, up to their thighs, listening to the birds and luxuriating in the feel of the first few rays of sun on their cold limbs.

Presently Diva said, 'This is beautiful.'

'I don't suppose,' Priss said, 'that Kabir would think much of this sort of thing.'

Diva looked at her, a sharp, awake look. 'Oh ho,' she said. 'Trying to put me off, are you?'

For a moment Priss thought of denying it, but she and Diva were good enough friends to be honest about everything, including this. 'Yes,' she said. 'I thought you might realise that, well, that there was more to life than just getting married to Kabir and settling down.'

Diva smiled and sighed. Then she said, 'Priss, honey, it's the other way around. I want to get married to Kabir. He's a good man. I know you're suspicious, but honestly, it's OK. I'm thirty-five. It's time I settled down. I want to start a family, and he'll be a good father.'

Priss couldn't reply. She felt the size of a gnat, and horribly bereft. Diva made a face, then reached over and kissed her cheek. 'Listen,' she said, 'I'm not saying I haven't had a good time. I have. But this is playing, Priss. It's not real life. Don't worry, we can still be friends. And when I have a baby you can be its auntie. You'll be a great auntie.'

Well, she had given it her best shot, and it hadn't worked. She could stand there feeling lonely and left out, or she could make the best of it. She said eventually, 'Are you sure you want an old reprobate like me to be your baby's auntie? I'm sure I'll be a bad influence.'

'Children need all sorts of influences,' said Diva.

The sun was fully up now and they waded out of the pool and found a broad flat rock in full sun and sat down on it, arms wrapped around their knees, waiting to be warm. Presently the door of the hut opened and TJ emerged, rubbing his hand through his dishevelled hair. He nodded to them and walked straight over to the stream and into the pool, where he went to the waterfall and ducked his head underneath it. The water cascaded down over his smooth dark skin and caught in the ridges of tattoos on his buttocks, running through them and off in little sprays. Priss and Diva watched him with grave concentration. The combination of the flowing water and the sunlight on his wet muscled body was superb. Priss tried to engrave it on her memory, because she easily forgot things, and she really wanted to remember this.

After a while TJ climbed out of the pool and came and sat down next to them. He was magnificent, but there seemed to be an unspoken agreement that the time for sex was over. He just sat with them in the sun, drying off, combing his fingers through his hair.

After a while Diva said, 'You said this was a holy place. I hope we won't have offended any gods, after all that.'

TJ smiled. 'Well,' he said, 'this was a place for

fertility rites. So perhaps it was the gods entering into us, after all.'

Priss laughed. Then she stopped laughing, because she thought that she could see something on the track above the trees. 'Hush,' she said, and pointed. 'Do you see that?'

It was difficult to make out what it was because the sun was bright and very low and made her eyes glitter with sharp tears. She turned her head, but still couldn't see. TJ held up his hand and gazed and eventually said, 'That's John and Sarah.'

'Really?' Diva hissed. 'Wow!'

'Ssh,' Priss said again. 'Maybe they won't see us.'

So they sat very still and quiet on their rock and watched the dark speck moving down through the trees, coming closer and closer, until even Priss's dazzled eyes could see that it was two people walking together with a blanket wrapped around them, so that they were like one person.

'You owe me twenty quid,' she hissed to Diva.

'Ssh,' Diva retorted, 'not proven.'

Still they waited, and John and Sarah came closer and closer, until they were standing between the tall trees that marked the boundary of the area around the hut. Then they stopped and faced each other and stood for long minutes with their foreheads touching, shapeless under the blanket, still and in silence.

Presently they kissed, a long, slow, tender kiss, and after a while the blanket fell off. Beneath it they were naked, and their bodies touched all along their length, Sarah's pale gold, ascetic thinness a pleasing contrast with John's darker muscled bulk. Then they stopped, and John lifted the blanket and wrapped it around them again, and they walked on towards the stream.

'*Definitely* twenty quid,' Priss whispered, and John

saw them. His hand tightened around Sarah's shoulder and she too looked up and saw them.

Priss expected her to react badly. But her face looked different, calm, happy. Instead of complaining or throwing a wobbly, she lifted her eyebrows and smiled. 'Hello,' she said. 'Lovely morning, isn't it?'

'Certainly is,' said Priss, because it was.

There was a silence, during which John and Sarah waded the stream, stopping in the pool to cup water to their lips. Eventually Diva said, 'Did you have a good night?'

Sarah's smile was like the sunrise. 'Oh yes,' she said. 'We spent it on the top of the hill. TJ, I'm sure you're right that this place is sacred.'

TJ nodded but didn't say anything, and Sarah went on, 'Priss, I held it against you that you – concocted all those goings-on. But now I'm glad you did.' She looked at John, her face shining. 'You see, I've decided to stay here with John. And if you hadn't done all that, I might not have found out that that's what I need to do. So I wanted to say thank you. And if ever you come back to New Zealand, and you want a place to stay, you'll find us somewhere around here.'

'You're welcome,' Priss said faintly. She thought she ought to feel pleased with herself, but at present she was probably in shock.

TJ turned his head, eyes fixed on the distance. 'Listen,' he said.

They listened, but Priss couldn't hear anything.

'The bus,' TJ said. 'I can hear it coming up the track. It makes a meal of it. It'll be here in maybe ten minutes. We need to wake people up.'

'Right.' Diva bounded off the rock and ran naked back towards the hut, her hair a black cloud behind her, looking like an Amazon, and TJ hurried after her.

Priss followed them, but before she reached the hut she turned to look back.

Sarah and John had let the blanket fall and they were standing together in the pool, splashed by the spray from the waterfall, kissing deeply. The sunlight poured over them and turned the leaves of the surrounding beeches to discs of golden green, and a bird was singing.

Priss watched them and her heart hurt her, and she knew that this was something she would remember without having to try.

BLACK LACE NEW BOOKS

Please note that publication dates given here are for UK only. For other territories, check with your retailer.

Published in December

GOING TOO FAR
Laura Hamilton
£6.99

Spirited adventurer Bliss van Bon is set for three months travelling around South America. When her travelling partner breaks her leg, she must begin her journey alone. Along the way, there's no shortage of company. From flirting on the plane to being tied up in Peru; from sex on snowy mountain peaks to finding herself out of her depth with local crooks, Bliss doesn't have time to miss her original companion one bit. And when brawny Australians Red and Robbie are happy to share their tent and their gorgeous bodies with her, she's spoilt for choice.

An exciting, topical adventure of a young woman caught up in sexual intrigue and global politics.

ISBN 0 352 33657 9

COMING UP ROSES
Crystalle Valentino
£6.99

Rosie Cooper, landscape gardener, is fired from her job by an over-fussy client. Although it's unprofessional, she decides to visit the woman a few days later, to contest her dismissal. She arrives to find a rugged, male replacement behaving even more unprofessionally by having sex with the client in the back garden! It seems she's got competition – a rival firm of fit, good-looking men are targeting single well-off women in West London. When the competition's this unfair, Rosie will need all her sexual skills to level the playing field.

A fun, sexy story of lust and rivalry . . . and landscape gardening!

ISBN 0 352 33658 7

THE STALLION

Georgina Brown

£6.99

Ambitious young horse rider Penny Bennett intends to gain the sponsorship and the very personal attention of showjumping's biggest impresario, Alistair Beaumont. The prize is a thoroughbred stallion, guaranteed to bring her money and success. Beaumont's riding school is not all it seems, however. Firstly there's the weird relationship between Alistair and his cigar-smoking sister. Then the bizarre clothes they want Penny to wear. In an atmosphere of unbridled kinkiness, Penny is determined to discover the truth about Beaumont's strange hobbies.

Sexual jealousy, bizarre hi-jinks and very unsporting behaviour in this Black Lace special reprint.

ISBN 0 352 33005 8

Published in January

DOWN UNDER

Juliet Hastings

£6.99

Priss and Diva, 30-something best friends, are taking the holiday of a lifetime in New Zealand. After a spell of relaxation they approach the week-long 'mountain trek', brimming with energy and dangerously horny. It's Fliss's idea to see if, in the course of one week, they can involve every member of the 12-person trek in their raunchy adventures. Some are pushovers but others present more of a challenge!

A sexual relay race set against a rugged landscape.

ISBN 0 352 33663 3

THE BITCH AND THE BASTARD

Wendy Harris

£6.99

Pam and Janice, bitter rivals since schooldays, now work alongside each other for the same employer. Pam's having an affair with the boss, but this doesn't stop Janice from flirting outrageously with him. There are plenty of hot and horny men around to fight over, however, including bad-boy Flynn who is after Pam, big time! Whatever each of them has, the other wants, and things come to head in an uproar of cat-fighting and sexual bravado.

Outrageously filthy sex and wild, wanton behaviour!

ISBN 0 352 33664 1

ODALISQUE
Fleur Reynolds
£6.99

Beautiful but ruthless designer Auralie plots to bring about the downfall of her more virtuous cousin, Jeanine. Recently widowed but still young wealthy and glamorous, Jeanine's passions are rekindled by Auralie's husband. But she is playing into Auralie's hands. Why are these cousins locked into this sexual feud? And what is the purpose of Jeanine's mysterious Confessor and his sordid underground sect?

A Black Lace special reprint of a cult classic of the genre.

ISBN 0 352 32887 8

LOOK OUT FOR THE NEW-STYLE BLACK LACE BOOKS COMING IN FEBRUARY!

GONE WILD
Maria Eppie
£6.99

At twenty-six, Zita's a babe on the way up: live-in cameraman lover, urban des-res, stupendous media job. It seems she can do no wrong. But somehow the volume gets turned up a little too loud and she ends up wrestling naked one night with her girl pal and now they're not just pals anymore. She is also becoming obsessed with Cy, the beautiful tai-chi naturist. And then the nude rave scene in the music promo she supervises gets totally out of hand! And what's her boyfriend up to in Cuba? If Zita thinks she has all the rules sussed, how come everyone else is playing a different game?

A hot and horny story of urban girls on the move.

ISBN 0 352 33670 6

RELEASE ME
Suki Cunningham
£6.99

Jo Bell is a feisty journalist with just one weakness – her boss, Jerome. When he sends her on an assignment to a remote stately English home, she finds herself sucked into a frenzied erotic battle of wills with the owners of the mansion. The decadent Alicia will go to any lengths to prove her sexual superiority and her seemingly shy brother is keeping his own proclivities too quiet for Jo's liking. Jerome becomes a pawn in the siblings' games, too, and boundaries are pushed to the limit as degradation and punishment are firmly fixed on the agenda.

Past and present mingle in this compelling tale of modern-day aristos up to no good.

ISBN 0 352 33671 4

JULIET RISING

Cleo Cordell

£6.99

Nothing is more important to Reynard than winning the favours of the bright and wilful Juliet, a pupil at Madame Nicol's exclusive but strict 18th-century ladies' academy. Her captivating beauty tinged with a hint of cruelty soon has Reynard willing to do anything to win her approval. But Juliet's methods have little effect on Andreas, the real object of her lustful obsessions. Unable to bend him to her will, she is forced to watch him lavish his manly talents on her fellow pupils. That is, until she agrees to change her spoilt ways.

This sophisticated, classic novel is a Black Lace special reprint of one of the earliest titles in the series – by an author who pioneered women's erotic fiction.

ISBN 0 352 32938 6

BLACK LACE BOOKLIST

Information is correct at time of printing. To avoid disappointment check availability before ordering. Go to www.blacklace-books.co.uk

All books are priced £5.99 unless another price is given.

Black Lace books with a contemporary setting

THE TOP OF HER GAME	Emma Holly ISBN 0 352 33337 5	☐
IN THE FLESH	Emma Holly ISBN 0 352 33498 3	☐
A PRIVATE VIEW	Crystalle Valentino ISBN 0 352 33308 1	☐
SHAMELESS	Stella Black ISBN 0 352 33485 1	☐
TONGUE IN CHEEK	Tabitha Flyte ISBN 0 352 33484 3	☐
INTENSE BLUE	Lyn Wood ISBN 0 352 33496 7	☐
THE NAKED TRUTH	Natasha Rostova ISBN 0 352 33497 5	☐
ANIMAL PASSIONS	Martine Marquand ISBN 0 352 33499 1	☐
A SPORTING CHANCE	Susie Raymond ISBN 0 352 33501 7	☐
TAKING LIBERTIES	Susie Raymond ISBN 0 352 33357 X	☐
A SCANDALOUS AFFAIR	Holly Graham ISBN 0 352 33523 8	☐
THE NAKED FLAME	Crystalle Valentino ISBN 0 352 33528 9	☐
CRASH COURSE	Juliet Hastings ISBN 0 352 33018 X	☐
ON THE EDGE	Laura Hamilton ISBN 0 352 33534 3	☐
LURED BY LUST	Tania Picarda ISBN 0 352 33533 5	☐
LEARNING TO LOVE IT	Alison Tyler ISBN 0 352 33535 1	☐
THE HOTTEST PLACE	Tabitha Flyte ISBN 0 352 33536 X	☐

THE NINETY DAYS OF GENEVIEVE	Lucinda Carrington ISBN 0 352 33070 8	☐
EARTHY DELIGHTS	Tesni Morgan ISBN 0 352 33548 3	☐
MAN HUNT £6.99	Cathleen Ross ISBN 0 352 33583 1	☐
MÉNAGE £6.99	Emma Holly ISBN 0 352 33231 X	☐
DREAMING SPIRES £6.99	Juliet Hastings ISBN 0 352 33584 X	☐
THE TRANSFORMATION £6.99	Natasha Rostova ISBN 0 352 33311 1	☐
STELLA DOES HOLLYWOOD £6.99	Stella Black ISBN 0 352 33588 2	☐
UP TO NO GOOD £6.99	Karen S. Smith ISBN 0 352 33589 0	☐
SIN.NET £6.99	Helena Ravenscroft ISBN 0 352 33598 X	☐
HOTBED £6.99	Portia Da Costa ISBN 0 352 33614 5	☐
TWO WEEKS IN TANGIER £6.99	Annabel Lee ISBN 0 352 33599 8	☐
HIGHLAND FLING £6.99	Jane Justine ISBN 0 352 33616 1	☐
PLAYING HARD £6.99	Tina Troy ISBN 0 352 33617 X	☐
SYMPHONY X £6.99	Jasmine Stone ISBN 0 352 33629 3	☐
STRICTLY CONFIDENTIAL £6.99	Alison Tyler ISBN 0 352 33624 2	☐
SUMMER FEVER £6.99	Anna Ricci ISBN 0 352 33625 0	☐
CONTINUUM £6.99	Portia Da Costa ISBN 0 352 33120 8	☐
OPENING ACTS £6.99	Suki Cunningham ISBN 0 352 33630 7	☐
FULL STEAM AHEAD £6.99	Tabitha Flyte ISBN 0 352 33637 4	☐
A SECRET PLACE £6.99	Ella Broussard ISBN 0 352 33307 3	☐
GAME FOR ANYTHING £6.99	Lyn Wood ISBN 0 352 33639 0	☐
FORBIDDEN FRUIT £6.99	Susie Raymond ISBN 0 352 33306 5	☐
CHEAP TRICK £6.99	Astrid Fox ISBN 0 352 33640 4	☐
THE ORDER £6.99	Dee Kelly ISBN 0 352 33652 8	☐
ALL THE TRIMMINGS £6.99	Tesni Morgan ISBN 0 352 33641 3	☐

PLAYING WITH STARS £6.99	Jan Hunter ISBN 0 352 33653 6	☐
THE GIFT OF SHAME £6.99	Sara Hope-Walker ISBN 0 352 32935 1	☐
GOING TOO FAR £6.99	Laura Hamilton ISBN 0 352 33657 9	☐
COMING UP ROSES £6.99	Crystalle Valentino ISBN 0 352 33658 7	☐
THE STALLION £6.99	Georgina Brown ISBN 0 352 33005 8	☐
ODALISQUE £6.99	Fleur Reynolds ISBN 0 352 32887 8	☐
THE BITCH AND THE BASTARD £6.99	Wendy Harris ISBN 0 352 33664 1	☐

Black Lace books with an historical setting

PRIMAL SKIN	Leona Benkt Rhys ISBN 0 352 33500 9	☐
DEVIL'S FIRE	Melissa MacNeal ISBN 0 352 33527 0	☐
WILD KINGDOM	Deanna Ashford ISBN 0 352 33549 1	☐
DARKER THAN LOVE £6.99	Kristina Lloyd ISBN 0 352 33279 4	☐
STAND AND DELIVER	Helena Ravenscroft ISBN 0 352 33340 5	☐
THE CAPTIVATION £6.99	Natasha Rostova ISBN 0 352 33234 4	☐
CIRCO EROTICA £6.99	Mercedes Kelley ISBN 0 352 33257 3	☐
MINX £6.99	Megan Blythe ISBN 0 352 33638 2	☐
PLEASURE'S DAUGHTER £6.99	Sedalia Johnson ISBN 0 352 33237 9	☐

Black Lace anthologies

CRUEL ENCHANTMENT Erotic Fairy Stories	Janine Ashbless ISBN 0 352 33483 5	☐
MORE WICKED WORDS	Various ISBN 0 352 33487 8	☐
WICKED WORDS 4	Various ISBN 0 352 33603 X	☐
WICKED WORDS 5	Various ISBN 0 352 33642 0	☐

Black Lace non-fiction

THE BLACK LACE BOOK OF WOMEN'S SEXUAL FANTASIES	Ed. Kerri Sharp ISBN 0 352 33346 4	☐

-------✂---------------------

Please send me the books I have ticked above.

Name ....

Address ....

....

....

.... Post Code ....

Send to: **Cash Sales, Black Lace Books, Thames Wharf Studios, Rainville Road, London W6 9HA.**

US customers: for prices and details of how to order books for delivery by mail, call 1-800-343-4499.

Please enclose a cheque or postal order, made payable to **Virgin Books Ltd**, to the value of the books you have ordered plus postage and packing costs as follows:

UK and BFPO – £1.00 for the first book, 50p for each subsequent book.

Overseas (including Republic of Ireland) – £2.00 for the first book, £1.00 for each subsequent book.

If you would prefer to pay by VISA, ACCESS/MASTERCARD, DINERS CLUB, AMEX or SWITCH, please write your card number and expiry date here:

....

Please allow up to 28 days for delivery.

Signature ....

-------✂---------------------